UNDEAD
REVELATIONS

2 SLEEPS

Isla Reid

This edition first published in paperback by
Michael Terence Publishing in 2026
www.mtp.agency

ISBN 9781805881889

Cover design (AI)
Michael Terence Publishing

Michael Terence
Publishing

PROLOGUE

Spotify Apple Music Amazon Music

Track: AILSA

Eighteen Years Earlier – 2003

The Isle of Druichmachon had a way of making time move differently. Slower, perhaps, or maybe just more deliberately. On the mainland, people rushed from place to place, always late, always stressed. But here, on this small Scottish island where everyone knew everyone, time was something to be savoured, not conquered.

The school playground sat on a gentle slope overlooking the harbour, where fishing boats bobbed on water that shifted between slate grey and brilliant blue depending on the mood of the Scottish sky. Ancient stone walls, weathered by centuries of Atlantic winds, enclosed the yard where generations of island children had played. The air carried the perpetual scent of salt and seaweed, mixed with the earthy smell of peat smoke from nearby cottages.

Alexander McRae, ten years old and gangly with it, sat alone on the playground during lunch break. He was reading a book about marine biology—not because it was assigned, but because he thought Ailsa Campbell might find it interesting.

Ailsa Campbell. Just thinking her name made his stomach do strange things.

She was nine years old, nearly ten, but somehow seemed older, more confident, surer of herself than the other children. She had auburn hair that caught the light like copper, and green eyes that seemed to see right through all his carefully constructed defences.

And she was walking toward him right now.

"Still reading during lunch, Alexander?" Ailsa's voice was teasing but not unkind. "The book's not going anywhere."

Alexander looked up, flustered. "It's… it's about marine biology. I thought you might find it interesting since you're always going on about the seals."

Ailsa sat beside him, genuinely interested. "You were listening when I talked about the seals?"

"I listen to everything you say, Ailsa Campbell."

She bumped his shoulder playfully, and Alexander felt his face flush. They sat there for a while, Ailsa asking questions about the book, Alexander explaining things he'd learned, both of them aware of something shifting between them but too young to name it.

Around them, other children played and shouted, but Alexander and Ailsa existed in their own bubble, a space where only they existed.

It was the beginning of something that would define both their lives.

The years passed in a blur of shared moments. Walking home from primary school together, Alexander carrying both their bags. Ailsa teaching Alexander to skip stones by the harbour, laughing when his stones sank immediately. Moving on to secondary school together, then to college. The college dance where Alexander nervously asked Ailsa to dance, his palms sweating, his heart hammering.

"About time," Ailsa had said with a smile, taking his hand.

They danced badly, stepping on each other's feet, but neither cared. They were together, and that was all that mattered.

College completion came in 2013. Alexander was twenty, Ailsa nineteen. They stood with their families outside the college, proud and excited and terrified of the future.

"What now?" Ailsa asked as they walked along the harbour afterward.

"Now?" Alexander stopped, his heart pounding. "Now I ask you something I've been wanting to ask for years."

He pulled out a simple ring, nothing fancy, just a silver band he'd saved for months to buy.

"Ailsa Campbell, will you…"

"If you're about to propose to me standing on this smelly harbour wall, I swear I'll push you in," Ailsa interrupted, but she was smiling, tears in her eyes.

"Well, I was going to wait for somewhere more romantic, but…"

Ailsa squealed and threw her arms around him, nearly knocking them both into the water. "Yes, you daft man! Of course, yes!"

They kissed as the sun set behind them, and Alexander thought his heart might burst with happiness.

The wedding was small, held two years later in the island's church with the entire community in attendance. Ailsa wore a simple but beautiful dress, and when she walked down the aisle with her father, Alexander felt tears streaming down his face.

"Do you, Alexander, take Ailsa…"

The minister's words washed over him as he stared at Ailsa, unable to believe his luck. This beautiful, brilliant, fierce woman had chosen him. Had said yes to spending her life with him.

"I do," he said, his voice strong and clear.

"I do," Ailsa echoed, squeezing his hands.

They exchanged rings, kissed, and walked back down the aisle as husband and wife, their community cheering and throwing rice.

It was perfect.

The years that followed were filled with the ordinary magic of married life. Moving into their cottage, making it their own. Alexander's work as a safety consultant, Ailsa's job at the island school. Quiet evenings on the porch, watching the sun set. Arguments about whose turn it was to do the dishes, resolved with kisses and laughter.

And then, in 2019, everything changed.

Ailsa showed Alexander the positive pregnancy test with shaking hands. "We're going to have a baby."

Alexander stared at the test, then at Ailsa, then back at the test. "We're going to have a baby."

"That's what I just said."

"We're going to have a BABY!"

He picked her up and spun her around, both of them laughing and crying at the same time.

Nine months later, Magsy was born. Margaret Ailsa McRae—Magsy for short. She came into the world screaming, red-faced and furious, smelling of warmth and new life, and Alexander fell in love all over again.

Holding his daughter for the first time, feeling her tiny hand wrap around his finger, Alexander made a silent promise: I will always protect you. I will always come home to you. No matter what.

It was a promise he would be tested on in ways he couldn't imagine.

But for now, in this moment, with his wife beside him and his daughter in his arms, Alexander McRae was the happiest man alive.

1

The Island Life – Present Day

Spotify Apple Music Amazon Music

Track: SCOTTISH JOY

The morning mist clung to the Isle of Druichmachon like a lover reluctant to let go. Alexander McRae stood at the window of his cottage, coffee mug warming his hands, watching the sun burn through the grey veil to reveal the harbour below.

At twenty-eight, Alexander was tall and lean, just over six feet, with the wiry build of someone who spent more time walking island paths than sitting at desks. His dark brown hair was perpetually windswept—a losing battle against the Atlantic winds—and his grey-blue eyes held the calm steadiness that came from growing up on an island where everyone depended on everyone else. His face was weathered in the way of men who worked outdoors, with fine lines at the corners of his eyes from squinting against the sun and sea spray. He had his father's strong jaw and his mother's gentle expression, a combination that made him approachable despite his height.

The cottage sat at the very top of the hillside—the highest point on Druichmachon—positioned perfectly to catch both sunrise and sunset. Below, the village of Braelin lay two miles distant, a cluster of whitewashed cottages with slate roofs, their chimneys already sending up thin columns of peat smoke. The smell drifted up the hill, that distinctive Scottish scent that meant home, warmth, and centuries of tradition. The harbour stretched in a natural crescent, the stone pier jutting into water that lay calm as glass, reflecting the pearl-grey sky. Beyond the harbour, the Atlantic extended to the horizon, a vast expanse of shifting blues and greys that changed with every passing cloud.

Three fishing boats were already heading out—he recognised them all. The Bonnie Jean belonged to old Malcolm Fraser, the Selkie's Song to the Morrison brothers, and the smallest one, the Wee Beastie, to young Jamie Campbell, who'd bought her last spring.

Alexander knew every boat in the harbour. He knew every person on this island. That was the nature of Druichmachon—a community of three hundred souls where everyone's business was everyone's business, where a sneeze in the morning meant soup delivered by afternoon, where children grew up knowing they were watched over by an entire village.

Behind him came the soft padding of small feet on the wooden floor.

"Daddy?"

He turned to see Magsy standing in the doorway, her blonde hair a wild tangle, one of his old T-shirts serving as her nightgown. At two years old, she was all chubby cheeks and curious eyes—Ailsa's eyes, that particular shade of brown that turned amber in the sunlight.

"Good morning, my darling," Alexander said, setting down his coffee and scooping her up. "You're up early."

"Hungry," Magsy announced, as if this explained everything.

"Hungry, are we? Well, we can't have that. Let's see what we can find for breakfast."

He carried her to the kitchen, where Ailsa was already moving about, her auburn hair pulled back in a messy bun, wearing the old jumper she favoured for weekend mornings. She looked up as they entered and smiled—that smile that had captured Alexander's heart twenty years ago and never let go.

"Morning, you two. Porridge is almost ready."

"Porridge!" Magsy clapped her hands. "With honey?"

"With honey," Ailsa confirmed. "But only if you eat all your fruit first."

Alexander set Magsy in her high chair and moved to stand behind Ailsa, wrapping his arms around her waist and resting his chin on her shoulder. "You're up early too."

"Couldn't sleep. Kept thinking about you leaving tomorrow."

"It's only three days, love."

"I know. But still." She turned in his arms to face him. "I don't like you being away."

"I don't like being away either. But it's just a conference. Boring PowerPoint presentations about workplace safety protocols. I'll be bored out of my mind and wishing I was here."

"Promise you'll call every day?"

"Every day. Morning and night if the signal holds."

They stood there for a moment, foreheads touching, while Magsy babbled happily to herself about honey and porridge and the "big doggy" she'd seen yesterday (Mrs Henderson's cow, which had escaped again).

This was Alexander's life. This was his world. The cottage with its creaky floorboards and draughty windows, the view of the harbour, the smell of porridge and coffee, the weight of his daughter in his arms and his wife in his embrace. It was simple, ordinary, perfect.

He had no way of knowing that in forty-eight hours, this world would be nothing but a memory. That he would spend days fighting through hell just to get back to this moment, this feeling, this life.

But for now, everything was exactly as it should be.

After breakfast, Alexander drove down to the harbour. It was his routine on Saturdays—check in with the fishermen, make sure the safety equipment was up to code, have a chat with Captain Hamish about the ferry schedule. The two-mile journey from the cottage to Braelin was a winding single-track road that switch backed down the steep hillside.

The old Land Rover handled the familiar curves with practised ease. Dry stone walls lined both sides of the road, covered in moss and lichen that glowed emerald in the morning light. Wild heather grew in purple patches between the stones, and the ever-present wind carried the cries of gulls wheeling overhead. As he descended, the view opened up—the harbour spread below like a painting, fishing boats rocking gently at their moorings, their masts a forest of verticals against the horizontal expanse of sea. The water was that particular shade of grey-green that meant good weather coming, and the air tasted of salt and possibility. As the island's safety consultant, it was technically his job. But really, it was just an excuse to be part of the community, to feel connected to the rhythms of island life.

"Morning, Alex!" Malcolm Fraser called from the deck of the Bonnie Jean. "Heard you're off to the mainland tomorrow."

"Just for a few days. Conference in Loonswrath."

"Loonswrath, eh? Rather you than me, lad. Too many people, too much noise. Give me the open sea any day."

"I'll be back before you know it."

"Aye, well. Safe travels. And mind you don't let those mainlanders talk you into staying. We need you here."

Alexander smiled. This was what he loved about Druichmachon—the sense of belonging, of being needed, of being home.

He continued along the harbour, stopping to chat with the Morrison brothers about their new nets, with young Jamie Campbell about his boat's engine (which was making a worrying sound), with Mrs Henderson about her escaped cow (found, thankfully, before it could swim to the mainland).

By the time he reached Captain Hamish's office, the sun was fully up, and the mist had burned away, revealing a perfect Scottish morning—the kind that made you believe summer might actually come this year.

"Alex!" Hamish looked up from his paperwork. "Come in, come in. Tea?"

"Always."

Hamish poured tea so strong it could stand a spoon, then set two oatcakes on the chart like improvised coasters. They sat in his cluttered office, surrounded by ferry schedules and maritime charts, drinking in the warmth and talking about nothing in particular. This was another island ritual—the morning tea, the comfortable silence between old friends, the sense that time moved differently here than it did on the mainland.

"So, this conference," Hamish said eventually. "Health and safety, is it?"

"Industrial safety standards. Riveting stuff."

"And you're taking the morning ferry tomorrow?"

"If I can make it on time. You know how Magsy is in the mornings."

Hamish chuckled. "Aye, that wee one has you wrapped around her finger. Just like her mother did."

"Still does."

"Well, you'll make the ferry. I'll hold it for you if I have to. Can't have our safety man missing his important conference."

They finished their tea and Alexander drove back up the hill toward home. The climb back up the winding single-track road gave him a perfect view of the island spread out around him—the small school where he and Ailsa had met as children, the pub where they'd had their first date, the church where they'd married, the cottage where they'd brought Magsy home from the mainland hospital.

Every stone, every tree, every building held a memory. This island was woven into his DNA, part of his identity in a way people who'd grown up in cities could never understand.

As he drove, he passed other islanders—Mrs Campbell with her shopping, young Tommy Morrison on his bike, old Angus MacLeod walking his dog. Everyone waved, everyone stopped to chat, everyone asked about his trip to the mainland. He pulled over to talk to old Angus, whose collie was chasing sheep that weren't there.

This was community. This was home. This was everything that mattered.

The Land Rover crunched up the gravel driveway to the cottage at the hill's summit. He found Ailsa in the garden with Magsy, planting vegetables for the summer. Magsy was "helping" by digging holes in random places and filling them with stones.

"How's the planting going?" Alexander asked.

"Well, we've planted three carrots, two potatoes, and approximately seventeen stones," Ailsa said with a laugh. "So, I'd say we're making excellent progress."

Alexander sat on the grass beside them, watching Magsy work with intense concentration, her little tongue poking out as she dug. The sun was warm on his face, the smell of earth and growing things filled the air, and somewhere in the distance, gulls cried.

Perfect. Everything was perfect.

"Daddy, look!" Magsy held up a worm. "Wiggly!"

"Very wiggly. That's a good worm. He helps the garden grow."

"Helps garden grow," Magsy repeated seriously, carefully placing the worm back in the soil.

Ailsa caught Alexander's eye and smiled. This was their life—simple moments, small joys, the everyday magic of being a family.

That afternoon, they walked to the beach. It was Magsy's favourite place—she loved the sand, the waves, the shells she could collect in her little bucket. Alexander and Ailsa sat on a blanket while Magsy played at the water's edge, never quite brave enough to get her feet wet but fascinated by the foam and spray.

They sat in comfortable silence for a few moments, just watching their daughter. Then Ailsa suddenly laughed, stripping off her socks and shoes and rolling up her jeans to her knees.

"Come on, baby girl!" she called, running toward the water. "Let's show Daddy how brave we are!"

Magsy's eyes went wide with delight as her mother splashed into the shallows. Alexander watched as Ailsa's movements became fluid and graceful, her running looking almost like a dance against the backdrop of the setting sun. She'd always moved that way—natural and beautiful, as if the rhythm of the ocean was in her blood.

Magsy finally found her courage, toddling into the water after her mother, shrieking with laughter as the cool waves splashed against her legs. Ailsa swept her up, spinning her around in the shallows as both of them screamed with delight.

Alexander laughed watching them, his heart so full it felt like it might burst. They played in and out of the water, chasing each other along the shoreline, their laughter carrying across the beach like music. He could get up and join them before the sun went down, but for now, he was content just to watch this perfect moment.

Eventually, Ailsa and Magsy came running back to the blanket, collapsing onto it out of breath and laughing. Magsy, having caught her second wind, continued tearing around the beach, chasing gulls and collecting shells while her parents sat together getting their breath back.

"I'm going to miss this," Alexander said quietly, watching Magsy dance along the shoreline.

"It's only three days."

"I know. But still. I hate being away from you two."

Ailsa leaned against him, her hair still damp from the sea. "We'll be here when you get back. We'll always be here."

The sun was starting to descend, painting the sky in shades of gold and pink.

"Two sleeps," Ailsa said suddenly.

"What?"

"That's what you should tell Magsy. When she asks when you're coming back, tell her two sleeps. She can count that. It makes it real for her."

"Two sleeps," Alexander repeated. "I like that."

"Promise her two sleeps, and she'll be okay."

"Two sleeps," Alexander said again, testing the words. "I promise."

He had no idea how much weight that promise would come to carry. How those two words would become his mantra, his motivation, his reason for surviving when everything else fell apart.

Two sleeps. Such a simple promise. Such an impossible distance to cross.

But in that moment, sitting on the beach with his family, watching the sun set over the ocean, it seemed like the easiest promise in the world to keep.

That evening, after Magsy was in bed, Alexander and Ailsa sat on the porch with glasses of wine, watching the stars come out. The island was quiet except for the distant sound of waves and the occasional bark of a dog.

"Do you ever think about leaving?" Ailsa asked suddenly.

"Leaving? Druichmachon?"

"Sometimes I wonder what it would be like. Living on the mainland. More opportunities, more excitement."

"Do you want to leave?"

"No," she said immediately. "No, I love it here. This is home. I just… sometimes I wonder, you know?"

"I know. But I can't imagine living anywhere else. This island, this community, this life—it's everything I want."

"Even with the gossip and everyone knowing your business?"

"Even with that. Because it means people care. It means we're not alone."

Ailsa smiled and squeezed his hand. "You're right. We're lucky, aren't we?"

"Very lucky."

They sat in silence for a while longer, and then Ailsa said, "Promise me something."

"Anything."

"Promise me that no matter what happens, you'll always come home. That this will always be home."

"I promise," Alexander said, not knowing how prophetic those words would become. "I'll always come home. Always."

Later that night, as Alexander lay in bed beside Ailsa, listening to her breathing slow into sleep, he thought about the next few days. The ferry ride, the flights, the hotel, the conference. It all seemed so far away, so disconnected from this life, this reality.

But it was only three days. Two sleeps for Magsy. Then he'd be back, and everything would return to normal.

He fell asleep thinking about the beach, about Magsy's laugh, about Ailsa's smile. He fell asleep in his perfect life, in his perfect world, not knowing that he would spend the rest of his life trying to get back to this moment.

Not knowing that the world was about to end.

2

The Departure

Spotify Apple Music Amazon Music

Track: DEPARTURE

Sunday morning arrived too quickly. Alexander woke before dawn, his internal clock refusing to let him sleep despite knowing he had a long day ahead. He lay in bed for a moment, listening to Ailsa's breathing beside him, feeling the warmth of her body, trying to memorise this feeling of peace and safety.

In the next room, he could hear Magsy stirring—she was an early riser, always had been. Soon she'd be calling for them, ready to start her day with the boundless energy only two-year-olds possessed.

"You're awake," Ailsa murmured, not opening her eyes.

"Can't sleep."

"Nervous about the trip?"

"No. Just… I don't want to leave."

Ailsa rolled over to face him, her eyes still heavy with sleep. "It's only three days."

"I know."

"Two sleeps for Magsy."

"Two sleeps," he repeated, the words already becoming a talisman.

They lay there for a few more minutes, holding each other, until Magsy's voice called out: "Mummy! Daddy! Wake up!"

The morning routine began—breakfast, getting dressed, packing last-minute items. Alexander had packed his overnight bag the night before, but he kept finding things he'd forgotten: his phone charger, his conference materials, the book he'd been reading.

By eight o'clock, Alexander was sitting on the living room floor with Magsy, building a tower out of coloured blocks. Toys were scattered everywhere—evidence of a two-year-old's domain.

"And the tower gets bigger… and bigger… and…" Alexander said in a silly voice, carefully placing another block on top.

Magsy giggled and knocked it down with one enthusiastic swipe. "Again, Daddy! Again!"

Ailsa entered from the kitchen, coffee in hand, watching them with a warm smile. "You're going to be late for the ferry."

Alexander checked his watch and jumped up in panic. "Bloody hell! Sorry, love, I—" He started rushing around, gathering papers and checking his bag.

"Language, Alexander," Ailsa said, amused. "Little ears."

From the floor, Magsy looked up at them both and repeated something that sounded distinctly like "bloody hell."

Alexander and Ailsa exchanged horrified looks.

"She didn't get that from me," Alexander said quickly.

Ailsa raised an eyebrow. "Really?"

"I mean… not intentionally…"

Despite the situation, they both laughed. Magsy, pleased with the reaction, repeated her new phrase with even more enthusiasm.

"We'll work on that while you're gone," Ailsa said, shaking her head.

Alexander grabbed his overnight bag and kissed Ailsa quickly. "It's only three days. One day there, conference tomorrow, back the day after."

"We'll miss you."

Magsy tugged at Alexander's leg, her face suddenly serious. "Daddy stays!"

Alexander's heart broke. He knelt down to her level. "Daddy has to go to work, sweetheart. But I'll be back in two sleeps, I promise."

"Two sleeps?"

"Two sleeps. You count them, okay?"

The taxi horn honked outside.

"That's my ride," Alexander said, standing. "I love you."

"Love you too. Be safe," Ailsa replied.

Another quick kiss. Alexander headed for the door, then turned back. "Take care of Mummy, Magsy!"

Magsy waved enthusiastically. Alexander forced himself to walk out the door.

As the taxi pulled away, he looked back to see them standing in the window—Ailsa holding Magsy, both of them waving. He waved back until the cottage disappeared around a bend in the road.

"Harbour?" the driver asked.

"Yes, please."

The driver—Donald MacKenzie, who Alexander had known since childhood—glanced at him in the rear-view mirror. "Hard leaving the wee one, eh?"

"Always is."

"Aye, well. You'll be back before you know it. It's not like you're going to war or anything."

Alexander smiled at the comment, not knowing how prophetic it would become. "Just a boring conference."

"Rather you than me, lad. I couldn't stand being cooped up in some hotel listening to people drone on about regulations."

Spotify Apple Music Amazon Music

Track: HIGHLANDS FAREWELL

They drove through the quiet Sunday morning streets of Druichmachon. The island was just waking up—smoke rising from chimneys, a few early risers out walking dogs, the Morrison brothers heading down to their boat.

Everything looked so normal, so peaceful. Alexander tried to memorise it all—the way the morning light hit the stone buildings, the smell of peat smoke and salt air, the sound of gulls crying overhead.

This was home. This was where he belonged. And in three days, he'd be back.

The ferry terminal was quiet when they arrived. The Caledonian Spirit sat at the dock, her engines already rumbling, ready for the morning crossing to the mainland.

The terminal building was a simple stone structure, weathered by decades of salt spray and Atlantic gales. Its windows looked out over the harbour, where the ferry waited like a patient beast. The Caledonian Spirit was a working vessel, not elegant but sturdy—white paint faded to cream, rust stains around the anchor chains, but her engines strong and her hull sound.

The morning air was crisp, carrying the diesel smell of the ferry's engines mixed with the ever-present scent of the sea. Gulls perched on the terminal roof, their yellow eyes watching for any dropped food, their cries echoing off the stone walls of the harbour.

Captain Hamish was standing at the gangway, checking his watch with exaggerated impatience. "Cutting it fine, Alex!"

"Sorry, Hamish. Magsy wouldn't let me leave."

The old captain's expression softened. "Aye, well. Get aboard then. We've got a schedule to keep."

Alexander paid Donald and grabbed his bag. As he walked up the gangway, he turned back for one last look at Druichmachon. The island sat peaceful in the morning light, his cottage visible on the hill, smoke rising from the chimney.

Home.

He'd be back in two sleeps.

The ferry was half-empty—a few commuters heading to the mainland for work, some tourists with cameras, an elderly couple who nodded politely as Alexander passed. He found his usual spot by the window and settled in, watching as the crew cast off the lines.

The engines changed pitch, and the ferry began to move. Slowly, steadily, Druichmachon began to shrink away.

Alexander pulled out his phone and looked at the wallpaper—the photo of Ailsa and Magsy at the beach, both of them laughing, the sun setting behind them. He'd taken it just last week, but it already felt like a lifetime ago.

The crossing took forty-five minutes. Alexander spent most of it staring out the window, watching the island disappear and the mainland grow larger. Other passengers read newspapers, dozed, chatted quietly. Everything was normal, routine, mundane.

On the mainland, Alexander caught a taxi to Achanshelloch Airfield. The driver was chatty, talking about the weather, the fishing, the latest football scores. Alexander made appropriate noises but wasn't really listening. His mind was already at the hotel, already counting down the hours until he could call home.

The airfield was small and regional, serving the scattered communities of the Highlands. The twin-engine aircraft that would take him to Glengail sat on the tarmac, looking smaller and more fragile than Alexander would have liked.

He'd never been comfortable with flying—too much could go wrong, too many systems that could fail. But it was the fastest way to reach Loonswrath, and the faster he got there, the faster he could come home.

The flight was bumpy, the small plane tossed by Highland winds. Alexander gripped the armrests and tried not to think about all the safety regulations he knew were supposed to prevent crashes. Knowing how things could go wrong didn't make flying any easier.

Beside him, a businessman in a suit was reading a newspaper. Alexander caught a glimpse of the headline: "CONTROVERSY AS MILITARY RECEIVES 'SUPER-SOLDIER' DRUG TRIALS."

"Excuse me," Alexander said. "Could I see that article?"

The businessman passed him the paper. Alexander read quickly:

"The Ministry of Defence has come under fire after approving widespread distribution of an experimental performance-enhancing drug to military personnel across Scotland. The drug, manufactured by VitaGenix Corporation, claims to enhance soldier capabilities by reducing the need for sleep by 80%, increasing strength and speed by 40%, and decreasing food requirements while maintaining peak operational readiness.

Defence Secretary James Richardson defended the programme, calling it 'a necessary evolution in modern warfare.' However, medical experts have expressed concern about the long-term effects of the drug, codenamed 'VIGOR-7.' Dr Eleanor Chen of the Royal College of Physicians warned that 'tampering with fundamental human biological needs without extensive testing could have catastrophic consequences.'

Several soldiers have reportedly been hospitalised with severe side effects, including extreme aggression and psychotic episodes. VitaGenix insists the incidents are isolated and unrelated to their product, citing the drug's 'perfect safety record' in initial trials."

Alexander felt a chill run down his spine. A drug that let soldiers go without sleep, made them stronger and faster, and reduced their need for food? It sounded like something out of a science fiction film. And the side effects—extreme aggression and psychotic episodes—that was deeply concerning. But the article was dated three days ago, and there'd been no follow-up coverage, so presumably the military had everything under control.

He handed the paper back and tried to put it out of his mind.

The plane landed at Glengail Military Airfield with a thump that made Alexander's stomach lurch. He disembarked with the other passengers and went through a brief security check—nothing too invasive, just a quick scan and a check of his identification.

Another taxi, another twenty-minute drive, this time into Loonswrath proper. The town was larger than he'd expected—not quite a city, but substantial enough to have traffic and crowds and all the noise and bustle that came with mainland life.

Alexander found himself missing Druichmachon already. Missing the quiet, the space, the sense of knowing everyone you passed on the street.

The Grand Caledonian Hotel loomed ahead, and Alexander felt a strange sense of foreboding as the taxi pulled up to the entrance.

The building was a Victorian monstrosity of grey granite, all turrets and bay windows, built in an era when grandeur meant imposing rather than welcoming. Single-glazed windows reflected the afternoon light like dead eyes. The brass plaque beside the entrance—"EST. 1887"—had turned green with age, and the stone steps leading to the door were worn into shallow bowls by more than a century of footsteps.

Around the hotel, Loonswrath spread out in typical Scottish town fashion—narrow streets lined with stone buildings, shop fronts with hand-painted signs, church spires rising above slate roofs.

The streets were quiet for a Sunday afternoon, the few people visible moving with purpose rather than leisure.

It was just a hotel, just a conference, just three days. But something felt off, though he couldn't put his finger on what.

"Here we are," the driver said. "That'll be fifteen pounds."

Alexander paid and grabbed his bag. The hotel looked old but well-maintained, its granite facade speaking of Victorian grandeur and faded elegance.

He took a deep breath and walked inside.

The lobby was busy with conference attendees—people in business casual attire, all wearing name badges, all looking slightly resigned to the next two days of presentations and networking.

Alexander checked in, collected his room key and conference materials, and headed for the elevator. In the lift, he met two other attendees—James and Sarah, both friendly enough, both clearly veterans of these kinds of conferences.

"First time?" James asked.

"Second. You?"

"Fourth. They're usually quite good. Bit dry, but useful."

The elevator dinged. Floor two. Alexander's floor.

"See you at the reception," Sarah said as he exited.

His room was standard hotel fare—clean, comfortable, impersonal. Alexander dropped his bag on the bed and went straight to the window.

The view showed Loonswrath spread out below, the bay beyond, and somewhere far beyond that, Druichmachon. He couldn't see the island from here, but knowing it was out there, knowing Ailsa and Magsy were there, made him feel slightly less alone.

He checked his watch: 2:47 PM. Magsy would be napping now. Ailsa would be reading or working in the garden or doing any of the hundred small tasks that filled her days.

Alexander pulled out his phone and called.

"Hi, it's me… Yes, I'm here safe… The hotel's nice, bit old-fashioned…"

Ailsa's voice was warm and familiar, grounding him in reality. She told him about Magsy's morning, about Mrs Henderson's cow (which had escaped again), about the weather (typical—rain, then sun, then probably rain again).

Normal things. Safe things. Home things.

"I miss you both already," Alexander said.

"I know. But it's only two sleeps, remember?"

"Two sleeps."

They talked for a few more minutes, and then Ailsa had to go—Magsy was waking up from her nap. Alexander hung up and stared at the phone for a long moment.

Two sleeps. Forty-eight hours. Then he'd be home.

He unpacked methodically, organising his things the way he always did—conference materials on the desk, clothes in the wardrobe, toiletries in the bathroom. Everything neat, everything in its place.

When he was done, he lay back on the bed and closed his eyes. Just for a moment, he told himself. Just a quick rest before the evening reception.

He must have dozed off, because when he opened his eyes again, the light had changed. His phone showed 6:30 PM. Time for the video call he'd promised Magsy.

Spotify　Apple Music　Amazon Music

Track: DISTANCE BETWEEN US

Alexander set up his laptop and dialled. The connection was fuzzy but good enough. Ailsa's face appeared on screen, Magsy bouncing on her lap.

"Can you see us okay?" Ailsa asked. "The connection seems a bit fuzzy."

"Perfect. You both look beautiful."

"Daddy! Daddy in the box!" Magsy reached toward the camera, trying to grab it.

Alexander laughed. "I'm in the box, sweetheart. How was your day?"

"Tell Daddy what we did today, Magsy," Ailsa prompted.

Magsy launched into an enthusiastic story. "We saw… we saw… big doggy!"

"A big doggy? Where?"

Ailsa smiled, amused. "Mrs Henderson's cow got loose again. Magsy thought it was a very big dog."

"A cow-dog. That's a new one."

Magsy suddenly got distracted by something off-camera and wriggled off Ailsa's lap.

"Magsy, come back and talk to Daddy!" Ailsa called after her.

The sound of Magsy's footsteps running away.

"And she's gone," Ailsa said to Alexander. "She's been like this all day—can't sit still for two minutes."

"She gets that from you."

"Excuse me?" Ailsa sat rigidly upright, hands folded, staring at the camera with exaggerated stillness. "I can sit perfectly still."

Alexander laughed. "Very convincing."

Ailsa broke character, laughing. Magsy ran back into frame, now wearing one of Alexander's old jumpers that was far too big for her. The sleeves hung past her hands, the bottom dragged on the floor.

"Look! Daddy's jumper!" Magsy announced proudly.

Alexander's voice caught slightly. "You look just like Daddy."

"She missed you today," Ailsa said gently. "Kept asking where you were and when you'd be home. We've just had a wee bedtime story."

"Daddy, when you come home?" Magsy asked, suddenly serious.

"Two sleeps, remember? Tonight is one sleep, tomorrow night is two sleeps, then Daddy comes home."

Magsy held up two fingers, but it was actually three.

"Two sleeps!"

"That's three, sweetheart. This is two." Ailsa helped Magsy hold up the correct number.

"That's right. Two sleeps."

Magsy suddenly ran off again. Ailsa shook her head.

"I swear she's had too much sugar today. Mrs Campbell brought over shortbread this afternoon."

"That woman's shortbread could power a small village for six weeks on the amount of sugar in it!"

Ailsa laughed. "She asked about you. Wanted to know if you were eating properly."

"Tell her I had a proper meal. Well, I will have. There's a reception and dinner downstairs."

"Ooh, fancy. Try not to fall asleep in your soup."

"That was one time!"

"At our wedding reception!"

"I was nervous! And exhausted! And your uncle kept buying me whisky!"

They were both laughing now. Magsy returned, this time with a stuffed rabbit.

"Mrs Bun Bun says hi!" She held up the rabbit and made it wave at the camera.

"Hello, Mrs Bun Bun. Are you taking care of my Magsy for me?"

Magsy made the bunny nod seriously, then hugged the rabbit tightly.

"Mrs Bun Bun helps me sleep and she loves big cuddles. Just like you, Daddy!"

Alexander's expression softened. "That's good. Mrs Bun Bun will keep you safe."

The connection started to pixelate slightly.

"The signal's getting worse," Ailsa said, frowning.

"I can still see you. How's the weather there?"

"Typical. Rained on and off all morning, sunny this afternoon, it'll probably snow tonight knowing Scotland. All four seasons in one day and if you're lucky… all within an hour."

The connection froze for a moment, then came back.

"You're breaking up a bit."

"Can you hear me?" Ailsa's voice was slightly distorted.

"Just about. Listen, I should let you get Magsy ready for bed."

"No bed! Talk to Daddy forever!" Magsy protested.

"Daddy needs to go to his work dinner, sweetheart," Ailsa said to Magsy.

"I'll call you tomorrow, okay? After the conference finishes."

"We love you."

"Love you, Daddy!" Magsy blew kisses at the camera.

"I love you both so much. Sweet dreams, Magsy. Be good for Mummy."

The connection started to cut out more.

"See you… too… love…" Ailsa's voice broke up.

The call dropped. The screen showed "CONNECTION LOST."

Alexander stared at the blank screen for a moment, then closed the laptop.

"Two sleeps," he said quietly to himself.

He got ready for the reception, putting on a fresh shirt, checking his appearance in the mirror. His dark hair was still damp from the shower, and he ran a hand through it, trying to tame the natural wave that Ailsa always said made him look younger than his twenty-eight years old. He looked tired, he realised—the grey-blue eyes that usually held a calm steadiness now showed the strain of travel and separation from his family. The journey had taken more out of him than he'd expected.

Or maybe it was just the weight of being away from home.

Spotify   Apple Music   Amazon Music

Track: CONFERENCE HARMONY

Alexander headed downstairs to the Argyll Suite, where the welcome reception was already in full swing. The room was crowded with conference attendees, all making small talk over drinks and canapés.

He collected his name badge and headed to the bar. "Just a pint, please."

While waiting, James appeared at his elbow with Sarah. "Oh, it's you from earlier! I'm James, we met in the lift? I didn't manage to catch your name earlier…"

"Alexander. Nice to meet you."

They chatted about their backgrounds, their work, the conference schedule. It was all perfectly pleasant and perfectly forgettable—the kind of professional networking that Alexander had never been particularly good at.

At their assigned table, Alexander met the other attendees—Frank, a man in his fifties with the weathered look of someone who'd spent years on construction sites. Peter, younger and eager, fresh from university. Three others whose names Alexander struggled to remember.

The conversation flowed easily enough. Frank complained about phone signal—"Anyone else having trouble?"—and several others agreed. Alexander mentioned his video call cutting out but didn't think much of it.

The first course arrived, and with it, more wine. The conversation turned to tomorrow's agenda, to the emergency response workshop that everyone agreed would be useful but probably boring.

"Here's to boring, safe jobs where nothing ever goes wrong," Alexander said, raising his glass.

They toasted, laughing at the mundanity of their profession, at the idea that anything truly dangerous might happen to them.

If only they'd known.

Alexander checked his phone under the table. The signal had dropped from two bars to none. He frowned but pocketed the phone. Probably just the old building's thick walls interfering with reception.

The dinner continued, pleasant and forgettable. By ten PM, people were starting to drift away, heading back to their rooms. Alexander said his goodnights and took the elevator back to the second floor.

In his room, he immediately tried to call home. No signal. He tried the laptop—"CONNECTION FAILED." Even the hotel phone on the bedside table had no dial tone.

"That's odd," he muttered, but he wasn't particularly worried. Technical issues happened. He'd try again in the morning.

He got ready for bed, checking his phone periodically out of habit. Still nothing.

Outside his window, Loonswrath looked peaceful—streetlights casting pools of amber on wet cobblestones, a few cars passing with their headlights cutting through the evening mist, the town settling in for the night. The church clock struck ten, its bells echoing off stone buildings. Somewhere a dog barked. A couple walked past below, their laughter floating up to his window.

Everything seemed normal. Everything seemed fine. The town lay quiet under a sky heavy with clouds, the kind of peaceful Scottish evening that had played out for centuries.

Alexander got changed into his pyjamas, lay on the bed and started staring at the ceiling, thinking about Ailsa and Magsy. Tomorrow would be one sleep down, one to go. Then he'd be home, and this would just be another forgettable business trip, another story to tell about bad hotel phone service.

He closed his eyes and drifted off to sleep, unaware that he was living through the last normal night of his life.

Unaware that in a number of hours, everything would change.

Unaware that the promise he'd made—two sleeps—would become the only thing keeping him alive through the nightmare to come.

In his dreams, he was home. Magsy was laughing, Ailsa was smiling, and the sun was setting over Druichmachon in shades of gold and pink.

It was perfect.

It was the last perfect dream he would ever have.

3

The Grand Caledonian

Spotify Apple Music Amazon Music

Track: CONFERENCE BLUES

The morning of the conference dawned grey and drizzly—typical Scottish weather that made Alexander think of home. He'd slept reasonably well, his dreams filled with fragmented images of Ailsa and Magsy, of the cottage, of the harbour, of his ferry journey. He'd woken a couple of times and checked his phone hoping the signal had returned. It hadn't.

The hotel phone still had no dial tone. Alexander tried not to worry—technical difficulties happened, especially in old buildings like this. The signal would come back. It always did.

He showered and dressed in his conference clothes—business casual, the uniform of the professional safety consultant. As he knotted his tie, he caught sight of himself in the mirror and barely recognised the man looking back. He looked tired, older somehow, though it had only been one night away from home.

One sleep down, one to go.

The thought gave him comfort. By this time tomorrow, he'll be on his way home. By tomorrow night, he'd be sleeping in his own bed, Ailsa beside him, Magsy in the next room. This would all be over.

The conference breakfast was held in the same Argyll Suite where they had dinner. Long tables laden with pastries, fruit, coffee, and the full Scottish breakfast—eggs, bacon, sausage, black pudding, beans, toast. Alexander filled a plate more out of habit than hunger and found a seat near the window.

Outside, Loonswrath was waking up. People hurried along the streets, umbrellas up against the drizzle. Cars navigated the narrow roads. Everything looked normal, ordinary, mundane.

"Morning!" James sat down across from him, his plate piled high. "Sleep well?"

"Well enough. You?"

"Like a log. These hotel beds are always better than mine at home." He took a bite of sausage. "Looking forward to today's sessions?"

"About as much as anyone looks forward to PowerPoint presentations about risk assessment protocols."

James laughed. "Fair point. But the emergency response workshop this afternoon should be interesting. They're bringing in some new equipment to demonstrate."

Sarah joined them, along with Frank and Peter. The conversation flowed easily—small talk about the weather, the hotel, the schedule for the day. Normal conference chatter.

But Alexander noticed something odd. Several people were checking their phones with increasing frequency, frowning at the screens. The woman at the next table was arguing quietly with her husband about whether they should try to leave early.

"Still no signal," Frank muttered, staring at his phone. "This is ridiculous. I need to check in with my office."

"Same here," Peter said. "I've got a project deadline coming up."

"Probably just the old building," James suggested. "Thick walls, poor reception. It'll come back."

But Alexander wasn't so sure. He'd stayed in plenty of old buildings, and while reception could be spotty, it didn't usually disappear completely. And the hotel phones being down too? That seemed like more than just coincidence.

He pushed the thought away. He was being paranoid. Everything was fine.

The conference began at nine AM sharp. The opening session was in the main ballroom—a grand space with high ceilings and ornate moulding that spoke of the hotel's Victorian heritage. About sixty people filled the seats, all wearing name badges, all looking slightly resigned to the day ahead.

The keynote speaker was a man from the Health and Safety Executive, droning on about new regulations and compliance requirements. Alexander tried to pay attention but found his mind wandering. He kept thinking about Ailsa and Magsy, wondering what they were doing right now.

It would be mid-morning on Druichmachon. Ailsa would probably be at the shop, picking up groceries. Magsy would be with Mrs Campbell, who watched her on Mondays. They'd be playing in the garden, or reading stories, or doing any of the hundred small things that filled a toddler's day.

Alexander's phone buzzed in his pocket. He pulled it out hopefully, but it was just a low battery warning. Still no signal. He turned it off to conserve power.

The morning sessions dragged on. Risk assessment methodologies. Incident reporting procedures. Compliance documentation. All important, all necessary, all mind-numbingly dull.

Alexander sat through it all, taking notes when required, nodding at appropriate moments, his mind occasionally drifting to thoughts of home. But this was just another conference—boring but necessary, the kind of thing professionals in his field endured for the sake of continued education and networking requirements.

The lunch break was thoroughly ordinary. People mingled, exchanged business cards, complained about the quality of hotel coffee, discussed their respective companies' safety challenges.

Alexander found himself in a conversation with a woman from Glasgow about the complexities of implementing new EU safety regulations in Scottish manufacturing.

The afternoon sessions were much the same. The presenter was enthusiastic about workplace ergonomics, though most of the audience struggled to stay awake through the statistical analysis portion. Alexander saw a few people checking their phones, but that was normal behaviour at any conference—the constant need to stay connected to work emails and messages.

At three PM, the fire alarm went off, but it was quickly handled. A calm voice over the PA system announced it as a false alarm due to technical difficulties, and within five minutes, the presentation continued as if nothing had happened. A brief moment of disruption, nothing more.

By five PM, the conference wrapped up with the usual mixture of relief and mild satisfaction. People gathered their materials, some planning to head to the hotel bar for networking drinks, others making dinner plans. Alexander considered joining them but decided against it—he wanted to call Ailsa and Magsy before dinner.

Back in his room, Alexander tried the phone. Still no dial tone. He frowned—that was odd. He tried his mobile. No signal. He tried turning it off and on again. Still nothing. He turned on the television. Static on every channel.

Well, that was inconvenient. Technical difficulties, presumably. He'd try again in an hour. Maybe the storm he'd noticed gathering outside was affecting the signals.

Alexander made his way downstairs early for dinner and tried the hotel phone in the lobby. Still no dial tone. He asked the receptionist—Moira, the same woman who'd checked him in—about it.

"I'm terribly sorry," she said, looking genuinely distressed. "We're having some technical difficulties. The phone company says they're working on it."

"What about mobile signal?"

"That seems to be affected too. Something about a tower being down for maintenance. It should be back up soon."

"Soon" turned out to be relative. By dinner, there was still no signal, no dial tone, no way to contact the outside world. Alexander wasn't the only one getting anxious—he could see other attendees checking their phones obsessively, some looking genuinely worried.

"This is unacceptable," Frank said over dinner. "I have a family. They'll be worried sick."

"I'm sure it'll be fixed soon," Sarah said, though she didn't sound convinced.

The evening session was the emergency response workshop. Normally, Alexander would have been interested—this was his specialty, after all. But he couldn't focus. All he could think about was getting home, getting back to Ailsa and Magsy.

The instructor was demonstrating proper use of emergency equipment when someone's phone rang. The sound was so unexpected that everyone jumped. The woman who owned the phone—one of the attendees Alexander didn't know—grabbed it eagerly.

"Hello? Hello?" Her face fell. "It's just static. I can't hear anything."

But the fact that it had rung at all gave everyone hope. The signal was coming back. Soon they'd be able to call home, check in, reassure their families.

The workshop continued, but Alexander could tell no one was really paying attention any more. Everyone was too focused on their phones, waiting for that precious signal to return.

By the time the sessions ended at nine PM, there was still nothing.

"This is getting ridiculous," Frank said as they gathered in the lobby. "I'm going to walk into town, see if I can find a phone that works."

"I'll come with you," Peter said.

Alexander considered joining them, but something made him hesitate. The look on Moira's face when she'd talked about the technical difficulties. The way some of the hotel staff were whispering in corners, looking worried. The general sense of unease that seemed to be building in the hotel.

Something was wrong. He couldn't put his finger on what, but something was definitely wrong.

"I think I'll stay here," he said. "Try to get some sleep ready for tomorrow."

In his room, Alexander stood at the window, looking out at Loonswrath. The town looked normal enough—people going about their business, cars on the roads, lights in windows. But there seemed to be more activity than usual. More people hurrying, more cars moving quickly, more of a sense of urgency in the movements below.

He checked his watch: 10:15 PM. He should try to sleep. This time tomorrow he'd be home and back to normality.

He lay on the bed still fully dressed, staring at the ceiling, listening to the sounds of the hotel. Footsteps in the corridor. Doors opening and closing. The distant sound of sirens. When he finally drifted off to sleep, his last thoughts were of Ailsa and Magsy and how much he was looking forward to being home tomorrow.

Just one more sleep.

Spotify Apple Music Amazon Music

Track: AWAKENING

3:17 AM

Alexander was jolted awake by a sound that vibrated through the very walls of the hotel. A high-pitched, mechanical screech that went on and on, impossibly long, drilling into his skull with physical force. It wasn't human. It wasn't animal. It was something else, something utterly wrong.

He sat bolt upright in bed, his heart hammering against his ribs, his mind still fuzzy with sleep. What the hell was that? A faulty alarm system? Some kind of mechanical failure?

The screech finally ended, leaving a silence that was somehow worse. In that silence, he could hear other sounds now—shuffling footsteps in the corridor, muffled moaning. Probably just other conference-goers, disturbed by the noise like he was.

Alexander slid out of bed and crept to his door, pressing his ear against the wood. He could hear movement in the corridor—multiple figures, their footsteps uneven. Drunk people from the bar, maybe? It was late enough that people would be returning from their evening out.

Then another sound—that same horrible screech, but this time it was right outside his door. Close. So close he could feel the vibrations through the floorboards.

Through the crack under the door, he saw shadows moving. Multiple shadows, standing still in the corridor. One of them was taller than the others, unnaturally thin. It tilted its head, as if listening.

Then the screech came again, directly outside his room. Louder this time, so powerful it made his teeth ache and his eyes water. He covered his ears and fell to the floor. The pain was earth-shattering. He felt as though this sound would burst every cell in his body. He screamed in pain as blood started to run from his eyes, nose and ears. The sound suddenly stopped. He removed his hands from his ears and looked at them, saw blood—but he had no time to react.

BANG. BANG. BANG.

Something was pounding on his door. The whole frame rattled with each impact. Alexander stumbled backward, his mind refusing to process what was happening. This wasn't drunk people—this was something else entirely.

The door frame started to splinter. Whatever was out there was impossibly strong.

Alexander looked around frantically. No other exit. The window was too high to jump—four stories up, and even if he survived the fall, he'd be injured, helpless, easy prey for whatever those things were.

The bathroom had no windows at all. He was trapped.

CRACK—another piece of the door frame splintered away.

Alexander grabbed the only weapon he could find—a heavy table lamp, yanking the cord from the wall. It wasn't much, but it was better than nothing.

CRACK. Another piece of the door frame gave way. The door burst open with a sound like a gunshot, wood splintering and flying inward.

The creature filled the doorway, silhouetted against the flickering emergency lights. Its hotel uniform was torn and stained with dark fluids. Orange veins covered every visible inch of skin, pulsing with sickly light. Its eyes were completely white, milky orbs that somehow seemed to see him.

Its mouth opened impossibly wide, and Alexander knew with absolute certainty that his world had just ended.

That the promise he'd made to Magsy—two sleeps—had just become the hardest promise he'd ever have to keep.

The creature screeched again and lunged toward him.

Alexander didn't think. He swung the table lamp with all his strength, connecting with the creature's head. It staggered but didn't fall. It tried grabbing him but he dodged its hands and spotted a fire extinguisher on the wall.

With strength born of pure terror, Alexander yanked the extinguisher from its bracket and swung it like a club. The creature's head exploded in a spray of dark fluid and orange goo. It collapsed to the floor, twitching once, then lay still.

Alexander stood in the doorway, breathing hard, the fire extinguisher slick with blood in his hands. The corridor stretched before him like a scene from a nightmare—bodies crumpled against walls, dark stains spreading across floral carpet, more of those things shambling towards him with that terrible, uneven gait. And in the distance, echoing through the hotel, more screeches.

He thought of Magsy holding up two fingers. Two sleeps, Daddy.

He tightened his grip on the fire extinguisher and stepped into the corridor.

4

The Night Everything Changed

Spotify Apple Music Amazon Music

Track: THE SCREECHER

Alexander stepped back into the darkness of his hotel room, his heart hammering against his ribs, the fire extinguisher still clutched in his hands. He could hear them moving in the corridor—the shuffling footsteps, the wet moaning, the occasional screech that made his teeth ache. Doors were being torn open, furniture smashed, people screaming.

He had to get out. Had to escape. Had to get home to Ailsa and Magsy.

But first, he needed to know what he was really dealing with.

Moving as quietly as possible, Alexander approached his splintered doorway. The creature he'd killed lay in a heap just outside, orange fluids pooling around it. Very carefully, he peered around the shattered doorframe and into the corridor.

What he saw would be burned into his memory forever.

The corridor was a scene from hell. Bodies lay scattered across the carpet. More creatures shambled aimlessly, their movements jerky and unnatural. One of them wore a hotel uniform like the one he'd just killed, its face vacant, gaunt and unmistakably grey.

At the far end of the corridor, something large moved in the shadows. Eight feet tall, massively built, throwing furniture aside like it was made of paper.

The hallway was dimly lit by flickering emergency lighting that cast everything in a sickly yellow-green glow. Red stains spread across the carpet, dark in the emergency lighting but unmistakably blood.

And standing a little further down the corridor, their backs to him, were figures that looked human.

The closest one wore a hotel uniform—a porter, maybe, or maintenance staff. But the skin visible on his neck and hands was grey, mottled like meat left out too long. Dark orange veins spider-webbed across the surface, pulsing with a faint, sickly luminescence. His breathing was laboured, mechanical, like a broken engine trying to turn over.

As Alexander watched, frozen in horror, the figure slowly began to turn. It was another one of those screeching creatures. The face was worse than the body. The eyes were clouded, lifeless, like the eyes of a fish that had been dead for days. The skin was the same mottled grey, stretched tight over the skull. The mouth hung open, revealing blackened teeth and a tongue that looked swollen and wrong.

The creature's head tilted, as if listening. Its clouded eyes seemed to look right at Alexander. Alexander noted the creature had no ears—they were hanging lifelessly off either side of its head.

For a moment, neither moved. Alexander held his breath, not daring to blink, not daring to breathe, praying that the thing couldn't see him, couldn't hear his hammering heart.

Then the creature was in front of him. It moved unnaturally fast and accurately. It grabbed Alexander by the shirt with hands that were cold and impossibly strong, pulling him close. Up close, the smell was overwhelming—the sweet, sickly smell of decay mixed with something chemical, something wrong. The creature's mouth opened again, that horrible throat distending, and Alexander knew with absolute certainty that if it made that sound again at this distance, it would kill him. The sound would literally shake his brain apart.

With strength born of pure terror, Alexander broke free from its grip and dove for the extinguisher. The creature turned, mouth opening, and Alexander swung the extinguisher like a club.

It connected with the side of the thing's head with a wet crunch. The creature stumbled, momentarily stunned, but then it started to straighten up again, that horrible mouth opening.

Alexander panicked. He brought the extinguisher down again and again, smashing at the creature's skull with desperate, terrified strength. Blood—if it could be called blood—sprayed across the walls and carpet.

Finally, after what felt like an eternity but was probably only seconds, the creature collapsed.

Alexander stood over it, breathing heavily, the fire extinguisher raised and ready. The thing didn't move. Dark orange fluid pooled around its head, spreading across the carpet.

What he saw next when he looked up made him want to weep, curl up in a ball and hide forever.

The hallway was full of them. Bodies that had been lying still were now standing, moving with that same jerky, unnatural gait. He turned and began to move towards the staircase, but something made him stop with horror.

Alexander recognised one of the creatures shuffling towards him.

Sarah from the conference. Her name badge still hung from her torn blouse, but her face was grey, lifeless. She saw Alexander and let out a low moan, starting toward him with that horrible shambling walk.

"Sarah?" Alexander whispered, horrified.

She didn't respond to her name. She just kept coming, mouth hanging open, hands reaching.

Alexander heard shuffling behind him and turned to see James emerging from a doorway. Half his face was torn away, revealing muscle and bone underneath. The same grey skin, but noticeably no orange veins. He moaned and reached for Alexander with blood-stained hands.

Alexander was trapped between them. Sarah in front, James behind, and more of those things emerging from rooms all along the corridor.

He looked at Sarah—yesterday she'd been laughing at dinner, talking about her kids, making jokes about boring conferences. Now she was this… this thing, reaching for him with grey hands, moaning with a voice that was no longer human.

Alexander closed his eyes and swung the fire extinguisher.

It connected with Sarah's head with a sickening crunch. She dropped instantly, her body crumpling to the carpet.

Alexander stared at her body, at the blood spreading around her head, at the name badge that still read "Sarah Chen - Construction Safety Board."

"I'm sorry," he whispered, his voice breaking. "I'm so sorry."

James's moan snapped him back to reality. Alexander turned and swung again. James fell.

Alexander stood in the corridor, surrounded by the bodies of people he'd been having dinner with just hours ago. His hands shook as he gripped the fire extinguisher. His mind screamed at him that this couldn't be real, that this had to be a nightmare, that he would wake up any moment in his bed and laugh at the absurdity of it all.

But the weight of the fire extinguisher in his hands was real. The smell of blood and decay was real. The moaning echoing from the stairwell was real.

He looked down at James's body. James, who'd been so friendly in the lift. James, who'd told that story about preventing an accident at a chemical plant. James, who'd had a wife and kids waiting for him at home.

"I'm sorry," Alexander whispered. "I'm sorry I couldn't save you. I'm sorry I had to… I'm sorry."

But James was beyond hearing. Beyond caring. Whatever had made James human was gone, replaced by something that only looked like him.

Alexander thought about James's family. Did they know yet? Were they trying to call him, wondering why he wasn't answering? Or had this infection reached them too?

He thought about all the families of all the people in this hotel. Hundreds of people, all with loved ones waiting for them to come home. All those phone calls that would never be answered. All those promises that would never be kept.

Except his. He would keep his promise. He would get home to Ailsa and Magsy.

He had to.

More of them were coming. He could hear them, shuffling and moaning, drawn by the sounds of the fight.

Alexander wiped his eyes—when had he started crying?—and steeled himself.

"Two sleeps," he whispered to himself, like a mantra. "I promised."

He started moving towards the stairwell, stepping over bodies, trying not to look at their faces, trying not to think about who they had been just hours ago.

At the stairwell door, he paused, listening. Sounds of chaos from below—screaming, crashing, more of those inhuman screeches.

Alexander took a deep breath and opened the door.

He had to get out of this hotel. He had to get home. He had promised Magsy two sleeps, and he was going to keep that promise, no matter what.

Even if the world had ended while he slept.

Even if everyone around him had turned into monsters.

Even if he had to fight his way through hell itself.

Two sleeps. He'd promised.

And Alexander McRae always kept his promises.

The stairwell was a concrete and metal throat leading down into darkness. Emergency lighting flickered at irregular intervals, casting shadows that seemed to move with malevolent purpose. Alexander entered cautiously, fire extinguisher held ready, every sense straining for danger.

His hands were still shaking from what he'd just done. Sarah's face kept flashing in his mind—not the grey, dead thing she'd become, but Sarah from dinner. Sarah laughing at a joke. Sarah talking about her kids with such obvious love and pride.

"My boys are everything to me," she'd said. "Jack is seven, loves football. Ben is five, obsessed with dinosaurs. They're the reason I do this job—to make workplaces safer so other kids don't lose their parents to preventable accidents."

And now her boys had lost their mother anyway. Not to a workplace accident, but to something far worse. Something that had turned her into a monster that Alexander had been forced to kill.

He'd killed her. He'd smashed her skull with a fire extinguisher. The sound of it, the feel of it, the way she'd dropped—it was all burned into his memory.

"I'm sorry," he whispered to the empty stairwell. "I'm so sorry, Sarah."

But sorry didn't change anything. Sorry didn't bring her back. Sorry didn't help her boys, who were probably orphans now, or worse.

Alexander pushed the thoughts away. He couldn't afford to break down. Not now. Not when he still had so far to go.

He had to focus. Had to survive. Had to get home to Ailsa and Magsy.

Two sleeps. He'd promised two sleeps.

From below came the cacophony of the hotel's death throes—screaming, crashing, the wet sounds of violence, and underneath it all, that constant chorus of moaning that seemed to vibrate through the very structure of the building.

Alexander started down the stairs, moving as quietly as possible. His mind was still reeling, trying to process what he'd seen, what he'd done. Sarah's face kept flashing in his memory—first as she'd been at dinner, laughing and alive, then as she'd been in the corridor, grey and dead and reaching for him with those horrible hands.

He'd killed her. He'd killed James. He'd killed that thing in the doorway.

No, a voice in his head insisted. They were already dead. You just… stopped them from moving.

But the distinction felt meaningless when he could still feel the impact of the fire extinguisher connecting with Sarah's skull, could still see the way her body had crumpled, could still hear the sound—

A whimper from the landing below snapped him back to the present.

Alexander froze, listening. The whimper came again, definitely human, definitely alive.

He descended carefully to the landing between floors and found a man pressed against the wall, trembling. Frank—the man from dinner, the one who'd complained about phone signal. He was still in his pyjamas, his face pale with terror, his eyes wide and unfocused.

"Don't go down there," Frank whispered, his voice barely audible. "They're everywhere."

Alexander crouched beside him, keeping his voice low. "What happened? What are those things?"

"I don't know." Frank's eyes were wide, unfocused, seeing horrors that Alexander could only imagine. "People just… changed. Started attacking others. The screaming…" He trailed off, shaking his head.

A loud crash echoed up from the lobby, followed by more screaming.

"My wife," Frank continued, his voice breaking. "She came with me. I think she was one of the first. She tried to… to bite me." He showed Alexander scratches on his arm—not bites, just scratches from fingernails, but deep enough to bleed.

"Bite you?" Alexander felt his stomach turn. The scratches looked deep—angry red lines disappearing under Frank's sleeve. Was that enough? Could it spread that way?

"We need to get out of here," he said, not answering his own question.

"The lobby's full of them. And there's something else down there. Something big."

As if summoned by his words, a deep roar echoed up the stairwell. It was different from the moaning, different from the screeches. This was something primal, something that spoke to the most ancient parts of the human brain that remembered when humans were prey.

Both men froze, not daring to breathe.

Heavy footsteps started climbing the stairs towards them. THUD. THUD. THUD. Each step shook the metal stairs, sending vibrations through the walls.

"What the hell is that?" Alexander whispered.

"I told you," Frank said, his voice tight with terror. "Something big."

The footsteps were getting louder, closer. Whatever was coming was massive, taking the stairs three at a time, moving with terrifying speed for something so large.

"Is there another way out?" Alexander asked urgently.

"Fire exit. Third floor. But it's alarmed."

"I don't think anyone's going to complain about a fire alarm right now."

They started climbing back up the stairs, moving as quickly and quietly as they could. Behind them, something massive rounded the corner below.

Alexander glanced back and his blood turned to ice.

It was huge—eight feet tall at least, with shoulders so broad it had to turn sideways to fit in the stairwell. It wore the torn remains of what might have been a hotel security uniform, the fabric stretched to bursting over impossibly muscled limbs. The skin was the same mottled grey as the others, but the orange veins were thicker, pulsing with a brighter, more intense light. On its forehead was a glowing orange mark, like a target burned into its skull. The face was barely recognisable as human—the jaw had distended, the eyes had sunk deep into the skull, and the mouth was full of teeth that looked too large, too sharp.

It saw them and let out that bone-shaking roar.

The sound was physical, a wave of pressure that Alexander felt in his chest. The Bullseye started charging up the stairs, taking them three at a time, moving with impossible speed for something so massive.

"Move! MOVE!" Alexander shouted, all pretence of stealth abandoned.

They reached the third floor and Alexander yanked open the fire exit door. Alarm bells immediately started ringing throughout the hotel, adding to the chaos.

They burst out onto a metal fire escape overlooking the back alley. The view below showed more chaos—overturned bins, abandoned cars, bodies in the street. But it was quieter than the front of the hotel, and right now, quiet meant safe.

Behind them, the fire exit door exploded outward as the massive creature smashed through. It filled the doorway, too big to easily fit, roaring in frustration as it swiped at them with arms as thick as tree trunks.

"Down! Go down!" Alexander shouted.

They clattered down the metal stairs as fast as they could, the fire escape groaning and shaking under their weight. Behind them, the creature forced itself through the doorway and started pursuing them, each step making the entire structure shudder.

Alexander and Frank reached the bottom and dropped into the alley. The pavement was slick with something Alexander didn't want to identify.

"My car," Frank gasped, breathless. "It's in the hotel car park…"

"Forget the car. We go on foot."

Above them, the huge, hulking creature had reached the bottom of the fire escape. It didn't bother with the ladder—it simply jumped, landing in the alley with a crash that cracked the pavement and sent a shockwave through Alexander's bones.

Up close, the thing was even more terrifying. It stood at least eight feet tall, its massive frame blocking out the streetlight behind it. The orange veins pulsed with an almost hypnotic rhythm, and Alexander could see now that they weren't just on the surface—they seemed to writhe beneath the translucent grey skin, like molten fire trapped under flesh. On its forehead, the orange pulsing formed a perfect bullseye mark, glowing brightly like a target carved into its skull.

The Bullseye's eyes fixed on them, and Alexander saw something in those clouded depths that was worse than mindless hunger. There was intelligence there. Purpose. This thing wasn't just a mindless monster—it was hunting them.

"This way!" Alexander grabbed Frank's arm and they ran towards the mouth of the alley.

The Bullseye gave chase, but its size worked against it in the narrow space. It had to turn sideways to fit between the buildings, slowing it down just enough for them to reach the street.

They emerged onto the main road and Alexander's heart sank.

The street was a river of the dead.

5

The Streets of Loonswrath

Spotify Apple Music Amazon Music

Track: BULLSEYES' PURSUIT

The scene was apocalyptic. Crashed cars everywhere, fires burning, bodies scattered across the pavement. And among the wreckage, dozens of those shambling figures—the Aimless, Alexander found himself thinking, because they seemed to wander without purpose until they saw something living.

Several of them noticed Alexander and Frank and started shambling towards them with that horrible, jerky gait.

"Stay close to me," Alexander said, gripping the fire extinguisher tighter.

They moved carefully between abandoned cars, trying to avoid the creatures. Behind them, the massive Bullseye crashed out of the alley, its roar attracting every infected in the area. They all turned towards the sound, then towards Alexander and Frank.

"There's too many of them!" Frank's voice was rising with panic.

Alexander spotted a narrow side street between two shops. "There! Between those buildings!"

They ran for it, but Frank stumbled, his age and terror catching up with him. A former shop clerk with dark grey skin and half her face hanging off lunged at Frank.

Alexander swung the fire extinguisher and missed, the momentum nearly pulling him off balance. He growled in frustration and swung again, this time connecting with the clerk's head. She crumpled to the ground.

But more were closing in from all directions, drawn by the commotion. The Bullseye was getting closer, each of its footsteps shaking the ground.

"Frank, this way!" Alexander shouted.

They dodged between abandoned cars, Frank breathing heavily, struggling to keep up. Alexander saw a gap between two crashed vehicles—just wide enough to squeeze through.

"Through here!"

Alexander squeezed through first, the metal scraping against his shoulders. Frank followed but got stuck halfway, his larger frame wedged between the vehicles.

"I can't… I'm stuck…" Frank's voice was tight with panic.

The Aimless were closing in. Alexander grabbed Frank's arms, trying to pull him through. "Frank, calm down, I'll help you…"

Frank panicked, struggling violently, which only wedged him tighter. "Get me out! GET ME OUT!"

Then, suddenly, massive hands grabbed Frank from behind.

The Bullseye had caught up.

"Don't let it take me!" Frank screamed, his eyes wide with terror. "ALEX!"

Alexander tried to hold on, pulling with all his strength, but the creature was impossibly strong. He could feel Frank's hands slipping from his grip, could see the terror in the older man's eyes.

"I've got you, Frank! I've got—"

With a sickening sound that Alexander would hear in his nightmares for the rest of his life, the Bullseye tore Frank in half.

Blood sprayed everywhere, hot and sticky, covering Alexander's face and hands. Frank's screams cut off instantly, replaced by a wet, gurgling sound. The Bullseye held Frank's remains for a moment, then threw them aside like rubbish and let out a deafening roar of triumph.

Alexander stared in absolute horror, frozen, his mind unable to process what he'd just witnessed. Frank had been alive, had been talking, had been a person, and now he was… he was…

The Bullseye turned its attention to Alexander, those clouded eyes fixing on him with terrible purpose.

Alexander snapped out of his shock and ran. Pure terror drove him now, his mind blank except for one thought: survive. He ran towards a line of trees at the edge of town, his legs pumping, his lungs burning, Frank's blood still warm on his face.

Behind him, the Bullseye gave chase, and Alexander could hear it gaining, could hear its heavy footsteps getting closer, could hear its laboured breathing like a broken engine.

He reached the trees and crashed into the forest, branches tearing at his clothes and skin. Behind him, the Bullseye smashed through smaller trees like they were twigs, roaring with rage and hunger.

Alexander ran blindly through the forest, no idea where he was going, just trying to escape the image of Frank being torn apart, trying to escape the sound of that roar, trying to escape the feeling of Frank's hands slipping from his grip.

The Bullseye was fast—impossibly fast for something so large. Its roars were getting louder, not fainter. It was gaining.

Desperate, Alexander started weaving between trees, using them as obstacles. He ducked around a large oak just as the Bullseye charged past, missing him by inches. The displaced air from its passage nearly knocked him off his feet.

Alexander changed direction, zigzagging through the forest, using every trick he could think of. The Bullseye roared in frustration, trying to follow but struggling with the tight spaces between trees.

Alexander spotted a cluster of dense pines and dove into them, crawling on hands and knees through the low branches. Behind him, the Bullseye tried to follow but was too big—it got tangled in the branches, roaring and thrashing.

Alexander emerged on the other side and kept running, his lungs burning, his legs screaming in protest. He could hear the creature breaking free, could hear it crashing through the undergrowth behind him.

In the darkness, Alexander didn't see the hole ahead—an old wartime bunker entrance, partially collapsed and overgrown with vegetation. His foot hit empty air and suddenly he was falling, tumbling down about eight feet into darkness.

He landed hard on an earthen floor, his ankle twisting beneath him with a sharp crack of pain. "Ahhhh! Fuck!" The cry escaped before he could stop it, and Alexander immediately clamped his hand over his mouth, realising his mistake.

He looked around frantically. He was in what appeared to be an old concrete bunker, mostly buried and forgotten. There was just enough space for him to sit up, and the air smelled of damp earth and decay.

Above him, heavy footsteps approached. The Bullseye crashed through the trees nearby, its massive silhouette blocking out the sky as it stopped directly above the bunker entrance.

Alexander pressed himself against the concrete wall, trying to make himself invisible, trying not to breathe, trying not to exist. His ankle throbbed with pain, but he didn't dare move.

The Bullseye sniffed the air, its head turning left and right. Alexander could see its massive form through the opening, could see the orange veins pulsing in the dim light, could hear its laboured breathing.

After what felt like an eternity, the Bullseye let out a frustrated roar and continued running past the bunker, its footsteps fading into the distance.

Alexander waited several more minutes before daring to move. He examined his ankle in the dim light filtering down from above—it was already swelling badly, the pain sharp and constant.

"At least I'm hidden," he whispered to himself, his voice shaking.

He sat back against the concrete wall, exhausted, terrified, covered in Frank's blood. His hands were shaking so badly he could barely hold his phone. He checked it—still no signal, battery down to 30%.

He looked at the wallpaper photo of Ailsa and Magsy, and something broke inside him. The tears came then, hot and unstoppable, his body shaking with silent sobs.

Frank was dead. Sarah was dead. James was dead. Frank's wife, whose name he'd never learned. Everyone at the hotel was probably dead. The world had ended while he slept, and he was alone in a hole in the ground, injured and terrified and so far from home.

"I'm going to find a way home to you," he whispered to the photo, his voice breaking. "I promise. I'm going to keep my promise."

Two sleeps. He'd promised two sleeps.

It had already been that, and he was no closer to home. But he was alive. Somehow, impossibly, he was alive.

And as long as he was alive, he could keep moving. He could keep trying. He could keep his promise.

Alexander closed his eyes, trying to rest his injured ankle, trying to push away the image of Frank being torn apart, trying to hold onto the memory of Magsy's laugh and Ailsa's smile.

Hours passed. Dawn started to break above, pale light filtering down into the bunker. Another day. Another chance. Another promise to keep.

Alexander opened his eyes. His ankle was worse—swollen and throbbing—but he couldn't stay here. He had to keep moving. Had to get north. Had to get home.

"Two sleeps," he whispered to himself, like a prayer, like a promise, like the only truth left in a world gone mad.

He grabbed the fire extinguisher—still clutched in his hand even after everything—and used it as a makeshift crutch. Slowly, painfully, he climbed out of the bunker and into the morning light.

The forest was eerily quiet. No birdsong, no rustling of small animals. Just silence.

Alexander picked a direction and started limping through the trees, using the fire extinguisher for support. Every step sent pain shooting up his leg, but he kept moving.

He had to keep moving.

He had promised.

6

The Forest

Spotify Apple Music Amazon Music

Track: REFLECTIONS IN THE SHADOWS

The morning sun filtered through the trees in shafts of golden light, beautiful and serene, completely at odds with the horror Alexander had just survived. He limped through the forest, each step a fresh agony, his mind still reeling from the night's events.

Frank's face kept appearing in his mind. Not the moment of his death—Alexander couldn't bear to think about that—but earlier moments. Frank at dinner, complaining about phone signal. Frank in the stairwell, terrified but still human. Frank's last words: "Don't let it take me."

But Alexander had let it take him. Had felt Frank's hands slip from his grip. Had watched, helpless, as that monster tore him apart.

"I'm sorry," Alexander whispered to the empty forest. "I'm so sorry, Frank."

He stopped to rest against a tree, his ankle screaming in protest. He needed to assess his situation, make a plan. He couldn't just wander aimlessly through the forest.

Alexander pulled out his phone and turned it on briefly—25% battery remaining. No signal. He switched it off to conserve power.

He pushed off from the tree and continued limping, using the fire extinguisher as a crutch. The forest stretched endlessly before him, a maze of trees and shadows that all looked the same.

Hours passed. The sun climbed higher. Alexander's throat grew dry, his lips cracked. He needed water.

As if in answer to his prayers, he heard it—the sound of running water. Alexander followed the sound until he found a small stream, clear and cold. He fell to his knees and drank handful after handful, the water so cold it made his teeth ache but tasting better than anything he'd ever had.

He splashed water on his face and neck, washing away the sweat and grime. His reflection in the water showed a man he barely recognised—stubble covering his jaw, dark circles under his eyes, a hardness in his expression that hadn't been there before.

Three days ago, he'd been Alexander McRae, safety consultant, husband, father. A man who worried about making the ferry on time and whether Magsy was eating enough vegetables.

He stopped to rest against a tree, his ankle screaming in protest. He needed to assess his situation, make a plan. He couldn't just wander aimlessly through the forest.

Alexander pulled out his phone and turned it on briefly—25% battery remaining. No signal. He switched it off to conserve power.

He pushed off from the tree and continued limping, using the fire extinguisher as a crutch. The forest stretched endlessly before him, a maze of trees and shadows that all looked the same.

Hours passed. The sun climbed higher. Alexander's throat grew dry, his lips cracked. He needed water.

As if in answer to his prayers, he heard it—the sound of running water. Alexander followed the sound until he found a small stream, clear and cold. He fell to his knees and drank handful after handful, the water so cold it made his teeth ache but tasting better than anything he'd ever had.

He splashed water on his face and neck, washing away the sweat and grime. His reflection in the water showed a man he barely recognised—stubble covering his jaw, dark circles under his eyes, a hardness in his expression that hadn't been there before.

Three days ago, he'd been Alexander McRae, safety consultant, husband, father. A man who worried about making the ferry on time and whether Magsy was eating enough vegetables.

Now he was… what? A survivor? A killer? A man who'd watched people die and somehow found a way to keep going?

He didn't know anymore. All he knew was that he had to keep moving.

As Alexander walked, his mind drifted to Ailsa. What was she doing right now? Did she know something was wrong? The phones had been down for two days now—she must have tried to call him, must be worried sick.

Or maybe the infection had spread to the islands. Maybe right now, Ailsa was fighting for her life, trying to protect Magsy from those things. Maybe—

No. He couldn't think like that. The islands were safe. They had to be safe. There was an ocean between them and the mainland. The infection couldn't cross water.

Could it?

Alexander pushed the thought away. He couldn't afford to think like that. He had to believe Ailsa and Magsy were safe, waiting for him. Magsy counting on her little fingers: "One sleep… two sleeps… where's Daddy?"

In the distance, Alexander heard something that made him freeze—the low moan of an Aimless. He pressed himself against a tree, listening. The sound was getting closer, shambling through the undergrowth with that distinctive jerky gait.

Alexander forced himself to move faster despite the pain, putting distance between himself and the sound. His breath came in ragged gasps, his vision swimming with exhaustion and pain.

Then, through the trees ahead, he saw something that made his heart leap: a roof. A chimney with smoke rising from it.

"Thank God," he whispered, his voice hoarse.

Alexander pushed through the last of the trees towards the cottage, hope surging through him for the first time since the nightmare began.

The cottage was small and old, built of grey stone with a slate roof. Warm light glowed from the windows, and the smoke rising from the chimney spoke of life, of normalcy, of safety. It looked like something from a postcard, a piece of the world that had existed before everything went wrong.

Alexander limped to the front door, exhausted and desperate. He could hear the Aimless moaning somewhere behind him in the forest, getting closer.

He tried the door handle—locked.

He knocked softly, trying not to make too much noise.

No answer.

The moaning was getting closer. Alexander could hear branches breaking as the Aimless shambled through the undergrowth.

He knocked harder, more urgently.

Still no answer, but he could hear movement inside—footsteps, the creak of floorboards.

Desperate now, Alexander tried the handle again and pushed. The door opened—it hadn't been properly locked after all.

Alexander quickly slipped inside and closed the door behind him, leaning against it with relief. He was safe. He was—

"Who the hell are you?! Get out of my house!"

Alexander looked up to find an old man in his eighties—Angus—coming down the corridor, shouting and pointing a double-barrelled shotgun directly at his chest.

7

Sanctuary and Loss

Spotify Apple Music Amazon Music

Track: FINDING SANCTUARY

Alexander dropped the fire extinguisher and raised his hands. "Please! Don't shoot! I'm not one of them!"

"Show me your arms. Roll up your sleeves." Angus's voice was hard, his hands steady on the shotgun despite his age.

"What?"

"Do it! Show me you haven't been bitten!"

Alexander quickly rolled up his sleeves, showing his arms, then his neck, turning so Angus could see. "Look—no bites, no scratches. I'm clean. I'm human."

An elderly woman—Morag—appeared behind Angus, her face drawn and haunted. "He looks alright, Angus."

"Turn around. Lift your shirt."

Alexander complied, showing his back. "Please, there are things in the forest. I'm trying to get home to my family. My name is Alexander McRae. I'm from the Isle of Druichmachon. I was at a conference at the Grand Caledonian when… when everything went wrong."

Angus slowly lowered the shotgun, though he kept it within reach. "Aye, we know about the things."

"You know?"

Morag's voice broke. "Our son Jamie came home yesterday morning. Something was wrong with him. Grey skin, those orange veins…"

"He tried to bite Morag," Angus said grimly. "I had to… I had to put him down."

Alexander saw the pain in their faces, the fresh grief that mirrored his own horror. "I'm so sorry."

"He was twenty-eight years old," Morag continued, tears in her eyes. "Worked at the power station near Veilwreck Bay. Our daughter Aileen lives in Cullen Bay—we haven't heard from her since this started."

"I was at the conference," Alexander said. "I woke up to chaos. I saw… I saw things I can't unsee. People who looked dead just… stood back up. They came back."

Morag nodded sadly. "Like Jamie. He died in our living room, then got back up. Angus had to shoot him. Had to shoot our own son."

"How many did you see?" Angus asked.

"Hundreds. The whole town was overrun. There are different types—some just wander and moan, others make this horrible screeching sound. And there are big ones. Really big ones. Eight feet tall, incredibly strong."

Angus and Morag exchanged worried glances.

"What about Aileen?" Morag asked, her voice trembling. "What if it's reached Cullen Bay?"

"We can't reach her," Angus said. "No phones, no way to know if she's safe."

"I need to get home," Alexander said, his voice desperate. "I need to find a way. Is there a ferry port or airport around here?"

"There's the ferry port in Belnahouthie," Morag said. "That's about twenty-two miles north of here, but I'm not sure if they'll still be running. Not if this has spread north too."

"Do you have a car? Any way for me to get there?"

Angus shook his head. "We're too old to drive, lad. Haven't had a car in five years. Besides, the roads might not be safe."

"I promised my daughter I'd be home in two sleeps." Alexander's voice cracked. "She's only two years old."

His legs gave out. He slid down the door to sit on the floor, the exhaustion and pain finally overwhelming him. Frank's blood was still on his clothes, still on his hands.

Morag's heart broke seeing his despair. "Angus, help him to the kitchen. He's hurt."

The kitchen was cosy and old-fashioned, the kind of room that spoke of decades of family meals and quiet evenings. Morag put the kettle on while Angus seated Alexander at the table, the shotgun still within reach.

"Let me look at that ankle," Morag said gently.

She examined Alexander's swollen ankle with practised hands. "It's badly sprained. I'll get you some ice."

"We've been barricaded in here since yesterday," Angus said. "Heard screaming in the night, gunshots from other houses."

"How many types have you seen?" Alexander asked.

"Just the one—Jamie. But we heard different sounds. Roaring and that horrible screeching."

"The screechers are the worst. The sound they make… it goes right through you. And the big ones—I saw one tear a man in half. Just… tore him apart like he was made of paper."

Morag wrapped ice in a tea towel and handed it to Alexander. "Our phone's been dead since yesterday. No television, no radio. We don't know what's happening out there."

"Same with my mobile. No signal anywhere. The whole communications network is down."

Alexander applied the ice, wincing. "I have to get home. My family doesn't know what's happening. What if this spreads to the islands?"

"It seems to be spreading fast, son," Angus said grimly. "But hopefully it's contained to the mainland. There's an ocean between here and the other islands. They should be safe."

"But you can't walk twenty-two miles on that ankle today, dear," Morag said firmly. "Look at the state of you."

Alexander looked down at himself—torn clothes, covered in dirt and blood. Frank's blood, he realised with a sick feeling.

"I have to try."

"You'll collapse before you make it five miles," Morag said. "Stay the night. Rest that ankle, get cleaned up. You'll have a better chance tomorrow."

"She's right, lad," Angus agreed. "You're no good to your family if you die on the road."

Alexander struggled with the decision. Every hour he waited was another hour away from Ailsa and Magsy, another hour they spent not knowing if he was alive or dead.

"Every hour I wait…"

"One night," Morag said gently. "Let me run you a bath, get you some of Jamie's clothes. You need to be strong for the journey ahead."

Alexander finally nodded, too exhausted to argue. "Alright. One night."

8

The Bath

Spotify Apple Music Amazon Music

Track: SHATTERED HOPE

The bathroom was small but clean, the tub already filling with hot water. Steam rose in the air, and for a moment, Alexander just stood there, staring at the simple miracle of hot running water.

After everything he'd been through—the hotel, Frank, the forest—this ordinary bathroom felt like a sanctuary.

He caught sight of himself in the mirror above the sink and barely recognised the man staring back. His face was gaunt, covered in dirt and scratches. His eyes were hollow, haunted. There was blood on his collar, dried and brown. Frank's blood. Or maybe Sarah's. Or James's. He couldn't remember anymore.

Alexander turned away from his reflection and began to undress. His clothes were ruined—torn, stained, reeking of sweat and fear and death. He dropped them in a pile on the floor, each piece a reminder of what he'd survived.

The conference badge was still clipped to his shirt. "Alexander McRae, Safety Consultant, Druichmachon." He stared at it for a long moment. That man—the safety consultant who worried about proper evacuation procedures and fire extinguisher placement—felt like someone from another lifetime.

He sat on the edge of the tub, staring at his hands. They were still stained with blood—Frank's blood, Sarah's blood, James's blood. The blood of people who had been alive just hours ago.

Alexander picked up a bar of soap and started scrubbing his hands vigorously. The water around his hands turned red, then pink, then cloudy. He scrubbed harder, trying to get the blood from under his fingernails, from the creases in his palms, from the lines on his wrists.

But he could still see it. Still smell it. Still feel Frank's hands slipping from his grip.

The memory hit him like a physical blow. Frank's terrified face. The sound of his screams. The wet, tearing sounds as that thing pulled him apart. And Alexander had run. Had left him there. Had saved himself.

"I'm sorry," he whispered to his hands. "Frank, I'm so sorry."

But sorry didn't bring Frank back. Sorry didn't change what had happened. Sorry was just a word, meaningless in the face of what he'd done—what he'd failed to do.

Alexander's breathing became ragged. The reality of what he'd seen, what he'd done, suddenly hit him all at once. The dam he'd built to hold back the horror finally broke.

His face crumpled. He started to cry—quietly at first, then building to deep, body-shaking sobs. He covered his face with his wet hands, not caring that they were still stained with blood.

"Sarah… I'm sorry… I'm so sorry…"

He thought of Sarah laughing at dinner, then saw Sarah's grey face, her mottled hands reaching for him. He'd killed her. He'd smashed her skull with a fire extinguisher.

The sound it had made. The way her body had crumpled. The way her eyes—those dead, orange-veined eyes—had finally gone still.

Alexander sobbed harder. "She had two boys waiting for her. A husband. How…"

What would happen to them now? Did they know their mother was dead? Were they safe, or had the infection reached them too? Were they alone, scared, calling for a mother who would never answer?

And James. Cheerful, friendly James who'd sat beside him during the keynote, making jokes about section 4.2.1. James, whose skull he'd crushed trying to save himself.

He slid down into the bath until the water reached his chin. The heat was almost painful against his cold skin, but he welcomed it. Anything to feel something other than the crushing weight of guilt and grief.

He stared at the ceiling, tears streaming down his face, mixing with the bathwater. The ceiling was old, with cracks in the plaster that formed patterns like rivers on a map. Alexander traced them with his eyes, trying to focus on anything other than the memories.

But they kept coming. The hotel. The broken doorframe. The screecher. Frank. The running. The forest. The cottage. Angus's shotgun pointed at his chest.

And through it all, one thought kept circling: What if I can't make it home? What if I never see them again?

Alexander pulled his phone from the floor beside the tub—he'd been carrying it in his pocket through everything. The screen was cracked now, a spiderweb of fractures across Ailsa and Magsy's faces, but it still worked. He pressed the button and the screen lit up: 18% battery remaining.

He looked at the wallpaper photo. Ailsa and Magsy on the beach, building sandcastles. Magsy was laughing, her face scrunched up with joy, sand in her hair. Ailsa was looking at the camera—at him—with that smile that had captured his heart twenty years ago.

They looked so happy. So safe. So impossibly far away.

"Daddy's trying to come home, sweetheart," Alexander whispered to Magsy's image, his voice breaking. "Daddy's trying so hard."

But was he? Or was he just surviving, running from one disaster to the next, getting further from home with each step?

Belnahouthie was still twenty-two miles away. Twenty-two miles through infected territory, with a sprained ankle and no real weapons. Even if he made it to the ferry, would it still be running? Would the other islands still be safe?

What if he got there and found the ferry abandoned, the dock overrun with those things? What if he made it all the way home only to find Druichmachon infected, Ailsa and Magsy already gone?

"No," Alexander said aloud, his voice echoing in the small bathroom. "No. They're safe. They have to be safe."

He held the phone to his chest and cried until there were no tears left, until his body was empty of everything except the determination to keep going.

Finally, he wiped his eyes and took a deep breath. "I'm getting home. I promised two sleeps."

But it had already been more than two sleeps. Three days since he'd left Druichmachon. Three days that felt like a lifetime. Magsy would have stopped counting by now. She'd think Daddy had broken his promise.

"I'm coming, baby girl," he whispered. "Daddy's coming home."

He started washing properly, cleaning off the dirt and grime and blood of the last day. The water turned dark, cloudy with filth. Alexander had to drain and refill the tub twice before he felt clean.

As he washed, he took inventory of his injuries. The sprained ankle was the worst—swollen and purple, painful to touch. There were cuts and scratches all over his arms and legs from running through the forest. Bruises on his ribs from where he'd fallen. His hands were raw from gripping the fire extinguisher.

But he was alive. Battered and traumatised and barely holding together, but alive.

He thought about the people who weren't. Frank. Sarah. James. The hotel staff. The people on the streets of Loonswrath. How many had died in the last day? Hundreds? Thousands?

And for what? What had caused this? Some kind of disease? A biological weapon? An accident?

Alexander thought about the speed of the infection. Yesterday morning, people had been normal. By nighttime, they were monsters. That wasn't natural. Diseases didn't work that fast.

Unless someone had made it that way.

The thought chilled him. If this was deliberate, if someone had released this on purpose, then the world he'd known was truly gone. This wasn't a disaster that could be contained, a crisis that could be managed. This was the end of everything.

But he couldn't think about that. Couldn't let himself spiral into despair. He had to focus on what he could control: getting home, getting to Ailsa and Magsy, keeping his promise.

One step at a time. One mile at a time. One day at a time.

When he was finally clean, Alexander pulled the plug and watched the dirty water drain away. He wished he could drain away the memories as easily, wash away the guilt and the horror and the fear.

But they remained, settling into his bones like a weight he'd carry forever.

He dried off with a towel Morag had left—soft and clean and smelling of lavender. Such a normal thing, a clean towel. It made him want to cry again.

Alexander looked at his reflection in the mirror, now clear of steam. The man looking back was cleaner but changed. Harder. There was something in his eyes that hadn't been there before—a darkness, a knowledge of what humans were capable of when pushed to the edge.

He thought about the man who'd left Druichmachon three days ago. That man had been soft, comfortable, used to a world that made sense. This man had killed. This man had watched people die. This man had survived when so many others hadn't.

This man would do whatever it took to get home.

He found the clothes Morag had left for him—jeans and a warm jumper that fitted well enough. Jamie's clothes. Clothes that belonged to a dead man, given to him by people who had lost their son.

Alexander held the jumper for a moment, feeling the weight of that gift. Morag and Angus had lost everything—their son, their old life, probably most of their friends and neighbours. And yet they'd taken him in, fed him, clothed him, given him shelter.

He would honour that gift. He would survive. He would make it home. And someday, when this was all over—if it was ever over—he would find a way to repay their kindness.

Alexander dressed slowly, his body protesting every movement. He was exhausted, physically and emotionally drained. But he was clean, warm, and safe. For now, that was enough.

He sat on the edge of the bed in the guest room, looking at his phone one more time. Battery at 16%. He turned it off to conserve power, but not before looking one more time at Ailsa and Magsy's faces.

"Two sleeps," he whispered. "I'm coming home."

Outside the window, he could hear birds singing. Normal, everyday birds, going about their lives as if the world hadn't ended. As if people weren't dying in the streets. As if everything was still the way it had always been.

Alexander envied them their ignorance.

He lay back on the bed, exhaustion finally catching up with him. For the first time in nearly twenty-four hours, he felt safe enough to close his eyes. Safe enough to let his guard down, just for a moment.

As he drifted off to sleep, his last thought was of home. Of the cottage by the harbour. Of Ailsa's smile and Magsy's laugh. Of the life he'd had before the world ended.

He would get back to that life. He had to.

Two sleeps. He'd promised.

And Alexander McRae always kept his promises.

Even if it killed him.

9

Morning After

Spotify Apple Music Amazon Music

Track: SANCTUARY LOST

Alexander woke to pale morning light filtering through the cottage window. His ankle throbbed—a dull, persistent ache that seemed to pulse in time with his heartbeat. He sat up carefully, wincing as he shifted his weight, and pulled back the blanket to examine the injury.

The swelling had gone down slightly overnight, though the bruising had deepened to an ugly purple-black that spread across his foot like spilled ink. He pressed gently around the bone, testing. Pain flared sharp and immediate, but nothing felt loose or grinding. Probably just a bad sprain, he told himself. He'd had worse playing football at school.

He could hear movement from the other room—the soft clink of crockery, the scrape of a chair. Morag must be up already. Alexander pulled on his trousers and shirt, then hobbled to the doorway, keeping his weight on his good foot.

The kitchen was warm, the fire already built up and crackling in the hearth. Morag stood at the counter, her back to him, working flour and water into dough with practiced efficiency. Angus sat at the table, his weathered hands wrapped around a chipped mug of tea. He looked up as Alexander entered.

"Morning, lad," Angus said. His voice was gruff but not unkind. "How's the ankle?"

"Better than yesterday," Alexander lied, lowering himself into a chair. The truth was it hurt like hell, but complaining wouldn't help anyone.

Morag glanced over her shoulder. "You should stay off it another day at least. Give it time to heal proper."

"I can't afford to wait," Alexander said. "I need to get back to the village. My family—"

"Your family will still be there tomorrow," Morag interrupted, turning back to her dough. "Dead men can't help anyone."

Angus took a slow sip of his tea, studying Alexander over the rim of the mug. "She's right, you know. Those things are still out there. More of them every day, seems like. You go limping through the forest on that ankle, you'll not make it half a mile."

Alexander wanted to argue, but he knew they were right. He'd barely made it here yesterday, and that was with adrenaline and terror driving him forward. In daylight, moving slowly, he'd be easy prey.

"Then what do I do?" he asked quietly.

"You rest," Morag said firmly. She shaped the dough into a round loaf and set it near the fire to rise. "You eat. You let that ankle mend. Then, when you're ready, we'll see about getting you home."

She moved to the larder and began pulling out ingredients—eggs, a bit of bacon wrapped in cloth, some withered potatoes. "Angus, stoke that fire up a bit more. I'll make us a proper breakfast."

Angus rose and added another log to the flames, then returned to his seat. For a while, the only sounds were the pop and hiss of the fire and Morag's quiet movements as she prepared the meal. Alexander sat in silence, his mind churning with worry. His mother would be frantic by now. His father would have organised search parties, probably. And Margaret—God, Margaret must think him dead.

"You're thinking too much," Angus observed. "I can see it on your face."

"How can I not?" Alexander replied. "Every hour I'm here is another hour they don't know if I'm alive or dead."

"Aye, that's hard," Angus admitted. "But you'll do them no good by getting yourself killed trying to rush back. Better to arrive late than not at all."

Morag cracked eggs into a pan, and soon the smell of frying bacon filled the cottage. Despite his anxiety, Alexander's stomach growled. He couldn't remember the last time he'd eaten—sometime yesterday morning, before everything went to hell.

"Tell me about your family," Morag said, not looking up from the stove. "What are they like?"

Alexander hesitated, then began to speak. He told them about his father, stern but fair, who ran the village shop. About his mother, who sang while she worked and always smelled of lavender soap. About Margaret, sharp-tongued and clever, who could argue theology with the minister and win. As he talked, some of the tension in his chest eased.

Morag listened in silence, occasionally nodding. When the food was ready, she brought it to the table—eggs and bacon, fried potatoes, thick slices of bread with butter. It was simple fare, but it looked like a feast to Alexander.

"Eat up," she said, settling into her own chair. "You'll need your strength."

They ate in companionable quiet for a few minutes. Then Angus set down his fork and pushed back from the table. "Wait here a moment," he said, and disappeared into the back room.

Alexander exchanged a glance with Morag, who merely shrugged and continued eating. A moment later, Angus returned, carrying something long and wooden. A walking stick, Alexander realised—beautifully crafted, with a smooth, worn handle and a sturdy shaft of dark wood.

Angus held it out to him. "This was my son's," he said quietly. "Jamie's. He made it himself, years back. Carved the handle and everything."

Alexander stared at the stick, not reaching for it. "I can't—"

"You can, and you will," Angus interrupted. "Jamie's gone. Has been for three years now. One of those things got him, out in the forest." His voice was steady, but Alexander could see the pain in his eyes. "This stick won't bring him back. But it might help keep you alive. And that's what he would have wanted."

Morag had stopped eating, her hands folded in her lap. She was looking at her husband with an expression Alexander couldn't quite read—grief and love and something like pride all mixed together.

"Take it, lad," Angus said again, pressing the stick into Alexander's hands. "It's a good, strong piece of ash. It'll take your weight off that ankle, and if you need to, well… it'll serve as a weapon too. Better than nothing."

Alexander's fingers closed around the smooth wood. It was heavier than he'd expected, solid and reassuring. The handle fit his palm perfectly, worn smooth by years of use. He could see the care that had gone into its making—the careful shaping, the attention to detail.

"Thank you," he said, his voice rough. "I don't know what to say."

"Don't say anything," Angus replied, returning to his seat. "Just make it count. Get yourself home to that family of yours. That'll be thanks enough."

Alexander nodded, unable to speak past the lump in his throat. He ran his hand along the stick's length, feeling the grain of the wood beneath his fingers. Jamie had held this, had carved it with his own hands. And now it was his, a gift from strangers who had every reason to turn him away but had instead taken him in.

"I'll make it count," he said finally. "I promise. And when this is over, when things are… normal again, I'll come back. I'll bring my family to meet you both. I'll—"

A tremendous crash from outside cut him off mid-sentence. The cottage shook, and dust rained down from the rafters. Morag's hand flew to her mouth. Angus was on his feet in an instant, moving to the window.

"Christ," he breathed. "It's one of them. A big one."

Alexander pushed himself up, grabbing the walking stick for support, and hobbled to join him. Through the small window, he could see it—a Bullseye, but larger than any he'd encountered before. It must have been seven feet tall, its body a mass of twisted muscle and bone. The red mark on its chest seemed to pulse with its own light.

As they watched, it charged the cottage again, slamming into the wall with enough force to make the entire structure shudder. Plates fell from the shelf and shattered on the floor.

"The rifle," Angus said, already moving. He grabbed the weapon from where it leant against the wall and checked the chamber. "Get away from the window, both of you."

Another impact. This time, Alexander heard wood splintering. The door wouldn't hold much longer.

Angus positioned himself in the centre of the room, rifle raised. "Morag, get to the back room. Take the lad with you."

"I'm not leaving you," Morag said firmly.

"Woman, for once in your life, do as I say!"

The door exploded inward in a shower of splinters. The Bullseye filled the doorway, its eyeless face turning towards them. It opened its mouth—too wide, impossibly wide—and released a sound that was part roar, part scream.

Angus fired. The shot caught the creature in the shoulder, spinning it sideways. Black blood sprayed across the wall. But it didn't go down. Instead, it lunged forward with terrifying speed.

Angus fired again, and again. Each shot found its mark, but the Bullseye kept coming. It was almost upon him when the fourth bullet finally struck something vital. The creature stumbled, its legs buckling.

But its momentum carried it forward. It crashed into Angus, and both of them went down in a tangle of limbs. Alexander heard the sickening crack of bone meeting stone as Angus was thrown against the wall.

"No!" Morag screamed, starting forward.

The Bullseye was getting up, shaking its head like a dog shedding water. Angus lay crumpled against the wall, not moving. The rifle had skittered across the floor, out of reach.

Alexander didn't think. He simply moved.

He stepped forward, the walking stick gripped tight in both hands, and swung with everything he had. The solid ash connected with the creature's skull with a satisfying crack. The Bullseye reeled, turning its eyeless face towards him.

Alexander swung again, this time catching it across the chest. The impact jarred his arms, but the stick held firm. The creature lunged at him, claws extended, and he brought the stick up in a desperate parry. Wood met bone with a sharp crack.

His ankle screamed in protest as he shifted his weight, but he couldn't stop now. The Bullseye was between him and the door, between him and any hope of escape. He had to keep it focused on him, had to give Morag time to get to Angus.

The creature swiped at him, and Alexander ducked, feeling the wind of its claws passing inches from his face. He jabbed forward with the stick, driving the end into the creature's midsection. It barely seemed to notice.

They circled each other in the confined space of the cottage. Alexander's breath came in ragged gasps, his injured ankle threatening to give out with every step. The Bullseye moved with predatory patience now, seeming to sense his weakness.

It feinted left, then lunged right. Alexander swung the stick in a wide arc, but the creature was faster. Its claws raked across his shoulder, tearing through fabric and flesh. Pain exploded across his back, hot and immediate.

He stumbled backward, nearly falling. The Bullseye pressed its advantage, coming at him in a rush. Alexander brought the stick up horizontally, catching the creature's arms as it reached for him. For a moment, they were locked together, the Bullseye's weight pressing down on him, its fetid breath hot on his face.

With a desperate heave, Alexander shoved the creature back. It stumbled, off-balance, and he swung the stick like a cricket bat, putting his full weight behind the blow. The wood connected with the side of the Bullseye's head with a crack that echoed through the cottage.

The creature went down hard, crashing into the table. The furniture splintered beneath its weight. Alexander didn't wait to see if it would get up again. He turned and ran—or tried to. His ankle gave out on the second step, and he went down on one knee.

Behind him, he heard the Bullseye stirring. Heard the scrape of claws on stone as it pulled itself up.

"The back door!" Morag's voice, sharp with urgency. "Go, lad! Go now!"

Alexander forced himself up, using the stick for support. He could see the back door, could see daylight beyond it. It seemed impossibly far away.

The Bullseye roared. Alexander didn't look back. He hobbled forward as fast as his injured ankle would allow, each step an agony. Behind him, he heard Morag screaming something, heard the creature's heavy footfalls.

He reached the door and yanked it open. Fresh air hit his face, cool and clean. He stumbled through, out into the morning light.

Behind him, the cottage erupted in chaos. He heard Morag's voice, high and desperate. Heard the Bullseye's roar. And then, cutting through it all, a sound that made his blood run cold—the whoosh of flames catching.

Alexander turned back, horror flooding through him. Through the open door, he could see fire spreading across the cottage floor, racing up the walls with unnatural speed. The lamp—someone must have knocked over the lamp.

"Morag!" he shouted. "Angus!"

Morag appeared in the doorway, her face streaked with soot and tears. "Run!" she screamed at him. "Run, you fool!"

She disappeared back into the smoke. Alexander took a step towards the cottage, but the heat drove him back. The flames were everywhere now, consuming the small building with terrifying speed.

He heard Morag scream again, a sound of pure anguish that cut through him like a blade. Then nothing but the roar of the fire.

Alexander stood frozen, the walking stick clutched in his hands, watching the cottage burn. He should go back. He should help them. But even as the thought formed, he knew it was too late. The entire structure was engulfed now, flames shooting through the roof.

A section of wall collapsed inward with a shower of sparks. The heat was intense, even from where he stood. Alexander took another step back, then another.

He couldn't help them. He couldn't save them. All he could do was honour their sacrifice by surviving.

With tears streaming down his face, Alexander turned and fled into the forest. His ankle screamed with every step, but he didn't slow down. He used the walking stick to support his weight, to propel himself forward, away from the burning cottage and the screams that still echoed in his ears.

Behind him, smoke rose into the morning sky, a dark pillar marking the place where two kind strangers had given everything to save him.

Alexander ran until his lungs burned and his legs threatened to give out. Only then did he allow himself to stop, collapsing against a tree trunk. He looked down at the walking stick in his hands—Jamie's stick, Angus had called it. Made by a son who was gone, given by a father who was now gone too.

"I'll make it count," Alexander whispered, his voice breaking. "I promise. I'll make it count."

He pushed himself upright and started walking again, limping through the forest with the stick as his only companion. The village was still two days away. Two sleeps, as his mother used to say when he was small. Two sleeps until he was home.

If he could survive that long.

Two sleeps.

He repeated it to himself like a prayer, like a promise, like the only thing keeping him moving forward through the endless trees.

Two sleeps.

10

The Long Walk North

Spotify Apple Music Amazon Music

Track: WHISPERS OF THE WOODS

The forest stretched endlessly before Alexander, a maze of trees and shadows that all looked the same. He walked steadily northward, using a fallen branch as a walking stick to help with his injured ankle. The fire extinguisher had been left behind at the cottage—too heavy, too cumbersome. Now he had only the kitchen knife tucked into his belt and the clothes on his back.

Jamie's clothes, he reminded himself. Clothes that belonged to a dead man, given to him by people who were now dead too.

The guilt was a physical weight in his chest. Angus and Morag had taken him in, fed him, cared for him. And he'd led that monster right to their door. If he hadn't gone there, if he'd just kept walking, they might still be alive.

But you would be dead, a voice in his head argued. *You couldn't walk twenty-two miles on that ankle yesterday. You would have collapsed in the forest and died, and then you'd never get home.*

The logic was sound, but it didn't make him feel any better.

The woods remained eerily quiet. No birdsong, no rustling of small animals. Just his footsteps on the forest floor and the occasional distant moan of an Aimless. Alexander had learned to recognise the sound now, to gauge the distance and direction, to know when to hide and when to keep moving.

He stopped frequently to rest, checking his phone's compass to maintain his northward heading. The battery was at 13% now. He'd have to turn it off soon, save it for emergencies. But first, he allowed himself one more look at the wallpaper photo.

Ailsa and Magsy smiled up at him from the screen, frozen in that perfect moment of joy. How long ago had that photo been taken? A week? It felt like a lifetime. It felt like looking at people from another world, a world where fathers went to conferences and came home on schedule, where the worst thing that could happen was missing the ferry.

"I'm coming home," he whispered to the photo. "I promise I'm coming home."

He turned off the phone and put it away, then continued walking.

Hours passed. The sun climbed higher, then began its descent. Alexander's ankle throbbed with each step, a constant reminder of his limitations. He'd been walking for hours now, and the pain was becoming harder to ignore.

His stomach growled—he'd eaten the food Morag had packed, but it was long gone now. His mouth was dry, his lips cracked. He needed water.

As if in answer to his prayers, he heard it—the sound of running water. Alexander followed the sound until he found a small stream, clear and cold. He fell to his knees and drank handful after handful, the water so cold it made his teeth ache but tasting better than anything he'd ever had.

He splashed water on his face and neck, washing away the sweat and grime. His reflection in the water showed a man he barely recognised—stubble covering his jaw, dark circles under his eyes, a hardness in his expression that hadn't been there before.

Alexander used his stick to heave himself back to his feet and continued north. His ankle screamed in protest. How much farther had he come?

Through the trees, he spotted a road sign: "BELNAHOUTHIE 17 MILES."

Seventeen miles. Alexander leaned heavily on his walking stick, doing the maths. The cottage had been about four miles from the hotel—he remembered the desperate limping journey through the forest that first day. And now, after this morning's escape and hours of walking, he'd managed maybe another mile. Just one more painful mile.

Five miles total since Monday. Seventeen miles still to go.

The numbers felt impossible. His ankle could barely handle another hour, let alone another three days of this.

But you have to, he told himself. *Magsy is waiting.*

As Alexander walked, his mind drifted to Ailsa. What was she doing right now? Did she know something was wrong? The phones had been down since Monday morning—she must have tried to call him, must be worried sick.

Or maybe the infection had spread to the islands. Maybe right now, Ailsa was fighting for her life, trying to protect Magsy from those things. Maybe—

No. He couldn't think like that. The islands were safe. They had to be safe. There was an ocean between them and the mainland. The infection couldn't cross water.

Could it?

In the distance, Alexander heard something that made him stop—a mechanical sound. Engines. Vehicles.

He moved cautiously towards the sound until he could see a road through the trees. On it, a convoy was moving north—sleek black trucks and armoured vehicles, all moving in military-style formation. But these weren't military vehicles. They were too clean, too corporate. Private security forces manned the vehicles, dressed in black tactical gear with full face respirators.

On the side of each vehicle was a logo: a twisted double helix with a butterfly emerging from the top.

Alexander stared at the logo, a nagging feeling of recognition tugging at his memory. He'd seen that symbol before, recently, but where? His exhausted brain couldn't make the connection, but something about it felt wrong. Pharmaceutical company? Biotech firm?

The convoy moved with precision, weapons visible, clearly prepared for combat. These weren't rescue workers. These were soldiers. Corporate soldiers.

He considered trying to flag them down, but something held him back. The way they moved—alert, aggressive, searching—made him feel like prey rather than someone who might be rescued. By the time he could have made the decision, they were gone anyway, leaving only dust and the fading sound of engines.

Alexander stood at the forest's edge, staring after them. Where was the actual military? Where were the police, the fire services, the emergency responders? Why was a private company running a military-style convoy through infected territory?

The questions unsettled him more than the silence that followed.

He continued walking, but each step was agony now. The brief rest by the stream had let the pain settle deeper into his ankle, and now it felt like walking on broken glass. He was limping badly, progress measured in yards rather than miles.

The sun was lower now, casting long shadows through the trees. Alexander knew he should find shelter before dark—the infected seemed more active at night, and he didn't want to be caught in the open. But he'd barely covered any distance today. At this rate, Belnahouthie was four days away. Maybe five.

Two sleeps, he'd promised Magsy. It had already been three days.

As the light faded, Alexander heard voices in the distance. Human voices. Alive voices.

He moved carefully towards the sound, gripping the kitchen knife, not sure if he should reveal himself or stay hidden. The voices grew louder, and through the trees, he could see a small group of people gathered around a makeshift camp—a tarp stretched between trees, a small fire.

There were four of them: a middle-aged man in torn business clothes, a young woman in hiking gear, an elderly woman, and a teenage boy. They looked exhausted, scared, but alive.

Alexander approached slowly, hands visible, trying not to limp too obviously. “Hello! I’m human! Don’t be afraid!”

The group immediately tensed. The middle-aged man picked up a cricket bat.

“Stop right there! Show us your arms!”

Alexander set down the knife and rolled up his sleeves, showing no bites. “No bites. I’m clean.”

The young woman approached cautiously. “Turn around. Lift your shirt.”

Alexander complied, showing his back.

“He’s clean,” she said to the others.

The group relaxed slightly. The man with the cricket bat lowered it. “Where did you come from?”

“Loonswrath. Spent last night with an elderly couple about four miles south. You?”

“We’re from Sheepsford,” the elderly woman said. “The whole town went mad yesterday morning.”

“My mum and dad…” the teenage boy said quietly. “They changed. Tried to bite me.”

The young woman put a protective arm around the boy. “We found Tommy hiding in a shop. Been travelling together since.”

“I’m David,” the man with the cricket bat said. “This is Sarah, Margaret, and Tommy.”

“Alexander. I’m heading to Belnahouthie. The ferry port. Trying to get home to my family.”

“Belnahouthie? That’s where we’re going too,” Margaret said. “How far?”

"I passed a sign about an hour ago. Seventeen miles." Alexander's voice was heavy with exhaustion. "I saw a convoy on the road heading north—looked like they were heading that way too. We could travel together if you want. Safety in numbers."

"A convoy?" David's eyes lit up. "Military?"

"I don't think so. Private security, maybe. Black vehicles, tactical gear. Had some kind of corporate logo on the side."

Sarah frowned. "Not military? Where the hell is the army? The police?"

"I don't know," Alexander admitted. "But someone's still organised out there. That's something."

The group exchanged uncertain glances. David spoke first. "What did you see back there? How bad is it?"

Alexander took a breath. "Bad. The whole of Loonswrath was overrun. There are different types—some just wander and moan, others make this horrible screeching sound. And there are big ones. Really big ones."

"Big ones?" Tommy's voice was scared.

"Eight feet tall, incredibly strong. I saw one tear a man in half. But if we stick to the forest, avoid making noise, we should be okay."

Tommy swallowed hard. "We need to name them. If we're going to survive, we need to know what we're talking about."

Sarah nodded. "He's right. Calling them 'those things' isn't helping." She looked at Alexander. "You've seen the most. What should we call them?"

Alexander thought for a moment. "The ones that just wander and moan—they don't seem to have much purpose. They just… drift. Like they're aimless. Let's call them the Aimless."

"The Aimless," Margaret repeated, testing the word. "That fits."

"What about the screeching ones?" David asked.

"The Screechers," Sarah said immediately. "Simple and accurate. We need to run when we hear a Screecher."

"And the big ones?" Tommy asked, his voice small.

Alexander thought about the monster that had killed Angus and Morag, the one that had chased him through the hotel. "The ones I saw—pure strength and relentless. Like they lock onto a target and won't stop. Let's call them Bullseyes."

"Bullseyes," David said grimly. "Good to know. Anything else?"

Alexander hesitated. "There were… children. But they looked no different to the Aimless in the end."

Tommy started shaking. "Children…"

"Hey," Sarah said, putting her arm around him. "We need to know. Knowledge keeps us alive." She looked at Alexander. "So we have the Aimless, the Screechers, and the Bullseyes. Is that all?"

"That's all I've seen," Alexander confirmed. "But there could be more."

"We haven't eaten since yesterday," Margaret said quietly.

"I ate a bit this morning before…" Alexander trailed off, not wanting to talk about the cottage, about Angus and Morag. "My stomach's been rumbling all day."

David nodded. "Alright. We'll travel together, but we need rules—no loud noises, we move as a group, and if someone gets bitten…"

He didn't finish the sentence, but everyone understood.

"Agreed," Alexander said. He looked down at his ankle, swollen and throbbing inside Jamie's boot. "Fair warning though—I've got a bad ankle. Twisted it on Monday. I can keep going, but I'm not fast."

Sarah noticed his limp for the first time. "How bad?"

"Bad enough. I managed about a mile today, maybe a bit more. It's getting worse."

"We're not exactly sprinters ourselves," David said, gesturing to Margaret. "We'll match your pace."

"We should rest here tonight," Sarah suggested. "Get some sleep. Start fresh in the morning."

Alexander wanted to argue, wanted to keep moving, but his body was screaming for rest. "Alright. But we leave at first light."

Tommy approached Alexander as the group settled in for the night. "Do you really think the ferries will still be running?"

Alexander looked at the boy—sixteen, maybe seventeen, already orphaned by this nightmare. "I have to believe they are. I promised my little girl I'd be home."

Tommy nodded, finding some comfort in Alexander's determination. "Seventeen miles. If we can do five or six miles a day, that's three days. Maybe four."

"Maybe four," Alexander agreed, though the thought of four more days of this pain made him want to weep.

As darkness fell, the group huddled around their small fire. Alexander sat with his back against a tree, his ankle elevated on his pack. Sarah had found some relatively clean cloth and wrapped it tightly—not much, but it helped.

"Get some sleep," she said. "You'll need your strength tomorrow."

Alexander closed his eyes, but sleep was elusive. Every time he drifted off, he saw the Bullseye smashing through the cottage door, heard Morag's screams, saw Angus flying across the room.

Five miles. Only five miles in three days.

Seventeen miles still to go.

Two sleeps, Magsy's voice echoed in his memory. *Promise, Daddy?*

I promise, sweetheart. I promise.

But that had been three days ago. Three days that felt like three lifetimes. And he was still so far from home.

Alexander opened his eyes and stared up at the darkening sky through the tree branches. Somewhere beyond those trees, beyond those seventeen miles, beyond the sea, his daughter was waiting.

He would get there.

No matter how much it hurt.

No matter how long it took.

He would keep his promise.

12

The Abandoned Village

Spotify   Apple Music   Amazon Music

Track: ECHOES OF THE BULLSEYE

They had camped overnight in the forest, taking turns keeping watch, no one sleeping more than an hour or two. As dawn broke on their fourth day since the outbreak, they continued north, following Alexander's compass.

By mid-morning, the forest opened up ahead, revealing the outskirts of a small village. Alexander held up his hand, signaling the group to stop. They crouched behind a fallen log, surveying the scene before them.

The village was small—maybe twenty buildings clustered around a single main street. A post office, a local shop, a pub called The Red Grous and a few houses with neat gardens. Everything was silent, still, abandoned.

"Looks empty," David whispered.

"Looks can be deceiving," Alexander replied, remembering the cottage, remembering Angus and Morag. "We need to be careful."

"But there might be food," Tommy said, his stomach growling audibly. "Supplies. We need supplies."

He was right. They'd been walking for hours with nothing to eat. Alexander's own stomach was a hollow ache, and he could see the exhaustion in the others' faces. If they were going to make it to Belnahouthie, they needed food, water, and rest.

"Alright," Alexander said. "But we do this smart. We stick together, we move quietly, and at the first sign of trouble, we run. Agreed?"

Everyone nodded.

They approached the village cautiously, moving from tree to tree, watching for any sign of movement. The silence was oppressive—no birds, no wind, just the sound of their own breathing and footsteps.

The first building they reached was the local shop. Its windows were intact, the door closed but unlocked. Alexander pushed it open slowly, the bell above the door tinkling softly in the silence.

Inside, the shop was a mess. Shelves had been knocked over, products scattered across the floor. But it hadn't been completely looted—there were still goods on some of the shelves, still supplies they could use.

"Spread out," Alexander said quietly. "Look for anything useful. Food, water, medical supplies, weapons. But stay where I can see you."

They moved through the store quickly and efficiently. Sarah found bottled water and filled her backpack. Tommy discovered canned goods—beans, soup, vegetables. Margaret found a first aid kit behind the counter, still sealed in its packaging. David grabbed a torch and spare batteries.

Alexander found a small camping section and took a compact sleeping bag, a box of matches, and a folding knife that was better than the kitchen knife he'd been carrying. He also grabbed energy bars, dried fruit, and a map of the local area.

Near the village entrance, he'd spotted a weathered road sign through the trees: "BELNAHOUTHIE 14 MILES."

Fourteen miles. They'd covered about three miles since breaking camp this morning. At this pace, with his ankle slowing them down, they'd reach the ferry in three or four more days.

If they survived that long.

Tommy was looking out the window, his face pale. "Guys? We need to go. Now."

Alexander moved to the window and felt his blood run cold. Shambling down the main street were at least a dozen Aimless, their jerky movements unmistakable even from this distance. And behind them, towering over the smaller infected, was a Bullseye—eight feet of twisted muscle and rage.

"Back door," Alexander hissed. "Move!"

They grabbed what they could carry and ran for the back of the store. Alexander found a door marked "Staff Only" and pushed through into a storage room. Another door led outside into an alley behind the buildings.

They emerged into the alley just as they heard the front door of the store crash open. The Aimless had found them.

"This way," Alexander whispered, leading them down the alley away from the main street. They moved as quietly as possible, but their footsteps seemed impossibly loud in the silence.

The alley opened onto a small courtyard behind the pub. Alexander was about to lead them across when he heard it—the heavy, thudding footsteps of the Bullseye. It was close, too close.

"In here," David said, pointing to a door marked "The Stag's Head - Cellar Entrance." He tried the handle—locked.

The footsteps were getting closer. They could hear the Bullseye's heavy breathing, the scrape of its feet on the pavement.

"Stand back," Alexander said. He raised his foot and kicked the door hard, just below the lock. The old wood splintered, and the door swung open.

They tumbled inside and Alexander pulled the door closed behind them, wedging a piece of broken wood under it to keep it shut. They were in a narrow stairwell leading down into darkness.

"Down," Alexander whispered. "Quietly."

They descended the stairs carefully, feeling their way in the darkness. At the bottom, David pulled out the torch he'd found and clicked it on. The beam revealed a typical pub cellar—barrels of beer, crates of bottles, boxes of supplies.

And in the corner, huddled behind a stack of crates, was a woman.

She screamed when the light hit her, a high-pitched sound of pure terror.

"It's okay!" Sarah said quickly, holding up her hands. "We're not infected. We're survivors, like you."

The woman stared at them with wild eyes. She was in her thirties, wearing what had once been a nice dress, now torn and stained. Her hair was matted, her face streaked with dirt and tears.

"They're everywhere," she whispered. "They killed everyone. My husband, my children, everyone."

Margaret moved forward slowly, her voice gentle. "What's your name, dear?"

"Claire. Claire Morrison. I've been hiding here for two days. I heard them upstairs, in the pub. I thought… I thought they'd found me."

"You're safe now," Margaret said, though they all knew it was a lie. None of them were safe.

Above them, they heard the heavy footsteps moving through the courtyard. The Bullseye paused near the cellar door, and they all held their breath. The door rattled as the creature tested it, but the wedge held.

After what felt like an eternity, the footsteps moved away.

"We can't stay here," Alexander said quietly. "If that thing comes back with more of them, we'll be trapped."

"But where do we go?" Tommy asked. "They're everywhere out there."

Alexander pulled out the map he'd taken from the store and studied it by torchlight. "There's a farm about a mile north of here. If we can make it there, we might be able to find a vehicle, maybe even a working phone."

"A mile through infected territory?" David said. "That's suicide."

"Staying here is suicide," Alexander countered. "At least if we're moving, we have a chance."

Claire spoke up, her voice stronger now. "I know the farm you mean. The Hendersons' place. They have a Land Rover, and old Donald always kept it in good condition. If it's still there…"

"Then we have a way out," Alexander finished. "Can you walk? Can you come with us?"

Claire nodded, standing on shaky legs. "I can't stay here. I can't hide anymore. If you're going, I'm coming with you."

"Alright," Alexander said. "We wait for a while, then we move. We need to give that Bullseye enough time to move on. If we're quiet and careful, we can make it."

They settled in to wait, sharing the food and water they'd gathered. Alexander gave Claire an energy bar and a bottle of water, which she consumed gratefully.

As they waited, Claire told them her story. She'd been at home with her family when the outbreak started. Her husband had gone to check on a neighbour and never came back. Then her children had started showing symptoms—the fever, the aggression, the orange veins spreading across their skin.

"I locked them in their rooms," she said, tears streaming down her face. "My own children, and I locked them away like animals. But I could hear them changing, hear them becoming those things. And then they broke down the doors, and I ran. I just ran."

Margaret put her arm around Claire, letting her cry. Alexander looked away, thinking of Magsy. What would he do if she started showing symptoms? Could he lock her away? Could he…

No. He couldn't think about that. Magsy was safe. She had to be safe.

As darkness fell, they prepared to move. Alexander checked his supplies—the knife, the matches, the map. David had his cricket bat. Sarah had found a heavy wrench in the cellar. Tommy had a broken bottle clutched in his hand, his knuckles white. Margaret had a rolling pin from behind the bar upstairs. Claire had nothing, but she was determined to come with them.

"Remember," Alexander said as they gathered at the bottom of the stairs. "Stay quiet, stay together, and if we get separated, head north. Always north. Belnahouthie is our goal."

They climbed the stairs slowly, Alexander in the lead. He removed the wedge from the door and opened it carefully, peering out into the courtyard.

It was empty. The Bullseye and the Aimless had moved on.

"Now," Alexander whispered.

They slipped out into the night, six survivors moving through a dead village, heading for a farm that might offer salvation or might be just another tomb.

The moon was bright, casting long shadows across the empty streets. They moved from shadow to shadow, avoiding the open spaces, always watching, always listening.

They were halfway through the village when they heard it—the moan of an Aimless, close by. Too close.

"Hide," Alexander hissed.

They pressed themselves against the wall of a house, barely breathing. An Aimless shambled past, not ten feet away, its head turning slowly from side to side as if searching for something.

It paused, sniffing the air. Alexander's hand tightened on his knife.

Then, from somewhere in the distance, came a loud crash—the sound of something falling, metal on stone. The Aimless's head snapped toward the sound, and it shambled off in that direction.

"Go," Alexander whispered. "Now, while it's distracted."

They ran, as quietly as they could, through the rest of the village and out into the fields beyond. Behind them, they could hear more moans, more footsteps, as the Aimless converged on the source of the noise.

They didn't stop running until they were well clear of the village, until the buildings were just dark shapes in the distance. Only then did they pause, gasping for breath, hearts pounding.

"Everyone okay?" Alexander asked.

They nodded, too breathless to speak.

"The farm should be just ahead," Claire said, pointing to a cluster of buildings silhouetted against the night sky. "Maybe half a mile."

"Then let's keep moving," Alexander said. "We're not safe yet."

They walked through the dark fields, the grass wet with dew, the night air cold against their faces. Above them, stars shone in a clear sky, beautiful and indifferent to the horror below.

Alexander thought about all the times he'd looked up at these same stars from Druichmachon, standing on his porch with Ailsa, pointing out constellations to Magsy even though she was too young to understand.

Those stars were still there, still shining, as if nothing had changed. As if the world hadn't ended.

But it had. And all Alexander could do was keep walking, keep moving forward, keep trying to get home.

The farm appeared ahead, dark and silent. They approached cautiously, watching for any sign of movement.

"There," Claire whispered, pointing to a barn. "That's where Donald kept the Land Rover."

They moved toward the barn, hope rising in their chests. A vehicle. A way to cover the remaining miles to Belnahouthie quickly, safely.

Alexander pulled open the barn door, and David shone his torch inside.

There, sitting in the middle of the barn, was a Land Rover. Old but well-maintained, just as Claire had said.

"Please have keys," Tommy whispered. "Please, please have keys."

12

The Farm

Spotify Apple Music Amazon Music

Track: THE FARM

Alexander climbed into the driver's seat and checked the ignition. No keys. He flipped down the sun visor—nothing. Checked the glove box—nothing.

"They might be in the house," Claire said. "Donald always kept a spare set in the kitchen."

Alexander looked at the farmhouse, dark and silent. They'd have to go inside, search for the keys, risk whatever might be waiting in there.

But they'd come this far. They couldn't give up now.

"Alright," he said. "Let's go find those keys."

They started making their way toward the farmhouse, moving cautiously across the open ground. Margaret led, with David close behind. Claire and Sarah followed, Tommy beside them, Alexander bringing up the rear.

They were maybe twenty yards from the front door when the first sound came.

A heavy thud from inside the house.

Everyone froze.

Another thud. Louder this time.

Then another.

Getting closer.

Getting faster.

"Back," Alexander said urgently, raising his hand. "Everyone back—"

The front door exploded outward in a shower of splinters.

A Bullseye charged through, its massive frame filling the doorway. The orange mark on its forehead pulsed like a warning beacon. Its eyes locked onto the group immediately.

And it roared—a sound so primal and rage-filled it seemed to shake the air itself.

For a split second, no one moved. They were all frozen in horror, staring at the seven-foot monster bearing down on them.

Then Claire screamed.

And everything erupted into chaos.

"RUN!" Alexander bellowed. "GO! GO! GO! GO!"

The group scattered. Margaret turned and sprinted back toward the barn, her age forgotten in pure terror. David was right behind her, Tommy at his heels.

Alexander spun around, looking for—

"Claire! CLAIRE, MOVE!"

But she was rooted to the spot, paralysed with fear. Staring at the approaching Bullseye like a deer in headlights.

The creature closed the distance in seconds—impossibly fast for something so large.

Alexander started running toward her, but he was too far away. Too slow.

The Bullseye reached Claire.

Its massive hands closed around her waist.

And then it pulled.

Claire's scream was cut short—horrifically, mercifully short—as her body came apart. The sound was worse than the scream. Wet. Tearing. Final.

The Bullseye tossed both halves aside like garbage. Claire's torso landed in the dirt, her legs crumpled several feet away. Blood spread across the ground in a rapidly expanding pool.

"ALEXANDER!" Margaret screamed from near the barn.

Alexander tore his eyes away from Claire's body. The Bullseye had already turned toward him, blood dripping from its hands. Its mouth opened in another roar.

"Shit. Shit!" Alexander turned and ran.

His injured ankle immediately protested, but adrenaline overrode the pain. He could hear the Bullseye behind him—the heavy thunder of its footfalls shaking the ground.

Getting closer.

Ahead, he could see the others had reached an old rusted car sitting near the barn—the skeleton of some ancient vehicle that had been left to decay. Margaret was yanking the door open, screaming at the others to get inside.

"THE CAR!" Alexander gasped as he ran. "GET IN THE CAR!"

David scrambled into the driver's seat. Sarah and Tommy piled into the back, cramming together. Margaret threw herself into the passenger seat.

They were slamming doors just as Alexander reached the vehicle.

He grabbed the rear door handle, yanked—

Locked from the inside.

"OPEN IT!" He pounded on the window. "OPEN THE DOOR!"

Inside, Sarah and Tommy were screaming, pointing behind him.

The Bullseye was fifteen yards away.

Ten.

David fumbled with the lock, but his hands were shaking too badly.

"There's no room!" Margaret screamed from inside. "There's no room!"

Five yards.

Alexander could see the creature's eyes—milky white, empty of everything except rage. Could smell the stench of rot coming off it.

No time.

He dropped.

Not gracefully—he basically threw himself at the ground. His shoulder hit hard, sending fresh pain through his injured body. He rolled—clumsily, desperately—toward the car.

Got his head under the chassis just as the Bullseye reached the vehicle.

Alexander scrambled the rest of the way underneath, his backpack catching on something. He had to twist awkwardly, scraping his back against the undercarriage, to get fully beneath the car.

His breath came in ragged gasps that he tried desperately to quiet.

Above him, he could hear the Bullseye's feet—heavy, deliberate.

Thud. Thud.

It stopped right beside the car.

Alexander could see its feet through the gap—massive, the toes splayed and broken.

Inside the car, someone whimpered.

"Quiet," Margaret whispered, barely audible. "Everyone quiet."

Silence fell.

Alexander lay frozen under the car, not daring to breathe. His face was pressed against the oil-stained ground, his arms pinned awkwardly beneath him. Every muscle in his body was screaming at him to move, to run, to do something.

But he didn't. Couldn't.

Above, the Bullseye's feet shifted. A wet snuffling sound—it was sniffing.

The creature could smell them. Alexander was sure of it. Could smell the sweat and fear and blood.

But it couldn't pinpoint exactly where they were.

The Bullseye moved around the car. Slowly. Methodically.

Its feet appeared on Alexander's right side, then disappeared. Reappeared on his left.

It was circling. Hunting.

More sniffing.

Then a sound that made Alexander's blood freeze—the scrape of claws on metal.

The car rocked slightly.

The Bullseye was touching it. Feeling it.

Inside, someone started crying—trying to muffle it but not quite succeeding.

The car rocked again, harder this time.

Alexander's hand slowly, carefully moved to his knife. If the creature found them, if it started tearing into the car… he'd have maybe one shot before it killed them all.

His fingers closed around the weapon.

The Bullseye's feet were visible again, right in front of Alexander's face. So close he could reach out and touch them. So close he could see the broken, bloodied nails.

The creature was leaning down, its face probably pressed against the car window.

Alexander could hear its breathing—harsh, rattling.

Then—

From somewhere in the distance, a cow mooed.

The Bullseye's feet shifted abruptly. Its head snapped toward the sound—Alexander could tell by the way its whole body reoriented.

Another moo, plaintive and oblivious.

For a moment, nothing happened. The Bullseye stood perfectly still, listening.

Then it moved.

Fast.

The creature took off in the direction of the sound, each footfall thundering against the earth. Within seconds, it was gone.

But no one moved.

Alexander remained frozen under the car, barely breathing. Inside the vehicle, the others were equally motionless.

Seconds ticked by.

Then a minute.

Still no one moved.

In the distance, there was a terrified moo that cut short. A crash. Then silence.

"Is it..." David whispered from inside the car. "Is it gone?"

"I don't know," Margaret replied, equally quiet. "I can't see anything."

"Don't. Move. Not yet." Alexander's voice was muffled from under the car.

He lay there in the dirt and oil, his heart pounding so hard he was sure the Bullseye would hear it even from wherever it had gone. His hands were shaking. His whole body was shaking.

Claire was dead. Ripped in half right in front of them.

And they'd almost joined her. Would have, if not for a cow.

Dumb luck. That's all that saved them. Dumb, random, impossible luck.

"Everyone…" Alexander whispered. "Everyone okay in there?"

"We're alive," Margaret said. "That's… that's something."

Silence fell again. No one seemed to know what to do next. How long did they wait? How did they know when it was safe?

They waited another five minutes before anyone dared to move.

Finally, Alexander carefully, quietly, began to shimmy out from underneath. Every movement sent fresh stabs of pain through his battered body. His back scraped against the undercarriage again, and he had to bite back a grunt.

When he emerged, he stayed low, scanning the area with wide eyes. The farmhouse sat silent in the distance. No movement. No sound except the wind rustling through the overgrown fields.

Claire's body lay where it had fallen, already attracting flies.

Alexander looked away.

The car doors opened slowly, cautiously. Margaret was the first to step out, her face pale, her hands still trembling.

"Is it safe?" Sarah whispered from the backseat, Tommy pressed close beside her.

"I don't know," Alexander admitted, keeping his voice low. "But we can't stay here. Not out in the open like this."

David climbed out of the driver's seat, his legs visibly unsteady. He looked toward the farmhouse, then back at the rusted car they'd hidden in. "We could… we could try to drive. Get out of here faster."

The old car was from the seventies, judging by the design. Rust had eaten through parts of the body, and the windscreen was covered in dust and grime. But it was a vehicle. Four wheels and an engine.

"You think it runs?" Margaret asked, moving closer.

David circled the car, examining it. "Could do. These old workhorses were built to last. Farmers used them for decades."

"We need keys," Sarah pointed out, she and Tommy emerging from the back seat.

They all looked around. Then Alexander remembered—the barn. The Land Rover.

"The barn," he said. "Donald's Land Rover. Claire said he kept it maintained. Maybe the keys are in there."

They moved cautiously back to the barn, constantly watching for the Bullseye's return. Alexander pulled open the door, and they slipped inside.

The Land Rover sat in the middle of the barn, exactly where they'd left it.

"Check the workbench," Alexander suggested. "Farmers usually keep everything accessible."

They spread out, searching. Alexander moved to the workbench near the back wall, rifling through drawers filled with nails, screws, and rusted tools. David checked the shelves. Margaret looked along the walls. Tommy helped Sarah search through boxes.

"Nothing," David said after a minute. "Maybe they're in the house?"

No one wanted to go into the farmhouse. Not after seeing the Bullseye emerge from there.

Alexander continued searching, his eyes scanning the pegboard above the workbench. Wrenches, hammers, screwdrivers all hung from hooks in some long-forgotten organizational system.

And there—near the top, almost hidden behind a coil of rope—

Key rings hanging from hooks, each with a faded tag attached.

"Here!" Alexander said, reaching up. His fingers closed around one of the rings. "Tractor… workshop… storage…" He moved to the next hook. "Land Rover."

He pulled the keys down—three keys on a worn leather fob with the Land Rover logo barely visible.

Everyone gathered around as Alexander held them up.

"We've got keys," he said, genuine hope surging through him for the first time in what felt like days.

David was already moving to the driver's side door of the Land Rover. "Let's see if she starts."

He pulled the door open and climbed into the driver's seat. Alexander handed him the keys through the window.

The others clustered around hopefully. David slid the key into the ignition.

"Here goes nothing," he muttered.

He turned the key.

Nothing. Not even a click.

He tried again, pumping the gas pedal. The engine made a weak clicking sound, then died.

"Come on," David said, trying a third time. "Come on, you old girl."

The engine turned over endlessly—

Then died completely with a sound like a death rattle.

The hope that had filled the barn moments before evaporated.

"She's dead," David said, slumping back in the seat. "Could be anything. This thing's been sitting here for God knows how long."

Alexander felt the disappointment settle over him like a weight. Of course it didn't work. Why would anything be easy?

"Maybe we could jump it?" Sarah suggested. "If we had another car—"

"We don't have another car," Margaret said quietly. "And even if we did, the noise… that thing could hear us from miles away. The Bullseye."

She was right. The sound of an engine—assuming they could even get it started—would be like ringing a dinner bell for every infected thing in the area.

"What about pushing it?" Tommy asked, though his tone suggested he already knew the answer. "Get it out of the barn, far enough away, then try to start it?"

Alexander looked at the Land Rover, then at the group. Five people now—Claire was gone. Most of them exhausted and terrified. Margaret was in her sixties at least. And Alexander himself could barely walk without his ankle screaming.

He walked around to examine the tires.

"Look at these," he said, pointing.

They all looked. Two of the four tires were nearly flat, the rubber cracked and degraded from years of sitting in the barn.

"We'd never get it moving," Alexander continued. "Not far enough to matter. And the effort would slow us down, tire us out. Make noise."

"So we just… leave it?" David sounded defeated as he climbed out of the driver's seat.

Alexander understood the feeling. The Land Rover represented safety, even if it was an illusion. Four walls and a roof, however rusted. Something between them and the horrors outside. A way to cover ground quickly.

But illusions didn't save lives.

"We have to," Alexander said. "Walking might be slower, but it's quieter. We can hide easier on foot. Can move through places a vehicle can't go."

"Walking means we're exposed," Margaret pointed out. "Vulnerable."

"We're vulnerable either way," Alexander replied. "At least on foot we can control how much noise we make."

He looked at each of them in turn. Saw the fear, the exhaustion, the desperate desire for this nightmare to be over.

"I know it's not what anyone wants to hear," he continued, his voice gentle but firm. "But that Bullseye is still out there somewhere. Maybe others too. The sound of us trying to fix this car, or even pushing it, would draw them straight to us."

David stood looking at the Land Rover like he was saying goodbye to a friend. "I really thought it might work."

"So did I," Alexander admitted, pocketing the keys—though he wasn't sure why. Force of habit, maybe.

They gathered what little they had—backpacks, weapons, water—and began to prepare for the long walk ahead.

Margaret walked to the barn door, then stopped. She looked back toward where Claire's body lay outside.

"What about Claire?" she asked quietly.

Everyone's eyes drifted toward the barn door, knowing what lay beyond it.

"We can't bury her," Alexander said, though it pained him to say it. "We don't have time. And digging would make noise."

"We can't just leave her," Sarah protested, tears in her eyes.

"We don't have a choice," Alexander said, more harshly than he intended. He softened his tone. "I'm sorry. I know it's not right. But Claire's gone. Our job now is to make sure the rest of us don't join her."

They moved to the barn door, pausing at the opening to scan the area outside.

The farmyard was quiet. The Bullseye was nowhere to be seen.

Margaret walked a few steps toward Claire's body, then stopped. She bowed her head for a moment, lips moving in what might have been a prayer.

Then she turned back to the group. "Let's go. Before I lose my nerve."

They set off, leaving the barn and the useless Land Rover behind. Leaving Claire behind. Moving on foot through hostile territory with nothing but luck and desperation to protect them.

Alexander took one last look at the barn as they walked away. Inside, the old Land Rover sat in the darkness, keys that worked for a vehicle that didn't.

For a brief moment, it had represented hope. Safety. A way out.

Now it was just another relic of the world that used to be.

He turned his back on it and kept walking, his injured ankle throbbing with each step, knowing that every mile ahead would be harder than the last.

But at least they were moving.

At least they were alive.

For now.

Fourteen miles to Belnahouthie. Three, maybe four more days of walking.

Three more days to keep his promise to Magsy.

Three more days to make it home.

Alexander limped forward into the darkness, and the others followed.

13

The Long March

Spotify   Apple Music   Amazon Music

Track: ECHOES OF HOME

They walked through the darkness for another hour before Alexander called a halt. “We need to rest. Find somewhere to shelter for the night.”

They found an abandoned car near the tree line—an old estate car with its doors still open, as if the occupants had fled in a hurry. The group huddled around it, taking turns keeping watch. Alexander took the first watch, sitting with his back against the vehicle, the folding knife in his hand, staring out at the dark forest. The others tried to sleep, but he could hear them shifting restlessly, unable to find comfort on the cold ground.

Sarah sat down beside him after a while. “Can’t sleep?”

“Someone needs to keep watch.”

“I’ll take over in a bit. You need rest too.”

They sat in silence for a moment, listening to the sounds of the night—distant moans, the rustle of wind through trees, the occasional crack of a branch.

“Tell me about your family,” Sarah said quietly. “Your daughter.”

Alexander smiled despite everything. "Magsy. She's two. Smart as a whip, stubborn as her mother. She has this laugh that just… it makes everything else disappear, you know? All the worries, all the stress. When she laughs, nothing else matters."

"She sounds wonderful."

"She is. And her mother, Ailsa… we've been together since we were kids. Grew up on the same island, went to the same school. I can't remember a time when she wasn't part of my life."

"That's beautiful," Sarah said softly.

"What about you? Do you have family?"

Sarah's expression darkened. "Had. My parents were in Sheepsford when it started. I was hiking in the hills, came back to find…" She trailed off, unable to finish.

"I'm sorry."

"We all lost someone," she said. "That's what makes us survivors, I guess. We're the ones who lived when others didn't."

They sat in silence for a while, watching the dark forest. In the distance, they could hear the occasional moan, the sound of something moving through the trees.

"Do you think it's everywhere?" Sarah asked. "Or just here?"

"I don't know. But I have to believe the islands are safe. There's an ocean between them and the mainland. That has to count for something."

"I hope you're right."

After a few hours, David took over the watch and Alexander tried to sleep. But every time he closed his eyes, he saw Claire being torn apart, saw the Bullseye's blood-covered hands, saw the cottage door exploding inward.

He gave up on sleep and sat up, checking his phone one more time. The battery was at 8%. He looked at the wallpaper photo—Ailsa and Magsy, smiling, happy, alive.

"Soon," he whispered to the photo. "I'll be home soon."

As dawn broke, they prepared to move. Margaret was stiff from sleeping on the ground, and Tommy looked exhausted, but they were all alive. That was something.

Alexander pulled out the map and traced their route with his finger. "If we keep heading north through these woods, we should hit the main road into Belnahouthie. From there, it's a straight shot to the ferry terminal."

"How far?" David asked.

"Maybe twelve, thirteen miles total. If we can cover six or seven today, we can rest tonight and make the final push tomorrow morning."

"Two days?" Tommy said, disappointment clear in his voice. "I thought we were almost there."

"We are," Alexander replied. "But my ankle's not going to make it if we try to do it all in one go. And Margaret needs rest. We all do."

Margaret nodded gratefully. "I'm not as young as I used to be. I can keep going, but I can't rush."

"Then we take it steady," Alexander said. "We've made it this far. One more day won't kill us."

The words hung in the air, heavy with irony. One more day could very well kill them. But they all knew pushing too hard would be just as dangerous.

They set off through the forest, moving more confidently now that they could see. The morning was clear and cold, their breath visible in the air.

As they walked, David told his story. He'd been at his office in Sheepsford when the outbreak started. "I heard screaming from the street. Looked out the window and saw people attacking each other. At first, I thought it was a riot or something. Then I saw one of them get up after being killed. Just… stood up and started attacking others."

"How did you escape?" Tommy asked.

"Fire exit. Ran to my car, but the roads were blocked. So I went on foot. That's when I found Margaret."

Margaret picked up the story. "I was in my garden when my neighbour came over the fence. Mrs. Patterson, lovely woman, we'd been friends for thirty years. But she wasn't herself. Her skin was gray, and she had those orange veins. She tried to bite me. I hit her with my garden spade and ran."

"I found her on the road," David continued. "She was in shock, didn't know where to go. So we travelled together."

"Then we found Tommy," Margaret said, her voice softening. "Poor dear was hiding in a shop, terrified."

Tommy's story was the hardest to hear. "Mum and Dad changed in the night. I woke up to hear them making these… sounds. Like moaning, but wrong. I went to check on them and…" He paused, swallowing hard. "Dad grabbed me. Tried to bite me. Mum was already dead on the floor, but then she got up. I ran. Just ran. Left them there."

"You did what you had to do," Sarah said gently. "You survived."

"But they were my parents," Tommy said, his voice breaking. "I left them."

"They weren't your parents anymore," Alexander said quietly. "Whatever those things are, they're not the people we knew. The people we loved are gone. We're just… stopping the things that are left."

It was a harsh truth, but it seemed to help Tommy. He nodded, wiping his eyes.

Sarah's story was similar to the others. "I was hiking in the hills above Sheepsford. Three-day solo hike, completely off the grid. When I came back down, the town was in chaos. I tried to find my parents, but their house was empty. Blood everywhere, but no bodies. I don't know if they escaped or if they… changed."

"I'm sorry," Alexander said.

"We're all sorry," Sarah replied. "But sorry doesn't change anything. We just have to keep moving."

They walked in silence for a while, each lost in their own thoughts, their own losses. The forest was thick here, the canopy above blocking out much of the morning light. Their footsteps were soft on the carpet of pine needles.

Around mid-morning, they reached a small stream. They stopped to refill their water bottles, using the purification tablets Alexander had taken from the general store. The water was ice cold and tasted faintly of minerals, but it was clean.

"How's the ankle?" Margaret asked as Alexander sat heavily on a fallen log.

"It's been better," he admitted. The truth was, it was agony. Every step sent jolts of pain up his leg. The makeshift splint had helped, but four days of walking on it had taken their toll. "But I can keep going."

"You're limping worse than yesterday," she observed.

"I'll rest when we reach the ferry."

They continued north, the forest gradually thinning. By early afternoon, they emerged onto a narrow country road. A faded sign pointed north: "BELNAHOUTHIE 7 MILES."

"Seven miles," Tommy said. "That's not far. We could make it by tonight."

But Alexander was already shaking his head. "Look at us." He gestured to the group. Margaret was leaning heavily on her walking stick, her face pale with exhaustion. David's cricket bat dragged on the ground. Sarah and Tommy looked ready to collapse. And Alexander himself could barely stand.

"We're spent," he continued. "If we push on now and run into trouble, we won't have anything left to fight with. Better to find shelter, rest properly, and make the final push tomorrow when we're fresh."

"He's right," Margaret said. "I hate to admit it, but I don't think I have seven more miles in me today."

David looked up and down the empty road. "So where do we shelter? Out here we're exposed."

They walked along the road, keeping to the tree line, watching for anywhere that might offer protection for the night. The road curved through farmland—fields of unharvested crops rotting in the fields, stone walls crumbling, gates hanging open.

After about half a mile, Sarah pointed ahead. "There. What's that?"

A small stone building sat back from the road, half-hidden by overgrown hedges. As they got closer, they could see it was an old chapel—one of those tiny rural churches that dotted the Scottish countryside. A wooden sign hung crooked near the door: "St. Columba's Chapel - All Welcome."

"A church," Margaret said softly. "Maybe that's a sign."

They approached cautiously. The chapel was small—maybe big enough for thirty people at most. Its stone walls were thick, the windows narrow and high. The heavy wooden door was closed but not locked.

Alexander pushed it open slowly, and they peered inside.

The chapel's interior was simple and austere. Wooden pews lined either side of a central aisle leading to a plain altar. Candles sat in holders, unlit. A small side room—probably a vestry—was visible through an open door. Everything was covered in a layer of dust, as if no one had been here in months.

"Looks empty," David said, stepping inside.

They searched the chapel thoroughly. The vestry contained some old hymnals, a few robes, and a cabinet with communion supplies. No food, but no infected either.

"It's defensible," Alexander said, examining the door. "One entrance, thick walls, high windows. And it's off the road—less likely to attract attention."

"I don't like the idea of only one way out," David countered. "If something gets in, we're trapped."

"If something gets in through that door," Alexander said, pointing at the heavy oak, "we'll hear it coming. And these walls will hold against Aimless. Maybe even a Bullseye."

They settled in, securing the door with one of the pews. They shared the last of the food from the general store—tinned beans, energy bars, dried fruit. It wasn't much, but it was something.

As the sun set, they lit a single candle and placed it on the altar. The flickering light cast long shadows across the chapel walls.

"Feels wrong to be in a church," Tommy said quietly. "After everything that's happened. Where was God when the world ended?"

"Maybe God's still here," Margaret said. She'd been sitting in one of the pews, her head bowed. "Maybe He's the reason we're still alive."

"Or maybe we're just lucky," David said, though his tone wasn't unkind.

"Luck or grace," Margaret replied, "I'll take either."

They established a watch rotation. Two hours each. David took the first shift, sitting near the door with his cricket bat across his knees.

Alexander sat in the back pew, his injured leg stretched out in front of him. He pulled out his phone—7% battery now. The wallpaper photo of Ailsa and Magsy glowed in the dim light.

Five nights.

He'd promised Magsy two sleeps. It had been five nights now. The cottage, the forest, the group's camp, the abandoned car, and now this chapel. Five nights, and he was still miles from home.

"I'm sorry, sweetheart," he whispered to the photo. "Daddy's trying. I'm trying so hard."

Sarah sat down beside him. "Talking to them?"

"Trying to. I don't even know if they're..." He couldn't finish the sentence.

"They're alive," Sarah said firmly. "You have to believe that. It's the only way to keep going."

"How do you do it? How do you keep going when you don't know?"

"Because the not knowing means there's still hope," she replied. "The moment I accept they're gone is the moment I give up. And I can't give up. None of us can."

They sat in silence for a while, listening to the old chapel creak and settle around them.

"Tomorrow," Alexander said finally. "Tomorrow we reach the ferry. Tomorrow I'm one step closer to home."

"Tomorrow," Sarah agreed.

As night deepened, the sounds began. Distant at first—the now-familiar moans of the Aimless, carried on the wind. Then closer. Footsteps on the road outside. Shuffling, dragging sounds.

Everyone was instantly alert. David gripped his cricket bat tighter. Alexander moved to the window, peering out through the narrow gap.

In the moonlight, he could see them—three Aimless, shambling down the road. They moved past the chapel without pausing, headed north toward Belnahouthie.

"They didn't see us," Margaret whispered.

"They're migrating," Alexander said. "Following something. Or being drawn somewhere."

"The ferry terminal?" Tommy suggested. "Maybe there are survivors there. Living people they can smell."

It was a disturbing thought. If the Aimless were converging on Belnahouthie, reaching the ferry would be even more dangerous than they'd anticipated.

"We'll deal with it tomorrow," Alexander said. "For now, we're safe. Everyone try to get some sleep."

But sleep was hard to come by. Every sound outside made them tense. Every creak of the old building sounded like footsteps. Tommy dozed fitfully, jerking awake every few minutes. Margaret prayed quietly, her lips moving in the darkness.

During Alexander's watch shift, around 2 AM, he heard something that made his blood run cold.

In the distance—maybe a mile away, maybe more—came a sound he'd heard only once before. High-pitched, piercing, inhuman.

A Screecher.

The sound cut through the night like a blade, rising and falling in an eerie wail. It lasted maybe ten seconds, then stopped. The silence that followed was somehow worse.

"What was that?" Tommy whispered, his voice shaking.

"Screecher," Alexander replied. "But it's far away. Not near us."

"What's it doing?"

"I don't know. Maybe calling to the others. Maybe marking territory. Or maybe…" He trailed off, not wanting to voice his fear.

"Maybe what?" Sarah asked.

"Maybe they're organizing," Alexander said quietly. "Maybe they're not as mindless as we thought."

It was a terrifying possibility. The Aimless were dangerous but predictable. The Bullseyes were powerful but straightforward. But if the Screechers could coordinate the others, could direct them somehow…

"Let's not jump to conclusions," David said, though he sounded uncertain. "We don't know anything for certain."

They heard the Screecher call twice more during the night, but it never came closer. By the time dawn began to lighten the narrow windows, the sounds had stopped.

They gathered their things as the sun rose, preparing for the final leg of their journey. Alexander's ankle had stiffened overnight, and the first few steps were agony. He gritted his teeth and kept moving.

Margaret looked exhausted, her face drawn and pale. David had dark circles under his eyes. Tommy moved like a sleepwalker. Sarah was the only one who seemed alert, though Alexander could see the strain in her eyes.

"Seven miles," Alexander said as they stood outside the chapel in the early morning light. "Maybe four or five hours of walking. We can do this."

"And then what?" Tommy asked. "What if the ferry's not running? What if it's like the farm—everything we need is there, but it doesn't work?"

"Then we find another way," Alexander said. "But we can't think like that. We have to believe we'll make it. Have to believe there's still a way out."

They set off down the road, the morning mist clinging to the fields around them. Behind them, St. Columba's Chapel stood silent and empty, one more sanctuary left behind in a world that no longer had room for sanctuaries.

Seven miles to go.

Seven miles to the ferry.

Seven miles closer to home.

Alexander limped forward, and the others followed. Together, they walked toward whatever waited for them in Belnahouthie.

14

The Survivors' Stories

Spotify Apple Music Amazon Music

Track: APPROACHING DARKNESS

The morning mist clung to the fields as they set off from St. Columba's Chapel. Alexander's ankle had stiffened overnight, and those first few steps were agony—sharp, shooting pains that made him grit his teeth and grip his walking stick until his knuckles turned white.

Seven miles. Just seven more miles.

He could do this. He had to do this.

Behind him, the others fell into line. Margaret moved slowly, her walking stick tapping a steady rhythm on the road. David carried his cricket bat over one shoulder, his other hand supporting Margaret's elbow when the ground was uneven. Tommy walked close to Sarah, both of them silent and watchful.

They were all running on fumes now. Five days of fear and flight and loss had worn them down to their cores. But they were still moving. Still fighting.

"Keep to the side of the road," Alexander said quietly. "Single file. If you hear anything—anything at all—we get off the road and into cover. Understood?"

Nods all around. They'd learned the hard way that survival meant caution, meant always having an escape route, meant never taking anything for granted.

The road wound through farmland—fields of unharvested wheat beginning to wilt in the late October cold, stone walls crumbling, gates hanging open. Every farm they passed was silent and abandoned. No smoke from chimneys. No lights in windows. Just empty buildings and the occasional lowing of cattle that had been left to fend for themselves.

"Do you think anyone's left?" Tommy asked after they'd been walking for an hour. "I mean, anywhere. Do you think there are still places that are… normal?"

"The islands might be," Alexander said, though he wasn't sure he believed it anymore. Five days ago he'd been certain Druichmachon was safe, that the ocean would protect them. Now he wasn't sure of anything.

"I heard on the radio," Margaret said, "before the broadcasts stopped. They said the Highlands were holding out. Something about the sparse population, easier to contain."

"Contain what, though?" David asked. "They never said what it was. What caused it."

"Does it matter?" Sarah said quietly. "Knowing what caused it won't bring anyone back. Won't make those things less dangerous."

"It matters if there's a cure," David replied. "If someone, somewhere knows what this is and how to stop it."

"Then we find those people," Alexander said. "But first we survive. We get to safety. Then we can worry about answers."

They walked in silence for a while, each lost in their own thoughts.

Around mid-morning, they crested a hill and saw it—Belnahouthie spread out below them in a valley that led down to the sea. The town was bigger than the village they'd passed through yesterday, with proper streets and shops and a small industrial area near the harbour. Beyond the town, the gray waters of the Sound stretched out toward the islands in the distance.

And there, docked at the ferry terminal, was a large vessel—the MV Hebridean, its white and blue paint gleaming even under the overcast sky. Its loading ramp was down, and the ship's engines were running. Alexander could see smoke coming from the funnel.

"It's there," Tommy said, wonder in his voice. "The ferry's actually there."

"And it's running," Sarah added. "Look at the smoke. The engines are on."

Hope surged through Alexander, so powerful it almost hurt. After everything—after Frank and Angus and Morag and Claire, after days of walking on a shattered ankle, after five nights of broken promises to his daughter—they were finally here. The ferry was right there. Waiting.

"Come on," he said, starting down the hill. "Let's not waste time."

But Margaret caught his arm. "Wait. Look at the town."

Alexander stopped and really looked. At first glance, Belnahouthie appeared quiet—no movement in the streets, no signs of life. But as he studied it more carefully, he began to see the details. Broken windows. Overturned cars. Dark stains on the pavement. And movement—subtle, slow, shambling movement in the shadows between buildings.

"It's not empty," David said quietly. "There are infected down there."

"Lots of them," Sarah agreed. "Look, there by the shop. And near that car park. And—oh God, there must be dozens."

She was right. The more Alexander looked, the more he saw. Aimless wandering through the streets in that distinctive jerky gait. Some alone, others in small groups. All of them moving with that same purposeless shuffle—until something caught their attention.

"The ferry terminal's on the far side of town," Alexander said, tracing the route with his eyes. "We'd have to go through the main street to reach it. Right through the densest part of the town."

"Could we go around?" Tommy suggested. "Along the coast maybe?"

Alexander studied the geography. The town was built in a narrow valley between steep hills. The coastal route would mean climbing down rocky cliffs, exposed and vulnerable. And it would take hours—hours they didn't have if that ferry was preparing to leave.

"We'd never make it in time," he said. "That ship could leave any minute. We have to go through."

"Through a town full of infected," David said flatly. "That's suicide."

"Maybe not," Sarah said. She was studying the streets below with narrowed eyes. "Look at how they're distributed. They're not evenly spread out. Most of them are concentrated around certain areas—the shops, the car parks, places where people would have gathered. But look at the residential streets. They're clearer."

She was right. The Aimless seemed drawn to the commercial centre of town, leaving some of the side streets relatively empty.

"If we stick to the residential areas," Sarah continued, "move quietly, avoid the main street entirely, we might be able to make it through without attracting too much attention."

"And if we're spotted?" Margaret asked.

"Then we run," Alexander said simply. "We're close enough to see the ferry. We're not turning back now."

He looked at each of them in turn. Saw the fear in their eyes, but also the determination. They'd come too far to give up now.

"Everyone check your weapons," he said. "Make sure you can draw them quickly if needed. We move fast but quiet. Stay close together. If someone falls behind, we all stop. Nobody gets left behind. Understood?"

"Understood," they chorused quietly.

They started down the hill, moving off the main road and into the fields that bordered the town. As they got closer, the full extent of the devastation became clear. Houses with their doors hanging open. Gardens trampled and destroyed. A children's playground with swings swaying gently in the wind, one of them stained with dried blood.

This had been someone's home. Hundreds of people had lived here, worked here, raised families here. And now it was a graveyard.

They reached the outskirts of town and paused behind an overturned delivery van. From here, they could hear the moans—low, constant, the sound of dozens of Aimless wandering somewhere nearby.

"Residential streets," Alexander whispered, pointing to the right. "That way. Quiet and quick."

They moved into the town.

The first street was narrow, lined with small terraced houses. Most of the windows were dark, but occasionally Alexander caught glimpses of movement inside—Aimless trapped in their own homes, too mindless to figure out how to open doors.

They passed a house where an Aimless stood at the window, its gray face pressed against the glass, orange veins pulsing. It saw them and began moaning, clawing at the window. But the glass held, and the group hurried past.

"Don't run," Alexander hissed as Tommy started to bolt. "Running makes noise. Just walk quickly."

They turned a corner and found themselves on a slightly wider street. Here there were Aimless outside—three of them, clustered around an abandoned car. They were paying no attention to the group, too focused on trying to get into the vehicle. Something inside—maybe a body, maybe just the smell of decay—had attracted them.

"Wide berth," Alexander whispered. "Give them space."

They crossed to the other side of the street, moving as quietly as possible. The Aimless didn't look up. The group slipped past and continued deeper into the town.

The moaning was getting louder now. They were getting closer to the commercial centre, where the bulk of the infected were gathered. Alexander could see them ahead—a whole crowd of Aimless in what looked like a town square, maybe fifty or sixty of them, all clustered together.

"This way," Sarah whispered, pointing down an alley. "We can cut through, avoid the square entirely."

The alley was narrow and dark, barely wide enough for them to walk single file. Bins lined one side, their contents rotting and rancid. The smell was overwhelming.

Halfway down the alley, something moved.

An Aimless stumbled out from behind a bin, almost directly in front of Margaret. She gasped—not loudly, but loud enough—and the Aimless's head snapped toward her.

David moved without thinking, swinging his cricket bat. The impact caught the Aimless on the side of the head with a sickening crack. It went down hard but immediately started trying to get back up.

"Move!" Alexander hissed.

They ran down the rest of the alley, emerging onto another residential street. Behind them, the Aimless was still struggling to rise, its moans echoing down the alley.

"Did it alert the others?" Tommy panted.

They listened. The general moaning from the town square continued unchanged. No sign that the horde had heard.

"We're okay," Alexander said. "But we need to move faster. We're running out of time."

They could see the harbour now, just a few streets away. The ferry was clearly visible, its white hull bright against the gray water. So close. So tantalizingly close.

"One more street," Sarah said. "Just one more and we're at the harbour road."

They hurried forward, caution giving way to desperation. Alexander's ankle was screaming, but he ignored it. Nothing mattered except reaching that ferry.

They turned onto the final residential street—and stopped dead.

Spotify Apple Music Amazon Music

Track: BELNAHOUTHIE FERRY

The street was full of Aimless. Not just a few, but dozens of them, all wandering aimlessly between the houses. There was no way through without being seen.

"Shit," David breathed.

"Back," Alexander said. "We'll find another—"

That's when they heard it.

From somewhere behind them, rising above the general moaning, came a sound that made Alexander's blood run cold.

A screech. High-pitched, piercing, inhuman.

A Screecher.

"Oh no," Margaret whimpered. "Not again."

The screech came again, closer now. And the Aimless in the street ahead of them suddenly became more animated. Their wandering took on purpose. They began moving faster, their heads turning, searching.

"The Screecher's directing them," Alexander said, his worst fear confirmed. "It's coordinating them."

"What do we do?" Tommy asked, panic rising in his voice.

Alexander looked around desperately. Behind them, the Screecher. Ahead, a street full of Aimless that were now alert and searching. To either side, more houses—but entering one could trap them.

Then he saw it. A shop on the corner, its windows broken but its door hanging open. And beyond it, just visible through the shattered glass—a back alley that led toward the harbour.

"There," he said, pointing. "The shop. We go through it, out the back, and make a run for the harbour."

"What about all those Aimless?" David asked.

The screech came again. The Aimless in the street ahead were now moving with purpose, shambling toward the sound—and toward the group.

"We don't have a choice," Alexander said. "We run. Now!"

They bolted for the shop, abandoning all pretense of stealth. Their footsteps pounded on the pavement. Behind them, the Screecher's cry rose to a fever pitch.

And then it appeared.

The Screecher came around the corner they'd just left, its pale, emaciated form moving with that horrible, jerky speed. Its jaw hung open impossibly wide, revealing rows of jagged teeth. Its eyes—milky white and empty—somehow still managed to fix directly on them.

It screeched again, and this time the sound was deafening.

Every Aimless in the street turned toward them.

"GO!" Alexander roared.

They crashed through the shop door into what had once been a small grocery store. Shelves lay toppled, their contents scattered across the floor. The group stumbled over cans and bottles, racing toward the back door that Alexander had spotted.

Behind them, the Aimless were pouring into the shop, their moans filling the air.

Sarah reached the back door first and yanked it open. "It's clear! Come on!"

They piled through into a narrow alley. The harbour was visible at the end—no more than fifty yards away. The ferry sat at the dock, engines still running.

"Don't stop!" Alexander yelled. "Straight to the ferry! GO!"

They ran.

Alexander's ankle gave out on the third step, and he went down hard, pain exploding through his leg. He tried to get up, couldn't, felt hands grabbing him.

"I've got you!" David had him under one arm, hauling him up. "Come on!"

They ran together, David half-carrying Alexander, the others just ahead. Behind them, the Aimless were spilling out of the shop and into the alley. The Screecher's cry echoed off the buildings.

They burst out of the alley onto the harbour road.

The ferry terminal building was just ahead—a small, modern structure with large windows. And beyond it, the MV Hebridean sat at the dock, its loading ramp still down.

But the area around the terminal was a nightmare.

Bodies littered the ground—some in ferry company uniforms, others clearly passengers. All of them showing the telltale signs of infection. And as the group watched in horror, the bodies began to move. Twitching. Rising.

"They're turning," Sarah gasped. "Right now, they're turning!"

"The ferry!" Alexander pointed. "Just get to the ferry! Ignore everything else!"

They ran across the terminal area, weaving between the rising Aimless. An infected ferry worker lunged at Tommy. David swung his cricket bat, connecting solidly, and the worker went down. But like all the others, it immediately started getting back up.

"They won't stay down!" David shouted.

"Don't try to fight them!" Alexander yelled back. "Just run!"

Sarah reached the boarding ramp first. "It's clear! The ramp is clear!"

Margaret was next, then Tommy, both of them racing up the metal ramp onto the ferry deck. David and Alexander were right behind them, Alexander's bad leg dragging, David practically carrying him.

They were almost there. Just a few more feet.

Then the Screecher appeared.

It came from inside the ferry terminal building, smashing through the glass doors in an explosion of shards. Its screech was so loud, so piercing, that everyone stumbled. Alexander felt his ears ring, felt his balance waver.

The Screecher fixed its empty eyes on them and charged.

It was impossibly fast. Crossing the distance in seconds. Its clawed hands reaching out.

David dropped his cricket bat, letting it clatter away, and used both hands to literally throw Alexander toward the ramp. "GO!"

Alexander hit the ramp hard, rolling, pain shooting through every part of his body. Above him, he could see Sarah and Margaret reaching down, grabbing his arms, pulling him up.

"DAVID!" he screamed.

David was backing up the ramp, but the Screecher was right there. It lunged, its claws raking across David's arm. David screamed and fell backward onto the ramp.

The Screecher started to follow him up.

And then Tommy was there.

The boy—because he was just a boy, barely sixteen—grabbed the ramp control lever and pulled.

The ramp began to rise.

Slowly. Too slowly.

The Screecher was still climbing, its claws scraping on the metal, its jaw opening wider, that horrible screech building again.

David kicked out desperately, catching the Screecher in the face. It recoiled, lost its grip, fell—

—and landed on the dock just as the ramp lifted clear.

The Screecher's final screech was one of rage and frustration. It leaped, clawed at the rising ramp, but couldn't reach. Below it, Aimless were gathering, dozens of them, all reaching up toward the ferry, all moaning in unison.

The ramp locked into its raised position with a heavy clank.

For a moment, nobody moved. They all just stood there on the vehicle deck of the MV Hebridean, breathing hard, bleeding, broken, but alive.

They'd made it.

Against all odds, through all the horror, they'd made it to the ferry.

Alexander lay on the cold metal deck, his vision blurring from pain and exhaustion. Through the gaps in the railing, he could see the dock below. The Screecher was still there, still screeching, still calling to its horde. The Aimless were gathering in their dozens, maybe hundreds, all clustered around the ferry.

But they were separated now. The water between the dock and the ferry was only a few feet, but it might as well have been an ocean.

"Is everyone…" Alexander managed to gasp out. "Is everyone okay?"

"David's hurt," Sarah said. She was kneeling beside him, examining his arm. "The Screecher got him. Deep cuts, bleeding badly, but…"

"But what?" Margaret asked.

Sarah looked up, and her expression was grim. "But I don't think it's infected. The wounds are clean. No orange veins. No discoloration."

David was sitting up, cradling his arm. Blood seeped between his fingers, but he was conscious and alert. "I'm okay," he said through gritted teeth. "Hurts like hell, but I'm okay."

Tommy was staring down at the dock, his face pale. "There's so many of them. So many."

He was right. The infected were still gathering, drawn by the Screecher's calls. The dock was becoming a mass of gray flesh and pulsing orange veins, all of them reaching toward the ferry, all of them moaning.

"We need to get this ferry moving," Alexander said, struggling to sit up. Every part of his body protested. "We need to get away from here before something else happens."

"How?" Margaret asked. "None of us know how to drive a ferry."

"Then we find someone who does," Alexander said. "There must be crew aboard. The engines are running. Someone has to be here."

They helped each other to their feet—Alexander leaning heavily on Sarah, David cradling his injured arm, Margaret and Tommy supporting each other. A group of battered survivors who should have been dead a dozen times over but somehow weren't.

It was late morning now, maybe eleven o'clock. Six hours ago they'd been leaving the chapel, facing seven miles of dangerous terrain and a town full of infected. Now they were standing on a ferry, about to attempt something none of them had ever done before.

Alexander pulled out his phone—5% battery left. One more look at the wallpaper photo. Ailsa and Magsy, frozen in that moment of happiness, before the world ended.

"I'm coming home," he whispered to the photo. "I swear to God, I'm coming home."

He put the phone away and turned to the others.

"Alright," he said. "Let's figure out how to sail this thing. We've got an hour to become a crew, and then we're getting the hell out of here."

Below them, the Screecher continued to call. The Aimless continued to gather. The dead world continued to die.

But Alexander was one step closer to home, to his family, to his whole world.

15

The Empty Ferry

Spotify Apple Music Amazon Music

Track: SOLITARY SEAS

The ferry's main deck was eerily empty, their footsteps echoing on the metal floor. Emergency lighting cast everything in a sickly yellow-green glow, creating shadows that seemed to move with malevolent purpose.

"This is wrong," Sarah whispered. "Where is everyone?"

Alexander looked around at the abandoned deck—life jackets hanging unused, safety information displays flickering, a coffee cup still steaming on a bench. He reached out and touched the cup. Still warm.

"Someone was here recently," he said, his voice low. "Very recently."

"Maybe they evacuated?" Tommy suggested hopefully, though his voice trembled.

"Or maybe they're like the ones outside," David said grimly, gripping his cricket bat tighter.

The ferry rocked gently beneath them, the sound of water lapping against the hull mixing with the hum of the engines. It should have been peaceful, normal. Instead, it felt like a trap.

Alexander noticed something else—a trail of dark stains on the deck, leading toward the stairs. He knelt down and touched one. His fingers came away red.

"Blood," he said quietly. "Still wet."

Margaret made a small sound of distress, her hand tightening on her walking stick.

"We need to get to the bridge," Alexander said, standing. "Figure out how to operate this thing."

"Can you drive a ferry?" Margaret asked.

"I've never operated anything this big. I grew up on boats, but nothing like this. But I have to try." He looked at each of them in turn. "Stay close. Stay quiet. And if something happens, if we get separated, the goal is the bridge. We meet at the bridge."

They moved cautiously toward the stairs leading to the upper decks, Alexander in the lead with his knife, Sarah behind him with her hand axe. David brought up the rear with his cricket bat. The blood trail continued up the stairs, a grim breadcrumb path leading them deeper into the ship.

The stairwell was narrow, forcing them to climb single file. Their footsteps clanged on the metal steps, impossibly loud in the silence. Alexander kept expecting something to lunge at them from above, kept imagining infected crew members waiting in the shadows.

But nothing came.

They reached the passenger deck, and Alexander held up his hand, signalling them to stop. The deck stretched before them—rows of seats, abandoned bags, a child's toy lying forgotten on the floor. A teddy bear, Alexander noticed, its button eyes staring at nothing.

He thought of Magsy's toys, scattered around their cottage. Would he ever see them again? Would he ever watch her play, hear her laugh, hold her in his arms?

"Alexander?" Sarah's voice pulled him back to the present.

"Sorry. Just… thinking." He shook his head, forcing himself to focus. "Let's keep moving."

The blood trail had disappeared now, or perhaps it had never continued this far. They moved through the passenger deck, checking behind seats, opening storage compartments, looking for any sign of life or threat.

"Look at this," Tommy said, pointing to a notice board near the cafeteria. Pinned to it was a handwritten note:

To anyone who finds this: The crew is infected. Captain tried to contain it but it spread too fast. We're abandoning ship. If you're reading this, get to the bridge and set course for Auld Strathdee. The autopilot knows the way. God help you. - First Mate Robertson

"At least we know the autopilot works," David said, trying to sound optimistic.

"And we know the crew is infected," Sarah added. "Which means they could still be on board."

They continued up toward the bridge level. A narrow corridor led to the bridge, with several doors lining the hallway—crew quarters, storage rooms. Each door was a potential threat, a place where something could be hiding, waiting.

One door was slightly ajar, a sliver of darkness visible through the gap.

Alexander approached it carefully, knife ready. He could hear something from inside—a soft, wet sound, like someone breathing through fluid-filled lungs.

He pushed the door open slowly.

Inside was a small room with bunk beds. On one of the beds lay a ferry worker in uniform. He was clearly dead—gray skin, orange veins spreading across his face like cracks in porcelain. But his chest was still moving, rising and falling with shallow, laboured breaths.

"Is he…?" Margaret whispered.

"Dead. But not turned yet, I think." Alexander watched the man's chest rise and fall. "The infection must take time. He's in transition."

"Should we…" David trailed off, not wanting to finish the sentence.

"Should we kill him?" Alexander finished. "Before he turns?"

They all looked at the dying man. He looked peaceful, almost serene, unaware of what was happening to him, unaware of what he was becoming.

"We can't just murder him," Sarah said. "He's still human."

"For now," David countered. "But in a few minutes, he'll be one of those things. And if we leave him, he could attack us later."

Alexander stared at the man, thinking about Frank, about Sarah from the conference, about all the people he'd seen change. The transformation was inevitable. This man was already dead; his body just didn't know it yet.

But could he kill someone who wasn't yet a threat? Could he cross that line?

Suddenly, the worker's eyes snapped open. They were clouded, unfocused, but there was something in them—a flicker of awareness, of fear, of understanding.

"Please," the man whispered, his voice barely audible. "Don't… let me… become…"

He couldn't finish the sentence. His body convulsed, his back arching, his hands clawing at the sheets. The orange veins spread faster now, racing across his skin like wildfire.

"Please," he gasped again, and this time there was no doubt what he was asking for.

Alexander stepped forward, knife in hand. "I'm sorry," he said quietly.

He drove the knife into the man's temple, quick and clean. The body went limp immediately, the convulsions stopping, the fear leaving his eyes.

Alexander pulled the knife free and stepped back, his hands shaking. Behind him, he heard Margaret's sharp intake of breath.

"You did the right thing," David said. "He asked you to."

"Did I?" Alexander looked at his hands, at the blood on the knife. "Or did I just murder a dying man?"

"He was already dead," Margaret said gently. "You gave him mercy. You gave him peace."

Alexander wanted to believe that. He needed to believe that. But the weight of what he'd done settled on his shoulders like a physical burden, adding to the guilt he already carried.

"Let's keep moving," he said, his voice hollow.

They continued toward the bridge, more cautious now, knowing that death could be waiting behind any door. They passed more crew quarters, a small galley, a storage room filled with life jackets and emergency equipment.

The bridge door was closed but unlocked. Alexander pushed it open, knife ready, expecting another infected crew member.

But the bridge was empty.

All the controls were still active, though. Navigation screens glowed, showing their current position. Radar displays swept in endless circles. The autopilot indicator blinked steadily: STANDBY MODE.

Alexander approached the control panel, his heart sinking at the complexity of it all. Dozens of screens, hundreds of buttons and switches, displays showing information he didn't understand.

"This is more complex than anything I've ever seen," he said.

Sarah pointed to an open logbook on the captain's desk. "Look—there's a logbook."

Alexander picked it up and read the last few entries aloud:

Day 1 of the crisis: Reports of violence in Belnahouthie. Evacuated 150 passengers to Auld Strathdee. Crew nervous but holding together.

Day 2: Situation deteriorating rapidly. Evacuated 200 more passengers this morning. Three crew members showing symptoms—fever, aggression, those damned orange veins. Quarantined them in the cargo hold. Returning for final run.

Day 2, Evening: Quarantine failed. Infected crew broke out. Captain bitten trying to contain them. Ordered evacuation. Strange sounds from below deck—scratching, scraping against the hull from outside. Something in the water? God help us all.

Final Entry: I'm the last one left. Everyone else is dead or turned or fled. I can hear them in the corridors, searching for me. The scratching from outside is getting louder. I think... I think there's something in the water. Something that followed us from Belnahouthie. I'm going to set the autopilot for Auld Strathdee and then... I don't know. Maybe I'll jump. Better to drown than become one of those things. To whoever finds this: I'm sorry. I'm so sorry we couldn't save everyone. – First Mate Morrison

The group stood in silence, absorbing the captain's final words.

"Scratching from outside?" Tommy's voice was small, frightened. "What could scratch the hull of a ferry?"

"What could scratch the hull of a ferry?" David repeated, looking out the bridge windows at the dark water surrounding them.

Margaret wrapped her arms around herself. "Maybe it's nothing. Maybe the captain was just… stressed. Hallucinating."

But Alexander remembered the scraping sounds they'd heard at the dock, the sense of something moving in the water. He didn't think the captain had been hallucinating.

He studied the navigation screen, trying to push away the unsettling thought. "According to this, we're still docked. The autopilot is engaged but set to 'standby'."

He found what looked like the main control panel, a touchscreen with various options. The interface was surprisingly intuitive—destination selection, speed controls, automated navigation.

"I think… if I change this setting to 'Auld Strathdee'…"

He touched the screen. A route appeared, showing a 10-mile journey across the water. Estimated time: 58 minutes.

"Can you do it?" Sarah asked.

"The computer seems to know the way. I just need to…" He pressed what appeared to be an 'engage' button.

Nothing happened for a moment. Then the ferry's engines changed pitch, deepening to a powerful thrum. They felt the vessel beginning to move, a subtle shift beneath their feet, the gentle pull of momentum.

"We're moving!" Margaret cried with relief.

Through the bridge windows, they could see the lights of Belnahouthie slowly pulling away. On the shore, the Screecher let out another piercing call, but it was getting fainter, less threatening.

"We did it," Alexander said, relief flooding through him. "We're heading to Auld Strathdee."

"How long will it take?" David asked.

Alexander checked the navigation display. "About an hour at this speed."

"What do we do for an hour?" Tommy asked.

"We search the ship. Make sure we're alone. And figure out what we're going to do when we reach Auld Strathdee."

As if summoned by the captain's log entry, they heard a faint sound from somewhere below—a soft scraping noise, rhythmic and deliberate.

Sarah tensed. "Did you hear that?"

They all listened. The sound came again—definitely scraping, but muffled, coming from deep within the ship. And beneath it, almost too faint to hear, that same soft knocking the captain had described.

"Could be anything," David said, though his voice lacked conviction. "Old ship, rough seas…"

"Right," Alexander said, though he didn't believe it either. "Let's search the ship. Stay together."

They left the bridge and began their systematic search of the ferry, starting at the top and working their way down. The upper passenger deck was clear—empty seats, abandoned belongings, but no people, no bodies, no threats.

But there were signs of panic. Overturned chairs. Scattered personal items. A woman's shoe lying in the middle of an aisle. A child's backpack, its contents spilled across the floor—crayons, a colouring book, a juice box.

"They ran," Sarah said quietly. "They were trying to escape something."

The main passenger deck was the same. They found the cafeteria, food still laid out behind the counter. Sandwiches under glass, pastries in display cases, a coffee machine still warm.

"There's food here," Tommy said, his voice tight with hunger. "Actual food."

"Take what you need," Alexander said. "We don't know when we'll eat again."

They didn't need to be told twice. They grabbed sandwiches, pastries, bottles of water and juice. It was the first real food any of them had eaten in over a day, and despite the circumstances and the fear that still gripped them, it tasted like heaven.

As they ate, the scraping sound came again, louder now, more insistent. It seemed to be moving along the hull, pacing them, keeping up with the ferry's speed.

"It's coming from below," David said. "The car deck."

Alexander stood, wiping his mouth. "We need to check it out."

"Do we have to?" Sarah asked, though she was already standing, already preparing to follow.

The scraping came again, followed by a sound that made Alexander's blood run cold—a soft knocking, as if something was tapping against the hull from outside. Tap. Tap. Tap. Rhythmic. Purposeful.

"Yes," Alexander said. "We need to know what's down there."

They descended to the car deck, a large open space designed for vehicles. Currently empty except for some maintenance equipment and a few cargo containers. The space was cavernous, their footsteps echoing off the metal walls.

The scraping sound echoed through the space, louder here, more distinct. And the knocking was clearer too—not random, not the sound of debris hitting the hull. It was deliberate, patterned, almost like…

"It sounds like it's trying to get in," Tommy whispered.

They moved toward the sound, toward the port side of the ship. Near a small porthole, they could hear it clearly now—something scraping against the metal hull, rhythmic and purposeful. And beneath it, that knocking, that tapping, as if something was testing the hull's strength, looking for a way inside.

Alexander looked through the porthole. Dark water rushed past, foam and spray obscuring his view. He couldn't see anything unusual. Just water, dark and cold and endless.

The scraping came again, and this time Alexander caught a glimpse of something—something dark moving in the water, something that didn't look like debris or foam. It was large, larger than a person, and it moved with purpose, keeping pace with the ferry.

"I thought I saw…" He trailed off, not wanting to voice his fear.

"What did you think you saw?" Sarah asked, though from her expression, she didn't really want to know.

"Nothing. Just tricks of the light."

But he had seen something. Something large, something that moved with purpose, something that was following the ferry through the dark water. And if the captain's log was right, it had been following them since Belnahouthie.

The scraping sound moved along the hull, as if whatever was making it was pacing them, keeping up with the ferry's speed. Twenty knots, the navigation display had said. Whatever was out there could swim at twenty knots.

"It's moving with us," Tommy said, his voice tight with fear.

"Debris can get caught in the wake," David said, but even he sounded uncertain. "It'll probably fall away once we change course."

Alexander checked his watch. "We've got forty minutes until we reach Auld Strathdee. Let's head back up. No point staying down here."

They climbed back to the passenger deck, but the scraping continued, sometimes loud, sometimes faint, but persistent. It followed them through the water, whatever it was, staying just out of sight, just beyond the reach of the light.

They gathered in the passenger lounge, sitting in a circle, trying to ignore the sounds from below. But it was impossible. Every few minutes, the scraping would come again, a reminder that they weren't alone, that something was out there in the dark water.

"Tell me about Druichmachon," Sarah said to Alexander, clearly trying to distract herself. "What's it like?"

Alexander smiled, grateful for the distraction. "It's small. Maybe three hundred people. Everyone knows everyone. There's one school, one pub, one shop. The kind of place where if you sneeze in the morning, someone's bringing you soup by afternoon."

"Sounds nice," Tommy said.

"It is. It's home. The air smells like salt and heather. You can see the stars at night, really see them, not like in the cities. And the sunsets…" He trailed off, remembering watching sunsets with

Ailsa, Magsy on his shoulders, the three of them silhouetted against the orange sky. “The sunsets are beautiful. The whole sky turns orange and pink and purple, and the water reflects it all, and for a few minutes, the whole world is on fire with colour.”

“You’ll get back there,” Margaret said gently. “You’ll see your family again.”

“I have to,” Alexander said simply. “I promised.”

They sat in silence for a while, each lost in their own thoughts. David thought about his office, his routine, the boring safety of his old life. Sarah thought about her parents, about hiking in the hills, about the moment she’d come home to find everything changed. Margaret thought about her grandchildren, wondering if they were safe, if they’d survived. Tommy thought about his parents, about the moment they’d changed, about running and hiding and being so terribly alone.

“Sounds nice,” Tommy said.

“It is. It’s home. The air smells like salt and heather. You can see the stars at night, really see them, not like in the cities. And the sunsets…” He trailed off, remembering watching sunsets with Ailsa, Magsy on his shoulders, the three of them silhouetted against the orange sky. “The sunsets are beautiful. The whole sky turns orange and pink and purple, and the water reflects it all, and for a few minutes, the whole world is on fire with colour.”

“You’ll get back there,” Margaret said gently. “You’ll see your family again.”

“I have to,” Alexander said simply. “I promised.”

They sat in silence for a while, each lost in their own thoughts. David thought about his office, his routine, the boring safety of his old life. Sarah thought about her parents, about hiking in the hills, about the moment she’d come home to find everything changed. Margaret thought about her grandchildren, wondering if they were safe, if they’d survived. Tommy thought about his parents, about the moment they’d changed, about running and hiding and being so terribly alone.

And Alexander thought about Ailsa and Magsy, about the cottage by the harbour, about the promise he'd made and the distance he still had to cross. Ten miles of water, then however many miles of land to the next ferry. And then home. Finally home.

The ferry continued its journey across the dark waters, carrying its small group of survivors toward an uncertain destination. And beneath them, in the cold depths, something followed, scraping and knocking, patient and persistent.

Waiting.

16

Auld Strathdee

Spotify Apple Music Amazon Music

Track: AULD STRATHDEE

The hour passed slowly, each minute marked by the steady thrum of the ferry's engines and the occasional scraping sound from below. Alexander stood at the bridge windows, watching the dark water ahead, shifting his weight off his injured ankle, looking for any sign of their destination.

"There," he said finally, pointing. "Auld Strathdee."

In the distance, lights were visible—a port, civilization, hope. As they drew closer, Alexander could see that the port was indeed active. People were moving around, vehicles were positioned strategically, and everything looked organised, controlled.

But something felt off.

"Those aren't army vehicles," Sarah observed.

She was right. The vehicles were sleek and black with tinted windows, more corporate than military. Men in black tactical gear moved between them with professional efficiency.

On the side of one van, barely visible in the dim light, was corporate lettering: "VitaGenix" with a logo showing a twisted double helix with a butterfly at the end.

"Private security?" David wondered. "Corporate?"

Alexander stared at the logo, that nagging feeling of recognition returning stronger now. He'd seen that logo before—on the convoy in the forest. VitaGenix. What was a private corporation doing running evacuation operations? Where was the military? Where was the government?

Before he could voice his concerns, a voice came through the ferry's external speakers, warm and reassuring.

"Welcome, survivors of the Belnahouthie ferry. You're safe now. We're here to help. Please exit the vessel calmly—we have food, medical care, and secure shelter waiting for you."

"Oh thank goodness," Margaret said with relief. "They sound like they're trying to help."

"Food and medical care," Sarah said. "That's exactly what we need."

Through the windows, they could see figures in black uniforms approaching the ferry, their body language non-threatening, almost welcoming.

"They seem… professional. Organised," David observed.

"Secure shelter sounds amazing right now," Tommy added.

The announcement continued, friendly and encouraging. "We know you've been through a terrible ordeal. Our teams are specially trained to help survivors like yourselves. We'll get you cleaned up, fed, and somewhere safe to rest."

"They sound so kind," Margaret said.

Alexander felt torn. Everything about this looked legitimate—organised, professional, helpful. But something in his gut told him to be cautious. Why was a private corporation running evacuation operations? And that logo—the twisted double helix. A DNA helix. A genetic company. And the infection, with its orange veins and gray skin, looked almost… engineered.

"You should go with them," he said finally. "Get somewhere safe."

Sarah looked at him sharply. "What do you mean? Aren't you coming?"

"I can't. I have to get north. My family is waiting for me."

"Alexander, be reasonable," David said. "You need rest, food, medical attention. Your ankle—"

"I need to get home. I promised my daughter two sleeps. It's already been longer than that."

"But they said it's safe," Tommy protested. "They can help you get to your family."

Alexander shook his head. "I can't risk getting stuck in some camp. I have to keep moving north."

"How will you get there?" Margaret asked. "You don't have transport."

"I'll find a way. I always do."

The ferry docked with a mechanical thud. The group moved toward the exit, but Alexander's resolve was clear—he wouldn't be going to any safe zone.

They walked down the boarding ramp together. At the bottom, several figures in black tactical gear waited for them. The lead figure removed his helmet, revealing a clean-shaven, professional-looking man in his forties.

"Welcome to Auld Strathdee. I'm Commander Hayes. I know you've been through hell, but you're safe now."

"Thank you," Margaret said, her voice breaking with relief. "We… we didn't think anyone was left."

"We're here to help. Our sanctuary has everything you need—hot meals, clean beds, medical care."

Alexander hung back slightly as the others moved forward. Hayes noticed.

"Sir, I understand your concern, but travel north is extremely dangerous right now. The infection has spread throughout the country including all the islands."

"I have to try," Alexander said.

"We can help you contact your family from our sanctuary. We have communication equipment."

Alexander shook his head. "No. I'm going north. Now."

The other survivors looked at Alexander with concern.

"Alexander, please," Tommy said. "Come with us."

"You'll die out there alone," Margaret added.

"I made a promise to my little girl," Alexander said firmly. "I'm keeping it."

Hayes signalled to his men, who began escorting the other survivors toward the vehicles. They went willingly, grateful for the promise of safety and care.

"If you change your mind," Hayes said to Alexander, "we'll be at the old VitaGenix facility outside Strathgarve. Just follow the helix markers."

"Alexander!" Sarah called as she was led away. "Please!"

Alexander watched as his companions were helped into the VitaGenix vehicles. David looked back one last time.

"Good luck, mate. I hope you make it home."

The vehicles drove away, leaving Alexander alone on the empty dock. He watched them disappear into the night, hoping he'd made the right decision, hoping they would be safe.

But something in his gut told him he'd made the right choice. Something about VitaGenix, about their too-perfect organisation, about their corporate efficiency in the midst of an apocalypse, felt wrong.

And that logo—the twisted double helix with a butterfly. He'd seen it on the convoy, seen it on the vehicles, seen it spray-painted on buildings. VitaGenix was everywhere, moving through the highlands like a well-oiled machine, collecting survivors and taking them… where?

Alexander didn't know. And right now, he didn't care. All that mattered was getting home.

"Right then," he said to himself. "Time to find a way north."

He looked around the deserted port, gripping his knife, and started walking toward the town centre. Somewhere in Auld Strathdee, there had to be a vehicle, a boat, something he could use to continue his journey.

Somewhere north, across hundreds of miles of infected territory, Ailsa and Magsy were waiting.

Two sleeps, he'd promised.

It had been four days now. Four days of horror and death and survival. But he was still alive. Still moving forward. Still keeping his promise, one step at a time.

He would get home.

No matter what it took.

Spotify Apple Music Amazon Music

Track: ALEXANDERS ESCAPE

Alexander walked through the empty streets of Auld Strathdee, his footsteps echoing off the buildings like lonely drumbeats in the silence, each step sending a dull throb of pain up his injured ankle. The town was larger than Belnahouthie but just as deserted, a ghost town frozen in the moment when the world ended. Street lights flickered intermittently, casting pools of light and shadow that danced across the abandoned pavement. Shop windows were dark, some shattered, their displays ransacked or left untouched—testaments to the chaos and confusion that had swept through here. Abandoned cars sat in the middle of the road, doors left open as if their drivers had simply vanished mid-journey, engines cold and dead.

His heart hammered against his ribs with each step, each sound he made feeling impossibly loud in the oppressive quiet. He approached the first car—a small hatchback, its driver's door slightly ajar. As he got closer, he heard a low moan from nearby, the sound sending ice through his veins. An Aimless emerged from between two parked cars, shuffling toward him with that characteristic zombie-like gait, its head tilted at an unnatural angle, its face a mask of gray skin and clouded eyes.

Alexander gripped his knife and moved around it, staying quiet, his breathing shallow, trying not to put too much weight on his bad ankle. The Aimless continued wandering aimlessly, not noticing him, its path taking it in the opposite direction. Alexander let out a breath he hadn't realized he'd been holding.

"Stay quiet," he whispered to himself, the words barely audible. "Just stay quiet."

He checked the car's ignition—empty, as expected. He searched the sun visor, the glove compartment, under the seats. Nothing. No keys, no hope.

He moved to the next car—a Ford Focus with a family's belongings still scattered across the back seat, children's toys and books lying abandoned. Two more Aimless were wandering near it, bumping into each other mindlessly, their movements slow but relentless. Alexander waited for them to move away before approaching the car, his heart pounding. Same result. No keys. Empty, useless, another dead end in a world full of them.

"Damn it," he whispered, the frustration mounting like pressure in his chest. Every moment he spent here was another moment Ailsa and Magsy were waiting, wondering, worrying.

From somewhere in the distance came that horrible, piercing screech—the sound that had haunted his nightmares since the hotel, the sound of the fast ones, the deadly ones. Alexander froze, every muscle in his body tensing. All the Aimless in the area suddenly became more alert, their movements gaining purpose, their heads turning toward the source of the sound. The aimless shuffling became directed, purposeful.

"Not good," he whispered, his voice tight with fear. "Not good at all."

He ducked behind a van as the Aimless started moving more purposefully, their coordination suddenly chilling. The screeching came again, closer this time, the sound cutting through the night air like a knife. Alexander spotted an alley between two buildings and made a run for it, ignoring the flare of pain in his ankle, his legs pumping, his breath coming in ragged gasps.

The alley was narrow, hemmed in by brick walls that rose stories above him. Alexander pressed himself against the rough brickwork, breathing hard, his chest aching. He put his back to the wall and lifted his injured foot slightly, giving it a moment's relief. Through the gap between buildings, he could see a Screecher moving down the main street. Its pale, emaciated form moved with unnatural speed, all coiled muscle and deadly intent. It let out another screech, and more Aimless emerged from buildings and doorways, drawn to the call like moths to a deadly flame.

Alexander waited until the sounds faded before moving, his legs trembling with adrenaline, his ankle throbbing with each heartbeat. He emerged onto a quieter back street, the air thick with the smell of decay and abandonment. He continued checking cars, his hands shaking, his hope dwindling with each empty ignition, his limp becoming more pronounced with each failed attempt. But the sound of heavy footsteps made him look up, made his blood run cold.

At the end of the street, a massive silhouette appeared—a Bullseye. Eight feet tall, gray skin with pulsing orange veins that seemed to glow with malevolent life. It was moving slowly but deliberately, searching, its heavy footsteps shaking the ground even from this distance.

"Oh fuck," Alexander breathed, the words barely escaping his lips. "Fuck. Fuck. Fuck."

Alexander ducked behind a van and waited, his heart hammering so hard he thought it might burst from his chest, his injured ankle screaming at him to rest. The Bullseye moved past, its massive form blocking out the streetlights, its heavy footsteps shaking the ground beneath him. Once it was gone, Alexander continued his search, his movements frantic, desperate, each step more painful than the last.

He reached a small garage at the end of the street, its sign reading "Mackenzie's Garage" in faded letters. The garage door was partially open, inviting, promising. Alexander checked for threats, then ducked underneath, his knife ready, grateful for a moment to take weight off his ankle.

The garage was dark, smelling of oil and metal and something else—something that might have been death. Alexander used his phone's flashlight sparingly, the beam cutting through the gloom, revealing tools scattered everywhere, workbenches covered in half-finished projects. A motorcycle sat in the corner, partially dismantled, its engine exposed like the entrails of some mechanical beast. On a pegboard, he spotted several sets of keys hanging like strange metal fruit.

"Finally," he whispered, the word a prayer of relief.

He grabbed the keys and headed back outside carefully, his senses heightened, every sound making him jump. He tried the keys on various cars parked nearby, constantly looking over his shoulder, expecting at any moment to see the Bullseye returning, to hear the screech of death approaching. In the distance, he could still hear the occasional moan and screech, the soundtrack of this nightmare world.

The third set worked—an old Land Rover, sturdy and reliable, exactly what he needed to get through the Highland roads.

Alexander got in, relief flooding through him as he took the weight off his injured ankle. His hands shook as he turned the key. The engine turned over but didn't start, coughing weakly.

"Come on… come on… quietly…" he whispered, his fingers crossed, his heart in his throat.

He tried again. The engine coughed to life, louder than he'd have liked, the sound echoing through the empty streets. Immediately, he heard responding moans from nearby, the sound of bodies stirring, of the dead awakening.

"Time to go," he said, his voice urgent with fear.

He checked the fuel gauge—quarter tank. Not great, but enough to get him.

He checked the fuel gauge—quarter tank. Not great, but enough to get him to Presthaven if he was careful. He couldn't afford to walk on it for the next 150 miles.

"I'm coming home, Magsy," he said aloud, his voice breaking. He was still coming home. He would always come home.

17

Glencore

Spotify Apple Music Amazon Music

Track: GLENCORE

The Land Rover's headlights cut through the darkness as Alexander drove north, the beams slicing through the night like knives. The road was narrow and winding, flanked by dense forest on both sides, the trees closing in like walls of some natural prison. His fuel gauge showed less than a quarter tank now, the needle edging dangerously close to empty. Alexander checked his phone—still no signal, battery at 1%, the screen dimming as if in surrender.

"Come on, just hold out a bit longer," he muttered to the device, though he knew it was futile.

In the distance, he saw the glow of a small town, a soft amber light that promised civilization, safety, maybe even fuel. Hope surged through him, sharp and painful.

A road sign appeared out of the darkness: "GLENCORE." The town appeared quiet as Alexander slowed the Land Rover, studying the scene with cautious optimism. Unlike the previous towns he'd passed through, this one didn't look completely abandoned. Candle lights flickered in some windows, warm and yellow, suggesting life, normalcy, people.

"Maybe they got lucky here," Alexander whispered, allowing himself to hope.

He drove slowly into the town centre, the engine's rumble seeming impossibly loud in the relative quiet. The street was empty, but Alexander could see movement behind curtained windows—shadows moving, people hiding, survivors. A few cars were parked normally, not abandoned in the middle of the road as in other places. He spotted a petrol station ahead—"MacLeod's Fuel & Supplies"—the sight of it making his heart pound with renewed hope.

"Please be open. Please have fuel," he prayed, the words barely audible.

He pulled up to the pumps, the engine still running, unwilling to turn it off in case it wouldn't start again. The station appeared closed, but there was a light on in the back office, a single bulb burning like a beacon in the night. Alexander got out of the Land Rover, testing his weight on his injured ankle—the compression bandage helping, but each step still sent a dull throb of pain up his leg. He gripped his knife in hand, his movements careful, deliberate.

Alexander approached the station cautiously, every sense heightened, his limp slight but noticeable. He tried the pump—it was locked, requiring payment first, a relic of a world that no longer existed. He walked toward the office, peering through the dirty window. Inside, he could see an elderly man sitting behind the counter, reading a newspaper by lamplight, the scene so normal, so mundane, that it felt surreal.

Alexander tapped gently on the glass, the sound loud in the silence.

The man looked up, startled, his newspaper dropping to the counter. "We're closed!" he called through the glass, his voice rough with age and suspicion.

"Please! I need fuel! I'm trying to get north!" Alexander replied, his voice urgent but not threatening.

The man studied Alexander for a long moment, his eyes narrow, assessing. Then, reluctantly, he unlocked the door, opening it just enough to speak. "You're not from around here."

"No, I'm from Druichmachon. Trying to get home to my family."

The man's expression softened slightly at the mention of the island. "Druichmachon? That's a long way north. You know what's happening out there?"

"The infection? Yes. I've seen it."

The man nodded grimly, stepping back to allow Alexander inside. "Aye. Started five days ago. We've been lucky so far—isolated enough that it hasn't reached us yet."

"Yet?" Alexander asked, his heart sinking.

"Radio reports say it's spreading fast. Military's disappeared. We're on our own."

Alexander pulled out what money he had—a few crumpled notes, his wallet nearly empty after days of survival. "I can pay for fuel. I just need enough to get to Shielingford."

The man shook his head, his expression grave. "Shielingford? You don't want to go there, lad."

"Why not?"

"Last radio contact we had said the whole area's overrun. Ferry port's been abandoned."

Alexander's heart sank, the hope that had sustained him suddenly feeling fragile, paper-thin. "There has to be another way to the islands."

"There might be. Old fishing boats up at Presthaven. About sixty miles northeast. But the roads…" He shook his head again. "They're saying the infected are everywhere between here and there."

Alexander looked at his nearly empty fuel gauge, the needle mocking him with its proximity to empty. "I have to try. My wife and daughter are waiting for me."

The man—Hamish, as Alexander would later learn—studied Alexander's determined face, seeing the desperation, the love that drove him. "Aye, I can see that. Come on then. Let's get you fuelled up."

Outside, Hamish walked with Alexander toward the pumps, the night air cool and crisp. "What kind of engine you got there?"

Alexander looked uncertain, his mechanical knowledge limited to checking oil and changing tires. "I… honestly, I'm not sure. I found it at a garage back in Auld Strathdee."

Hamish walked around to check the fuel cap, his movements practiced, efficient. "Let's have a look then." He opened the fuel cap and peered inside, then checked a small label near the cap. "You're in luck—petrol. Diesel would've been a problem. We're running low on that."

He activated the petrol pump, the sound of the machinery startling in the quiet night. "Fill her up. You'll need every drop."

As the fuel pumped, Alexander shifted his weight off his bad ankle, relief flooding through him at the brief respite. "What exactly are you hearing on the radio?"

Hamish leaned against the pump, his expression grim. "Government's calling it a 'biological incident.' Started down south, spreading fast. They're saying stay indoors, avoid contact with the infected." He spat on the ground, the gesture conveying his contempt. "Fat lot of good that does when there's nowhere left to run."

"What about the military? Police?"

"Military never showed up. Police made a stand in the bigger towns, but they went quiet about four days ago as well."

The fuel pump clicked off—tank full. "How much do I owe you?"

Hamish waved his hand dismissively. "Keep your money, lad. Won't do me much good if those things reach here."

Alexander put the nozzle back, gratitude warring with the guilt of taking something for nothing. "Thank you. Really."

Hamish disappeared into the office and returned with a cricket bat and a small rucksack. "Take these. Bat's got some weight to it. Bag's got some food, water, torch."

"I can't take your supplies," Alexander protested, though the thought of more food made his stomach ache with hunger.

"You've got further to go than I do. Besides…" Hamish looked around the quiet town, his expression sad, resigned. "If this place falls, I won't be needing them anyway."

Alexander took the bat and bag gratefully, the weight of them feeling like hope. "I don't know how to thank you."

"Get home to your family. That's thanks enough." Hamish extended his hand, and Alexander shook it firmly. "Good luck, lad. You're going to need it."

"What about you? Will you be alright here?"

Hamish glanced back at the petrol station, at the small town beyond. "We'll make our stand here if it comes to it."

In the distance, they heard a faint sound—like wind through trees, but wrong somehow. Both men tensed, listening.

"You'd best be going," Hamish said quietly.

Alexander nodded, climbing back into the Land Rover. As he drove away, he looked in the rearview mirror and saw Hamish standing outside the petrol station, a solitary figure against the coming dawn.

The Land Rover ate up the miles, the engine running smoothly now with a full tank. Alexander's hands gripped the wheel tightly, his knuckles white with tension.

Hamish leaned against the pump, his expression grim. "Government's calling it a 'biological incident.' Started down south, spreading fast. They're saying stay indoors, avoid contact with the infected." He spat on the ground, the gesture conveying his contempt. "Fat lot of good that does when there's nowhere left to run."

"What about the military? Police?"

"Military never showed up. Police made a stand in the bigger towns, but they went quiet about four days ago as well."

The fuel pump clicked off—tank full. "How much do I owe you?"

Hamish waved his hand dismissively. "Keep your money, lad. Won't do me much good if those things reach here."

Alexander put the nozzle back, gratitude warring with the guilt of taking something for nothing. "Thank you. Really."

Hamish disappeared into the office and returned with a cricket bat and a small rucksack. "Take these. Bat's got some weight to it. Bag's got some food, water, torch."

"I can't take your supplies," Alexander protested, though the thought of more food made his stomach ache with hunger.

"You've got further to go than I do. Besides…" Hamish looked around the quiet town, his expression sad, resigned. "If this place falls, I won't be needing them anyway."

Hamish pulled out a worn road map and spread it on the Land Rover's hood, the paper crinkling. "Take the A847 north, then west. Should be about two hours in normal times. But…" He traced a route with his finger, his movements precise. "You'll want to avoid the main towns. Muir of Howis, Cantsford, Strichenneth, and Cauldshame—radio says they're overrun. Stick to the back roads here, here and here. Take a left at Faewood Hollow—that'll keep you clear of the worst of it. Longer, but safer. And if you see any roadblocks…"

Alexander took the bat and bag gratefully, the weight of them feeling like hope. "The route to Presthaven—what's the best way?"

"Turn around?" Alexander guessed.

"Aye. Could be survivors, could be worse."

Alexander studied the map, memorizing the route, committing it to memory. “What about you? Your town?”

“We’ve got a few rifles and the odd shotgun, some folks around here used to be gamekeepers, they know how to use them. We’ll make our stand here if it comes to it.”

In the distance, they heard a faint sound—like a siren, but distorted, wrong somehow. Both men froze, the sound sending chills down Alexander’s spine.

“That’s not good,” Hamish said, his voice low.

“What is it?”

“Emergency broadcast system. Automated. Means there’s no one left to turn it off.”

The sound faded, leaving an ominous silence that felt heavier than before. Hamish looked at Alexander, his expression serious. “You’d better get moving, lad. Dawn’s not far off, and you don’t want to be caught on those roads in daylight.”

“Why not?”

“Easier for them to see you coming.”

Alexander got back in the Land Rover, settling into the seat with relief as the pressure came off his ankle. The engine’s hum was a promise of continued movement. “Thank you, Hamish. For everything.”

“Get home to your family. That’s thanks enough.”

Alexander started the engine and pulled away from the station, watching in the rearview mirror as Hamish stood there for a moment, then turned back to lock up the station, a solitary figure against the coming dawn.

FYLIE CASTLE

Spotify Apple Music Amazon Music

Track: FYLIE CASTLE

Alexander drove north on the A847, following Hamish's directions through the winding Highland roads. The Land Rover's engine hummed steadily, a comforting sound in the oppressive quiet. The road was empty, winding through dark Highland countryside, the landscape passing in shadowy blurs. Occasionally, he passed abandoned vehicles on the roadside—cars that had crashed, trucks that had stopped, the silent testimony of others' failed attempts to escape.

Alexander checked the fuel gauge—still three-quarters full, thanks to Hamish's generosity. "Just keep going. Stay on the back roads," he told himself, his voice barely audible above the engine's drone.

He passed a road sign: "MUIR OF HOWIS - 15 MILES." Alexander remembered Hamish's warning and looked for the turnoff to the back roads, his eyes scanning the darkness for the smaller lane Hamish had indicated on the map.

In the distance, Alexander could see the silhouette of an old castle on a hill, its dark shape standing against the sky like a sentinel from another time. A small sign read: "FYLIE CASTLE - HISTORIC SITE." The sight should have been comforting—a reminder of history, of permanence, of things that had lasted for centuries. But in this world, even ancient monuments felt vulnerable, felt like potential traps.

Suddenly, the Land Rover started making a grinding noise, a sound that sent fear through Alexander's heart. The engine began to sputter, the steady hum replaced by a series of concerning coughs.

"Come on, not now," Alexander pleaded, gripping the steering wheel tighter, his knuckles white.

Steam started rising from under the bonnet, a white plume that heralded disaster. The Land Rover began to lose power, the engine gasping for life like a drowning man.

"No, no, no!" Alexander cried, hitting the steering wheel in frustration, the sound loud in the cabin.

The Land Rover lost power completely and coasted to a stop on the side of the road, the engine dying with a final, pathetic cough. Alexander tried to restart it, turning the key again and again, but the engine wouldn't turn over, wouldn't even make a sound.

"Damn it!" he shouted, his voice raw with frustration and fear.

He got out, wincing as his injured ankle took his weight, and opened the bonnet. Steam poured out, obscuring his vision. He could see coolant leaking onto the ground, pooling beneath the vehicle like blood from a wound.

"Overheated. Probably blown a gasket," Alexander said to himself, the diagnosis feeling like a death sentence.

He looked around—the road was completely empty, stretching into darkness in both directions. In the distance, he could see lights from what must be Muir of Howis, but between him and the town, there was only dark countryside and the looming castle.

Alexander gathered his supplies—the cricket bat Hamish had given him, the rucksack with food and water, and his knife. He looked at the castle again, considering his options.

"Maybe I can shelter there until morning. Figure out what to do next." The castle looked solid, permanent, a place that had stood for centuries and would hopefully stand for a few more hours.

He locked the Land Rover—instinct, really, in a world where such things no longer mattered—and started walking toward Fylie Castle, his limp more pronounced now after hours of driving. The wind picked up as he walked, whipping around him, making eerie sounds through the Highland landscape, sounds that might have been the wind or might have been something else entirely.

The path to the castle was dark and treacherous, winding through dense woodland that seemed to close in around him. Alexander walked through the ancient forest, using his phone's dying flashlight to navigate, the beam weak and getting weaker with every passing minute. Ancient trees loomed overhead, their branches creating a canopy that blocked out most of the moonlight, turning the path into a tunnel of darkness. Each step on the uneven ground sent fresh jolts of pain through his ankle.

"Just get to the castle. Find shelter. Figure this out in the morning," Alexander told himself, the words a mantra against the rising fear.

His phone battery finally died, plunging him into near-total darkness, the sudden loss of light making him stumble and cry out as his ankle twisted slightly.

"Perfect," Alexander muttered, fumbling in the rucksack Hamish had given him. He found a small torch, its beam weak but better than nothing, a tiny circle of light in the overwhelming darkness.

As he continued through the woods, limping now more heavily, he began to hear a strange sound—a wallowing, crying, gurgling, wailing that seemed to come from everywhere and nowhere at once. The sound was unsettling, unlike anything he'd heard before, not the moan of an Aimless or the screech of a Screecher, but something else entirely, something more organic, more pained.

Alexander stopped, listening, his heart pounding. "What is that?" he whispered to the darkness.

The sound echoed through the trees, impossible to pinpoint, like the forest itself was in agony, like every tree, every leaf was crying out in pain. Alexander moved more cautiously now, his limp slowing him down, sweeping the torch beam across the forest floor, the light catching on twisted roots and fallen branches.

He saw what appeared to be several bodies lying motionless among the undergrowth, their forms barely visible in the weak torchlight.

"Poor bastards. At least they're at rest," Alexander thought, feeling a pang of sorrow for the dead.

He stepped carefully around what looked like a corpse—swollen chest, tattered clothing, lying on its back, appearing lifeless in the torchlight.

As his foot passed near the body, a massive, vein-covered arm shot up and clamped around his left ankle—his injured ankle—with crushing force. The grip was like steel, impossible to break, and the pain was immediate and blinding.

"AHHH! GET OFF ME!" Alexander screamed, the shock and pain making him cry out, his voice echoing through the forest.

The thing on the ground let out a horrible wallowing cry—a sound of pure agony and pain that blended with the ambient wailing, creating a chorus of suffering that seemed to come from all directions at once.

Alexander tried to pull free, but the grip was like a trap, unbreakable, crushing his already-injured ankle with terrible force. More arms emerged from other "corpses" around him, reaching and grasping, the forest floor coming alive with the dead and dying.

The wallowing, gurgling, wailing sound intensified, coming from all directions now, a symphony of agony that surrounded him, that seemed to seep into his very bones.

"They're not dead! They're not dead!" Alexander shouted, the realization hitting him like a physical blow.

He swung the cricket bat at the arm holding him, but it barely loosened the grip, the arm too strong, too determined. Black bile drooled from the creature's slack jaw as it made that terrible wallowing sound, the liquid thick and foul-smelling.

More of them were stirring, their clouded eyes staring blindly as they reached for him, their movements slow but relentless.

"The knife! The knife!" Alexander thought, desperation giving him clarity.

He dropped the bat and pulled out his knife, his hands shaking as he began sawing frantically at the wrist of the arm holding his ankle. The creature's wallowing became more intense—not anger, but pure anguish, the sound of something in terrible pain.

"Pleeeease… help… me…" the Wallower gurgled, the voice almost human, almost understandable, the plea making Alexander freeze for a moment, horrified by the humanity in the creature's cry.

"You can… you can talk?" Alexander asked, shocked, horrified, his knife stilling for a second.

But another Wallower's arm grabbed at his leg, the grip just as strong, just as desperate, and Alexander continued sawing with the knife, black blood spurting from the wound, covering his hands, his clothes. The blade cut through rotted flesh and bone, the resistance terrible, the effort immense.

Finally, the hand severed completely, and Alexander stumbled backward, the severed hand still clamped around his injured ankle like some grotesque bracelet, the pain excruciating. The Wallower continued its agonized crying, the sound of something trapped between life and death, aware of its torment.

"Kill… me… please… it hurts…" the Wallower whispered weakly, the plea breaking something inside Alexander.

Alexander backed away, horrified, as more Wallowers began to stir in the darkness, their wallowing, crying, gurgling, wailing filling the forest—an omnipresent sound of creatures trapped between life and death, aware of their suffering, conscious in their agony.

"I'm sorry… I'm so sorry…" Alexander whispered, his voice breaking, the guilt overwhelming him.

He turned and ran through the woods as best he could, his injured ankle screaming with every step, the severed hand still attached to his ankle, the terrible sounds of suffering echoing from every direction, following him, haunting him. The forest had become a place of nightmares, a place where the dead didn't rest, where they suffered endlessly, painfully, aware of every moment of their torment.

Alexander burst out of the woodland onto the castle grounds, gasping for breath, his lungs burning, his heart pounding, his ankle a mass of agony. He collapsed near the castle walls, breathing hard, trying to pry the severed hand from his ankle, the fingers locked in a death grip that wouldn't loosen, pressing into the already-injured flesh.

"What were those things?" he panted, looking back at the dark woods with terror. "They were… they were still human. Still aware."

He finally managed to break the fingers and remove the hand, throwing it aside with a cry of disgust and horror. Looking back at the dark woods, he could still hear the faint wallowing, crying, gurgling, wailing—impossible to locate, like the very air was weeping, like the forest itself was mourning its lost children.

He looked down at his ankle. The compression bandage was torn, soaked with fresh blood mixing with the black ichor from the Wallower. The joint was swelling rapidly, throbbing with each heartbeat.

"What kind of hell is this world becoming?" Alexander whispered, the question hanging in the air unanswered, the forest offering no response but its chorus of suffering.

He dragged himself to his feet and limped toward the castle entrance, each step an act of will. The ancient wooden door stood partially open, inviting him into the darkness beyond. Alexander stumbled inside, found a side chamber off the main hall, and collapsed onto the cold stone floor.

He pulled his jacket tighter around himself, checked that his knife was within reach, and let exhaustion claim him. The last thing he heard before darkness took him was the distant, fading wail of the Wallowers in the forest—a sound that would haunt his dreams.

18

The Armoury

Spotify Apple Music Amazon Music

Track: THE ARMOURY

Alexander woke to sunlight streaming through the narrow window of the side chamber. For a moment, he couldn't remember where he was, then the memories of the night before came flooding back—the Wallowers, their terrible pleas, the agony in his ankle.

He sat up, wincing, and listened. The wallowing sounds from the woods had stopped. The silence felt profound, almost unnatural after the night's chorus of suffering.

Alexander stretched carefully, testing his ankle. It was still swollen and painful, but the night's rest had helped. He unwrapped the torn bandage, examined the injury—bruised, swollen, but no signs of infection from the Wallower's grip. He rewrapped it as tightly as he could bear, then packed up his supplies.

"Right," he said to himself, his voice hoarse. "Time to see what this place has to offer."

He left the chamber and began exploring the castle more thoroughly.

The great hall was vast and shadowy despite the daylight outside. Alexander switched on his torch, the beam cutting through the gloom, revealing stone archways that led to different sections of the castle. Dust motes danced in the narrow shafts of sunlight that penetrated through arrow slits.

As he moved through the hall, limping slightly, he heard a strange sound echoing from somewhere deeper in the castle—a static hissing, like radio interference mixed with something organic.

Alexander stopped, listening, his hand moving instinctively to his knife.

"What the hell is that?" he muttered, wary.

He swept his torch beam around, but saw nothing. The hissing continued, impossible to pinpoint, seeming to come from everywhere and nowhere at once.

Alexander noticed a faded sign pointing down a corridor: "ARMORY & WEAPONS DISPLAY."

"Now that's promising," he said, hopeful but cautious.

He followed the signs down a stone corridor, the hissing sound growing fainter as he moved. His footsteps echoed off the ancient stones, and his injured ankle protested with each step.

The armory was even darker than the main hall, requiring the torch to see anything at all. Alexander's beam revealed a long chamber with stone walls lined with weapon displays. The static hissing was barely audible here, but still present, like a persistent whisper at the edge of hearing.

Most weapons were behind glass cases or secured with chains, but some appeared accessible. Medieval swords, axes, maces, and shields were mounted on the walls, their metal surfaces dulled by age but still solid. A placard read: "AUTHENTIC 14TH-16TH CENTURY WEAPONS COLLECTION."

"Christ, this is like a museum," Alexander said, impressed but alert, glancing over his shoulder as the hissing sound seemed to shift direction.

He examined the displays by torchlight, looking for something he could actually use. Many weapons were clearly replicas or too deteriorated, but some looked genuine and solid.

Alexander found a Scottish claymore mounted on the wall—the mounting was loose. He worked it free from its display and tried to lift it, struggling with the weight.

"Christ, this thing weighs a ton," he muttered, testing the balance. "Can't be running through the woods with this."

He put the claymore back and looked for something more practical. He spotted a smaller arming sword that was more manageable, its blade still straight and true despite the centuries. Next to it was a medieval dagger in a leather sheath, the leather cracked but functional.

Alexander took both, along with a small round shield that he could strap to his back.

In a corner display case, he found what appeared to be a crossbow with several bolts. The case was locked, but Alexander used a loose stone to break the glass. The sound echoed through the castle like a gunshot, and for a moment, the static hissing stopped completely.

Then it resumed, seeming closer, more focused.

"Hope this still works," Alexander said nervously, examining the crossbow.

He loaded one of the bolts and tested the mechanism—it seemed functional, the string still taut despite its age. He gathered the remaining bolts and placed them carefully in his rucksack.

Alexander strapped the sword to his back, put the dagger in his belt next to his kitchen knife, and carried the crossbow in his hands.

"Now I'm not going into those woods defenceless," he said, his voice more confident despite the unsettling hissing that continued somewhere in the castle's depths.

He headed back toward the main hall, better armed but still wary, his ankle throbbing with each step.

Alexander paused at one of the large windows overlooking the approach to the castle. The static hissing seemed to fade as he moved toward the exit, as if whatever made it preferred the deeper, darker parts of the castle.

In the distance, beyond the woods where he'd encountered the Wallowers, he could see his abandoned Land Rover sitting on the road like a reminder of how far he still had to go.

"Time to get moving," Alexander said, determined. "Presthaven's not getting any closer."

He emerged from the castle into the crisp Highland morning, adjusting the sword on his back and checking the crossbow. The weight of the weapons was reassuring, even if they were centuries old. The woods ahead looked less menacing in daylight, but he could still hear faint traces of that wallowing sound.

"Right," he said to himself. "Back through the woods to get to the Land Rover. Maybe I can fix it, or find another way."

He approached the edge of the woodland cautiously, his limp more pronounced now. In the daylight, he could see disturbed earth and claw marks where the Wallowers had been lying in wait. Some of them were still there, but they seemed sluggish, their movements lethargic.

Alexander moved carefully through the trees, following the path he'd taken the night before. The Wallowers were visible now in the filtered sunlight—their mottled skin blistering slightly where the light touched them, their movements slow and pained, more pained than before.

They moved sluggishly, their wallowing cries weaker, almost pitiful.

Alexander gave them a wide berth, crossbow raised and ready. One Wallower reached toward him half-heartedly, its fingers grasping at empty air, but its movements were slow and lacking the terrible strength from the night before.

"Sunlight," Alexander said quietly, remembering Hamish's warning. "Hamish was right about some of them being weaker in the light."

He continued through the woods, stepping carefully over roots and fallen branches. He spotted the cricket bat he'd dropped during his desperate escape, lying in a patch of disturbed earth. Alexander picked it up—it might still be useful, and after what Hamish had sacrificed to give it to him, it felt wrong to leave it behind.

He pressed forward, weapons ready, watching the Wallowers carefully as he navigated the nightmare forest in the revealing light of day.

Alexander emerged from the woodland onto the road where the Land Rover sat waiting, its battered form a reminder of how far he'd already come. He approached it cautiously, opening the bonnet to examine the damage in the morning light.

Coolant had leaked out completely, pooling beneath the vehicle in a dark stain. The radiator hose had burst—a clean split that explained the catastrophic failure.

"Damn it," Alexander muttered, examining the damage with growing frustration. "Even if I had water to refill it, that hose won't hold."

He closed the bonnet with a sense of finality. The Land Rover had brought him this far, but its journey was over.

Alexander looked at the landscape ahead, pulling out Hamish's map and tracing the route with his finger. Muir of Howis was about three miles north along the road—close enough to reach on foot, if his ankle held out.

He gathered what supplies he could carry: the medieval sword strapped across his back, the crossbow in hand, the cricket bat secured to his rucksack alongside the remaining food and water. The dagger sat comfortably in his belt next to his kitchen knife. He looked like something out of a fever dream—a modern man armed with medieval weapons, limping through the apocalypse.

"Right then," Alexander said to the abandoned Land Rover, patting its hood like saying goodbye to an old friend. "Thanks for getting me this far."

The walk to Muir of Howis took Alexander through some of the most beautiful and haunting landscape he'd ever seen. The Highland morning was crisp and clear, the air sharp with the scent of heather and pine. Rolling hills stretched away on either side of the road, covered in purple heather that swayed gently in the breeze. In the distance, mountains rose against a sky that was almost painfully blue—the kind of day that would have drawn tourists and photographers in the world that was.

But that world was gone.

Alexander limped along the empty road, his injured ankle throbbing with each step but manageable in the compression bandage he'd rewrapped. The sword bounced slightly against his back with each step, a constant reminder of the medieval arsenal he now carried. Birds sang in the trees—skylarks and thrushes, their songs unchanged by the horrors that had consumed humanity. It was surreal, this juxtaposition of natural beauty and human catastrophe.

He passed an old stone bridge that crossed a burbling stream, the water crystal clear and rushing over moss-covered rocks. In another time, he might have stopped to appreciate it, maybe even taken a photo. Now he barely paused, scanning the treeline for movement, for threats.

About a mile into his walk, Alexander came across an abandoned car on the roadside—a family sedan with the doors left open, personal belongings scattered on the ground. A child's teddy bear lay face-down in the dirt, one arm torn off. Alexander's chest tightened at the sight.

"Don't think about it," he told himself, forcing his eyes forward. "Keep moving."

The road wound through a section of dense forest, the canopy overhead blocking out much of the sunlight and casting everything in shadow. Alexander's grip tightened on the crossbow as he walked, remembering the Wallowers in the woods near Fylie Castle. Every rustle of leaves, every crack of a branch made his heart race.

But nothing emerged from the trees. The forest remained silent except for the sound of his own footsteps and laboured breathing.

As he emerged from the forest, the landscape opened up again into rolling farmland. Stone walls divided fields that had once held sheep or cattle, now empty except for the tall grass that swayed in the wind. An old farmhouse sat abandoned on a hillside, its windows dark and empty like the eye sockets of a skull.

Alexander could see smoke rising in the distance now—Muir of Howis, getting closer with each painful step. The smoke could mean survivors, people cooking, trying to maintain some semblance of normal life. Or it could mean destruction, buildings burning, civilization collapsing in slow motion.

The road curved around a small loch, its surface mirror-smooth and reflecting the mountains beyond. The scene was postcard-perfect, achingly beautiful in its serenity. Alexander paused for just a moment, allowing himself to appreciate it, to remember that the world still held beauty even as it fell apart.

"Ailsa would love this view," he whispered, thinking of his wife back on Druichmachon, wondering if she and Magsy were safe, wondering if he'd ever see them again.

He took a long drink from his water bottle, then continued on, his limp more pronounced now as fatigue set in.

Spotify Apple Music Amazon Music

Track: MUIR OF HOWIS

The final approach to Muir of Howis took him past more signs of hasty evacuation—cars abandoned with their boots open, suitcases spilled across the road, possessions deemed too heavy or too unimportant left behind in the rush to escape. A child's bicycle lay on its side in a ditch, one wheel still slowly spinning in the breeze.

And then he saw it—the barricade.

It stretched across the main road into town, a makeshift wall made of overturned cars, shop counters, mattresses, furniture, and anything else heavy enough to stop someone or something from getting through. This wasn't the work of people trying to escape; this was the work of people trying to defend themselves, people who had chosen to make their stand here.

As Alexander watched from a distance, catching his breath and assessing the situation, a group of survivors emerged from behind the barricade, working to reinforce it, dragging more debris into position. They looked organized, determined—and heavily armed.

Smoke rose from several points within the town—chimneys, Alexander hoped, rather than fires. Some of the buildings looked damaged, windows smashed, walls scarred with what might have been bullet holes or claw marks.

Alexander approached cautiously, his hands visible, carrying the crossbow but not aiming it, his movements deliberately non-threatening. His medieval arsenal must have made him look like a madman, but he hoped the survivors would see him as human, as someone in need rather than a threat.

"Hello?" he called out when he was close enough to be heard but still far enough to avoid being perceived as immediately dangerous. "I need help!"

A woman in her 40s looked up from her work on the barricade, her expression wary but not hostile. She held a rifle like someone who knew how to use it. "That's far enough! State your business!"

"I'm not infected," Alexander called, stopping and raising his hands slightly to show he wasn't a threat. "No bites, no scratches. I'm just trying to get to the coast."

A man in his 50s emerged from behind cover, holding a shotgun but not directly aiming it at Alexander. "Where have you come from?"

"Auld Strathdee, by way of Glencore."

The woman studied Alexander for a moment, her eyes taking in his strange assortment of weapons—the medieval sword, the crossbow, the cricket bat strapped to his pack. Then she lowered her weapon slightly. "We've got maybe twenty people left in the whole town. Holed up mostly in the library and the community centre."

"What happened to the rest?" Alexander asked, moving closer as they seemed to relax slightly.

The man gestured to the barricade, his expression grim. "First wave came four nights ago. Regular infected—what we're calling Aimless. Slow, but there were dozens of them."

The woman picked up the story, her voice tight with remembered fear. "We thought we'd handled it. Then the second wave hit." She pointed to deep claw marks gouged into a nearby building, the stone itself torn away by something with immense strength. "Screechers. Fast ones. They called in more Aimless from miles around."

Alexander nodded, understanding all too well. “And the Wallowers?”

“Found them last night,” the woman said, her voice dropping. “Lost three more people to them. Poor bastards didn’t even know they were there until it was too late.”

A younger survivor in his 20s approached carrying a toolbox. “Moira, we’ve got the radio working again.”

“Any word from the outside?” Moira asked hopefully.

“Nothing good. Every where’s gone dark. But there’s a broadcast from someone called Vitagenix saying there’s a safe zone at the old Strathgarve military barracks.”

Alexander stopped, his attention caught by the mention of Vitagenix. “Speaking of communication—does anyone have an iPhone charger? Mine died last night.”

The young man shook his head. “Phone networks went down six days ago. Even if you charge it, you won’t get through to anyone.”

Alexander sighed but kept his phone anyway. “Still, I’d like to try. My wife and daughter…”

Moira’s expression softened. “Check the library. Might be one in the computer section. What about the islands?”

“Nothing from there either,” the young man said. “Just this Vitagenix broadcast on repeat.”

“That’s where I’m heading,” Alexander said. “My family’s on Druichmachon.”

The older man looked at Alexander with sympathy. “Long way to go, mate, and getting trickier every day.”

Alexander wiped sweat from his brow, looking toward the town centre. “Do you have a working vehicle of any kind that I can use?.”

"There's an old pickup truck behind the garage," Moira said. "Engine's rough, but it runs. Owner won't be needing it anymore."

"What do you want for it?"

Moira looked at the barricade, then back at Alexander. "Help us get through today. These barricades won't hold forever, and we're planning to evacuate tomorrow morning."

"Evacuate to where?"

"North," the older man said. "Same as you. Figure there's safety in numbers."

Alexander considered this, weighing the risks of staying against the risks of going alone. "Alright. I help you today, you give me the truck and directions to avoid the worst areas."

"Deal," Moira agreed instantly.

Spotify Apple Music Amazon Music

Track: SURVIVAL BONDS

Suddenly the town shook as a deep, bullish roar ripped through the streets—one Alexander recognized, but now monstrous, vibrating through the air like a living force. Every building seemed to shudder beneath its power, and a cold, instinctive dread coiled in his chest. This was the sound he had feared, amplified beyond anything he had ever faced.

Everyone froze, looking around in confusion.

The young man's face went pale. "What the hell was that?"

"Bullseye," Alexander said grimly, already moving toward his weapons. "Big one, from the sound of it. Bigger than any I've seen."

"How big are we talking?" the older man asked, his voice tight with fear.

"Big enough to bring down that barricade in one charge," Alexander replied, loading his crossbow. "We need to be ready."

The roar came again, closer this time, and with it came the sound of heavy footfalls—each one like a drumbeat of approaching doom.

"Positions!" Moira shouted. "Everyone to your stations!"

The survivors scrambled to their posts, weapons raised, eyes scanning the streets for the source of that terrible sound.

Alexander positioned himself near the main barricade, his crossbow ready, his heart pounding. He'd faced Bullseyes before, but something about this one felt different. Bigger. Stronger. More dangerous.

"Here it comes," someone whispered.

And then they saw it.

The creature that rounded the corner was massive—easily twice the size of any Bullseye Alexander had encountered. Its bullseye marking glowed with an intense orange light, pulsing like a beacon. Its body was covered in thick, armoured plates that looked almost like natural body armour, and its arms were as thick as tree trunks.

"Jesus Christ," the older man breathed. "What is that thing?"

"Moira, is that you? Thank God." The relief in Thomson's voice was palpable even through the static. "We've got a situation here. Over."

Margaret's expression shifted, concern flickering across her features. "What kind of situation? Over."

"The boats… Margaret, three fishing vessels went out yesterday morning. None of them came back. We sent out a search party this morning—found two of the boats drifting, completely empty. No signs of struggle, no blood, just… empty. Like everyone just vanished. Over."

A chill ran through the crowd gathered around the radio. Alexander felt his stomach drop, a new fear taking root.

"And the third boat? Over," Margaret asked, her voice steady despite the worry in her eyes.

"Still missing. But Margaret, that's not the worst of it. The boats that we found—they were damaged. Not from weather or rocks. Something… something attacked them from below. Tore through the hulls like they were paper. Over."

Alexander's mind raced. Something in the water. Something that could sink boats, take entire crews without a trace.

"Thomson, are you saying there's something in the water? Some kind of infected? Over," Margaret asked, voicing what everyone was thinking.

"I don't know what it is, Margaret. But whatever it is, it's big, it's dangerous, and it's out there in the strait. We're advising all vessels to stay in port until we know more. Over."

Alexander felt his carefully constructed plans crumbling. The sea route to Druichmachon—his fastest, most direct path home—might not be safe anymore.

"Thomson, this is Alexander McRae. I'm trying to get to Druichmachon. What's the situation with the ferry routes? Over."

There was a pause, then Thomson's voice came back, heavy with regret. "Alexander, I know that name. You're Ailsa's husband, aren't you? Over."

"Yes. I'm trying to get home to my family. Over."

Another pause, longer this time. "Alexander… the ferry to Druichmachon stopped running four days ago. Last we heard, the island was… it was overrun. I'm sorry, lad. Over."

The words hit Alexander like a physical blow. Overrun. The island. His home. Ailsa. Magsy.

"No," he said, his voice barely a whisper. Then louder, "No. That can't be right. The islands were supposed to be safe. They were isolated, they had time to prepare—"

"I'm sorry, Alexander," Thomson said, his voice genuinely sympathetic. "But that's the last report we got. The infection spread faster than anyone expected. Even the islands couldn't stay clear. Over."

Alexander's hands were shaking. He gripped the edge of the table to steady himself, his mind refusing to accept what he was hearing.

"What about other boats?" he asked desperately. "Private vessels? Anything that could get me there? Over."

"Alexander, you're not listening," Thomson said, his voice firm but kind. "Even if you could find a boat, you'd be sailing into a death trap. And with whatever's in the water taking down experienced crews, you wouldn't make it halfway there. I'm sorry, but you need to accept that—"

"No." Alexander's voice was hard, final. "I made a promise. I'm going home."

He released the radio transmitter and stepped back, his jaw set, his eyes distant.

Margaret approached him carefully. "Alexander…"

"Don't," he said quietly. "Don't tell me it's hopeless. Don't tell me to give up. I've come too far, survived too much. I'm not stopping now."

"But if the island is overrun—"

"Then I'll deal with that when I get there," Alexander interrupted. "But I have to know. I have to see for myself. I can't just… I can't just assume they're gone."

Gordon had been listening from nearby. He approached now, his expression thoughtful. "There might be another way," he said slowly. "It's dangerous, probably stupid, but… there might be a way."

Alexander's attention snapped to him. "What way?"

"There's a small harbour about eight miles north of here. Cauldhame Cove. Used to be a smuggler's haven back in the day. There are usually a few small boats there—fishing dinghies, nothing fancy, but seaworthy. If you could get one of those…"

"I could sail it myself," Alexander finished, hope rekindling in his chest. "How far is Druichmachon from there?"

"Maybe twenty miles across open water," Gordon said. "In good conditions, in a small boat, you might make it in three or four hours. But Alexander, you need to understand—if Thomson's right about something in the water, if there really is something out there taking down boats…"

"I'll take that risk," Alexander said immediately. "I have to."

Margaret sighed, recognizing the determination in his eyes—the same determination that had carried him this far. "You'll need supplies. Food, water, warm clothes. The sea can be brutal, even in summer."

"And a weapon," Gordon added. "Something you can use if you encounter… whatever's out there."

"I have my crossbow," Alexander said. "And the sword."

"A sword won't do much good against something that can sink a fishing boat," Gordon pointed out. "But it's better than nothing."

Alexander looked around at the faces of the people who had taken him in, fed him, given him shelter and hope. "Thank you," he said simply. "All of you. For everything."

"You're leaving now?" Aileen asked, appearing from where she'd been helping with the children. "Tonight?"

"First light," Alexander said. "I need to rest, gather supplies, prepare. But yes, as soon as possible."

"Then let me help you get ready," she said. "It's the least I can do."

As the group dispersed to gather supplies and prepare for Alexander's departure, Margaret pulled him aside. "Alexander, I have to ask—what will you do if you get there and find… if you find that Thomson was right?"

Alexander was quiet for a long moment, staring out toward the western horizon where, somewhere beyond the hills and the sea, his home waited. "I don't know," he admitted finally. "But I have to try. I promised them I'd come home. I promised Magsy it would only be two sleeps."

"It's been more than two sleeps," Margaret said gently.

"I know," Alexander replied, his voice breaking slightly. "I know. But I'm still coming home. Even if I'm too late. Even if…" He couldn't finish the sentence.

Margaret squeezed his shoulder. "Then we'll make sure you have everything you need. And Alexander? If anyone can make it, it's you. You've survived this long against impossible odds. Don't give up now."

"I won't," Alexander promised. "I can't."

As night fell over Cauldhame, Alexander sat in the church hall, methodically checking his equipment, planning his route, preparing for what might be his final journey. Around him, the village settled into its nightly routine—guards posted, fires banked, children tucked into makeshift beds.

But Alexander couldn't sleep. Every time he closed his eyes, he saw Magsy's face, heard Ailsa's laugh, felt the weight of promises made and the desperate need to keep them.

Tomorrow, he would set out for the coast. Tomorrow, he would find a boat. Tomorrow, he would sail home.

And whatever he found there—whatever horrors or miracles awaited—he would face them.

Because he had made a promise.

And Alexander McRae always kept his promises.

19

Aileen

Spotify Apple Music Amazon Music

Track: WHISPER OF THE PAST

"One pickup won't carry twenty people," Duncan pointed out, looking at the group of survivors, at the faces of people who had been through hell together. "We need more vehicles."

"What if there are more of those things coming?" Jamie asked, his voice still trembling as he looked toward the direction the Bullseye had come from.

As if summoned by his words, another distant roar echoed from the south, deeper and more menacing than the first.

"Right. Everyone back to the library. Grab only essentials. We leave in thirty minutes," Moira ordered, taking charge.

"What other vehicles do you have?" Alexander asked, thinking about his own journey, his own need to keep moving north.

"There's a minibus at the school—seats about fifteen," Duncan said. "The pickup can take five more."

"What about fuel?"

"Petrol station's got a manual pump. We can siphon what we need."

Another roar, closer this time, made everyone jump.

"You still want to go north on your own, or travel with us?" Moira asked Alexander, her expression suggesting she hoped he'd stay, that his experience with these creatures might be valuable.

"That's completely the wrong direction for me. I need to get to Presthaven, on the coast."

Moira's face showed her disappointment. "That's a shame. Safety in numbers and all that."

"I understand, but my family's waiting for me. I can't go backwards."

Alexander looked at the dead Bullseye, then at the survivors—at the fear mixed with determination in their faces. He thought about what Hamish had said about safety in numbers, about how two people had better odds than one, but these people had each other. They were a community.

"You know what? Take the pickup. You need it more than I do—twenty people won't fit in just a minibus."

Duncan looked surprised by Alexander's generosity. "That's… that's decent of you, mate."

"Just get these people to safety."

Alexander headed toward the library, wanting to check for that phone charger before the group left, needing to maintain that fragile connection to his family, however tenuous.

The library showed signs of recent habitation—sleeping bags arranged in corners, food supplies stacked on tables, makeshift defenses at windows. Alexander headed to the computer section and searched through desks and drawers, looking for anything that could charge his phone.

Behind the librarian's desk, he found a charging station with multiple cables, a relic of a world where people could charge their devices freely, without fear. Alexander plugged in his phone, relief flooding through him as the screen lit up, showing it was charging. He turned it on properly, but no bars of signal appeared—no connection to the world beyond this town, this library.

Alexander tried calling Ailsa anyway—the call failed immediately, the silence of the phone mocking his hope.

"Come on… just one bar…" he muttered, moving around the library, holding the phone up, trying to catch a signal that wasn't there.

Outside, he could hear the survivors preparing to leave, the sounds of people loading vehicles, of families preparing for another journey, another escape.

Alexander kept his phone plugged in while he explored the library further, finding a local map section with detailed Highland road maps. He spread one out on a table, using his finger to trace potential routes north to Presthaven, to Ailsa and Magsy.

"If I avoid the main roads… stick to the back routes…" he murmured, planning, trying to find a path through this nightmare landscape.

His phone showed 15% battery now, still no signal. Alexander noticed the survivors had left behind some supplies—canned food, bottled water, a first aid kit. He packed what he could carry into his rucksack, the extra weight feeling like security.

From outside, he heard engines starting up.

"Alexander! We're leaving! Last chance!" Moira called from outside.

Alexander went to the window and waved. "Go! Get out of here! Good luck!"

He watched as the minibus and pickup truck pulled away, loaded with survivors, a small convoy of hope heading into an uncertain future. The convoy disappeared down the road, leaving Alexander alone in the town, alone with his thoughts and his mission.

His phone buzzed—now at 25% charge. He tried calling again, but still no signal.

"Damn it," he muttered in frustration, the feeling of helplessness overwhelming him for a moment.

He studied the map more carefully, looking for alternative routes, circling potential stops: Faewood Hollow, Cantsford, and smaller hamlets that might have vehicles or supplies.

"Find a vehicle in one of these places. Stay off the main roads."

Another distant roar echoed through the town, a reminder that he wasn't truly alone, that danger was always close. Alexander quickly unplugged his phone at 30% charge and pocketed the charger.

"Time to go."

He gathered his weapons—crossbow, sword, dagger—and headed for the library exit. As he reached the door, he paused and looked back at the makeshift shelter the survivors had created, at the evidence of their struggle to maintain normalcy in a world that had gone mad.

"Hope you all make it," he whispered to the empty room.

Alexander stepped outside into the empty town, the destroyed barricade and the dead Bullseye serving as grim reminders of what he was facing, of what he was running toward as much as running from.

He checked his map one more time, then started walking north toward the edge of town, toward the coast, toward his family.

Spotify Apple Music Amazon Music

Track: AILEEN

Behind him, he heard footsteps.

"Wait!" a woman's voice called out.

Alexander turned to see a woman in her 30s jogging toward him, carrying a small backpack, her expression determined but uncertain.

"I thought you all left," Alexander said, surprised.

"I heard you talking to Moira earlier. You said you came from the southeast?" the woman asked, her voice hopeful.

"That's right. Why?"

"Did you come through Braelinwoodshire by any chance?"

Alexander nodded, recognizing the name. "I did. Stayed there briefly."

The woman's face lit up with hope, her eyes bright with anticipation. "My parents live there. I've been trying to get word from them for days, but…" She gestured helplessly, the unspoken fear hanging between them.

"I hear your heading for Presthaven? I know it's not the quickest way, but if I stick with you, I can make it to the southwest coast by boat, cross the mainland, and catch another boat east. I don't want to face the longest part by myself—I need to get home to my family."

"It's dangerous traveling alone. Well, just the two of us," Alexander warned, thinking about the Bullseye, about the Wallowers, about all the dangers that lurked in the darkness.

"I can handle myself. And two people have a better chance than one," she said, her voice firm with conviction.

Alexander considered this, weighing the risks of companionship against the dangers of another mouth to feed, another person to protect. "What are your parents' names?"

"Angus and Morag MacLeod. They live in the cottage just south of Braelinwood."

Alexander's expression changed—recognition and sadness warring in his eyes. He remembered the couple from the village, remembered their kindness, their hospitality.

"Aileen… I'm sorry. I did meet them."

Aileen's face began to fall as she read his expression, as she saw the truth in his eyes before he even spoke it. "What happened?"

"They… they didn't make it. I'm so sorry."

Aileen staggered slightly, the news hitting her like a physical blow, like a punch to the gut. She wrapped her arms around herself, as if to hold herself together. "Both of them?"

"Yes. But they were brave. Your father… he helped me. Gave me directions, supplies. They were good people."

Aileen wiped tears from her eyes, the grief raw and overwhelming. "And what of my brother Jamie? Did they say anything about him?"

Alexander shook his head, his heart breaking for her. "He's gone too. I'm so sorry."

Aileen clamped a hand over her mouth, but the sound that escaped her was raw and broken, the kind of cry that came from somewhere deeper than breath. Her knees threatened to give as the truth settled in, hollowing her out piece by piece. When she finally lowered her hand, tears streaked her face unchecked, her eyes distant, unfocused—like she was already somewhere else. After a long moment, she wiped at her cheeks with shaking fingers and forced herself upright, but the effort showed in every rigid movement. Whatever hope had been keeping her standing was gone.

"Then there's no reason for me to go home now," she said, her voice hollow with loss.

"I'm sorry I had to tell you."

"No, I… I needed to know. Thank you for being honest."

Aileen looked toward where the other survivors had departed, toward the direction the convoy had gone. "I suppose I should catch up with the others then."

"Or… you could come west with me," Alexander said softly, his voice low. He thought of how utterly alone she was now, how everything she had loved was gone. "I couldn't save them… I couldn't save your parents. But I can help you. After everything they did for me, I want to give you something in return. I'm heading home to my wife and daughter, and I want you to come too. Ailsa would be glad to have you stay. At least you wouldn't have to face the world by yourself."

Aileen looked down, her voice quiet. "Are you sure your wife wouldn't mind? I don't want to intrude."

"Of course she'd be fine with it," he said, smiling faintly. "After everything Angus and Morag did for me, this is the least I can do. And my daughter? She's going to be excited to meet you."

Aileen nodded slowly, the decision settling in her eyes. "Alright then. Druichmachon it is."

Alexander unslung his sword with practiced ease, the leather straps sliding smoothly across his shoulder. The blade caught the dim light as he offered it to her, its steel worn but well-maintained, the grip wrapped in faded leather that had molded to his hand over countless hours of use.

"Here. You'll need something better than whatever you're carrying."

Aileen reached out and took the sword, her fingers wrapping uncertainly around the grip. The weight of it surprised her—heavier than she'd expected, the balance unfamiliar and awkward in her untrained hands. "I've never used one of these before."

"Hopefully you won't have to. But if you do, aim for the head and put your whole body behind it." Alexander's voice was matter-of-fact, the tone of someone who'd given—and received—such instructions before.

Spotify Apple Music Amazon Music

Track: SURVIVAL BONDS

Suddenly, another deep bullish roar tore through the morning air, reverberating off the stone buildings and rattling through their chests. It was much closer than before, close enough that they could feel the rage behind it.

Both Alexander and Aileen froze, their bodies going rigid with primal fear.

"That's the other one," Alexander said, his voice tight with urgency. "We need to move. Now."

The words had barely left his lips when they heard it—heavy footsteps that shook the ground beneath their feet, each impact accompanied by the sickening crunch of debris being crushed under immense weight. Around the corner of a building, another Bullseye appeared, its massive form filling the narrow street. It was slightly smaller than the first they'd encountered, but no less menacing. Thick plates of mutated flesh covered its body like armor, and steam rose from its nostrils in angry plumes. Its tiny, malevolent eyes locked onto them immediately, and it let out a challenging roar that showed rows of jagged teeth.

"What is that thing?" Aileen's voice cracked with terror, her newly acquired sword trembling in her grip.

Alexander grabbed her arm, his fingers digging in with desperate strength. "Something we can't fight. Run!"

They sprinted away from the library as the Bullseye charged after them, its roar of pursuit echoing off the empty buildings.

Alexander led Aileen through narrow alleyways between structures, his boots pounding against the cobblestones. His injured ankle, which had been a dull ache moments before, now flared with sharp, stabbing pain that shot up his leg with each stride. He gritted his teeth and pushed on, knowing that stopping meant death.

Behind them, they could hear the creature's relentless pursuit—the crash of wooden fences being obliterated, the screech of metal being torn apart, the thunder of its footfalls growing closer despite their desperate speed.

"The eyes!" Alexander shouted over his shoulder, his breath coming in ragged gasps. "If we have to fight, aim for the eyes!"

They burst from the alleyways and reached the edge of town where the road stretched north into open country. For a moment, hope flared in Aileen's chest—open ground, room to maneuver. But then the Bullseye crashed through a garden fence behind them, wooden posts exploding into splinters, and she realized with sinking dread that the creature was gaining on them.

"It's too fast!" she gasped, her lungs burning, legs already turning to lead.

Alexander's eyes frantically scanned their surroundings, searching for anything that could give them an advantage. Then he spotted it—an old farm tractor parked beside the road, its red paint faded and peeling, but its solid metal frame still intact.

"The tractor! Get behind it!"

They dove behind the heavy machinery, their bodies slamming against the cold metal just as the Bullseye charged past them in a blur of muscle and fury. The creature's momentum carried it several yards beyond their hiding spot before it realized its prey had vanished. Confused, it came to a grinding halt, its hooves tearing gouges in the dirt road. It turned around slowly, snorting angrily, hot breath misting in the cool morning air.

"Stay low," Alexander whispered, his lips barely moving, his body pressed flat against the tractor's wheel. "Move when I move."

The Bullseye paced back and forth like a caged predator, its massive head swinging from side to side. Those small, malicious eyes scanned the area, searching for any sign of movement, any hint of where its prey had disappeared to. Alexander could see the intelligence behind those eyes—limited perhaps, but present. This thing could think, could hunt.

Moving with agonizing slowness, Alexander raised his crossbow, his muscles screaming in protest at the careful, controlled movement. He lined up the shot, accounting for distance and the creature's constant movement. His finger found the trigger. He took a shallow breath, held it, and fired.

The bolt flew true, striking the creature's right eye with a wet, puncturing sound.

The Bullseye's roar of pain and rage was deafening, a primal scream that seemed to shake the very air around them. It thrashed wildly, its massive body spinning and crashing as it clawed at its ruined eye, blood streaming down its face.

"Now! While it's distracted!" Alexander grabbed Aileen and hauled her to her feet.

They sprinted away from the tractor as the blinded, enraged Bullseye crashed into the machinery behind them, its full weight slamming into the heavy metal with a sound like a car crash. The creature's roars—now tinged with confused agony—gradually faded behind them as they put precious distance between themselves and the town.

The country road stretched before them, empty and silent save for their labored breathing. Alexander and Aileen slowed to a fast walk, both gulping air, their hearts hammering against their ribs. Alexander's ankle finally forced him to stop. He sat heavily on a moss-covered stone at the roadside and pulled his left ankle into his hand, his fingers probing the swollen joint with practiced concern. That sprint had transformed the dull ache into something far worse—the tissue felt hot and inflamed beneath his touch.

"What were those things?" Aileen asked, still shaken, her eyes continuously darting back toward the town as if expecting another monster to appear at any moment.

"We call them 'Bullseyes' because of the mark on their heads," Alexander said, his voice grim, eyes hard. "But they're not natural. Nothing about this infection is."

Aileen adjusted the sword on her back, the unfamiliar weight still strange against her shoulders. The leather straps dug into her collarbone, and she wondered if she'd ever actually be able to use the weapon if the moment came. "Thank you. For the weapon, and for getting us out of there."

"We're not safe yet. We need to find transport and keep moving." Alexander pushed himself back to his feet with a grimace, testing his weight on the injured ankle. It would hold—for now.

They continued north along the empty road, their footsteps the only sound in the unnatural silence. Behind them, the distant sounds of destruction continued—crashes and roars and the death throes of a town consumed by something that defied explanation. But with each step, those sounds grew fainter, and the open countryside beckoned them forward into an uncertain future.

20

Cantsford

Spotify Apple Music Amazon Music

Track: WINDING PATHS OF CANTSFORD

By mid-afternoon, the sun had climbed higher in the pale sky, though its warmth seemed unable to penetrate the chill that had settled over the land. Alexander, still limping noticeably, and Aileen walked west along the empty Highland road, their shadows stretching long beside them.

The landscape rolled away on either side in gentle hills dotted with sheep farms and ancient stone walls that divided the land into irregular patches of green and brown. The sheep themselves were nowhere to be seen—either fled, taken, or hiding. The silence was profound and unsettling, broken only by the crunch of their footsteps and the occasional whistle of wind through gaps in the stone walls.

Abandoned vehicles appeared sporadically along the road like metal carcasses—some crashed into ditches or wrapped around trees, others simply left by the roadside as if their drivers had stepped out for a moment and never returned. Alexander checked each one they passed, his limp growing more pronounced as the day wore on. They stopped every thirty minutes to allow him to rest his ankle, each break a small mercy that he accepted with poorly concealed relief.

At one small car with its hood already popped open, Alexander peered at the engine compartment with the lost expression of someone staring at alien technology.

“I have no idea what I’m looking at,” he admitted, his hands hovering uselessly over the tangle of hoses and metal.

“You’re not much of a mechanic then?” Aileen asked, a hint of amusement creeping into her voice despite their situation.

“I’m a health and safety consultant. I spend my days writing risk assessments, not fixing engines.” He straightened up and wiped his hands on his trousers, leaving faint streaks of dust.

“What about that one?” Aileen pointed down the road to where a white delivery van sat askew on the shoulder, partially concealed behind an overgrown hedgerow.

They approached it cautiously, their footsteps slowing as details emerged. The driver’s door hung open at an awkward angle, and deep claw marks scored the white paint on the side—four parallel gouges that had stripped away the finish down to bare metal.

Alexander peered inside, his nose wrinkling at the stale, copper smell that wafted out. “Keys are still here, but…”

He pointed to dark stains on the driver’s seat—rusty brown patches that had soaked into the fabric and dried in irregular patterns that told a story neither of them wanted to imagine.

“Someone didn’t make it out.”

Despite the grim evidence, Alexander climbed into the driver’s seat, careful to avoid the stains. He turned the key in the ignition. The engine turned over with a grinding sound, coughing and sputtering, but it wouldn’t catch. He tried again, pumping the accelerator, but the result was the same—mechanical protest without ignition.

“Won’t start. Could be anything wrong with it.” Alexander’s frustration bled through his voice as he climbed back out, his injured ankle nearly giving way as he landed awkwardly on the road.

"Health and safety consultant? That must be useful now—assessing risks and all that," Aileen said, steadying him with a hand on his elbow.

"You'd think so, but none of my training covered 'zombie apocalypse protocols'." A bitter smile crossed his face as he gestured to his crossbow and the empty scabbard where his sword had been. "What about you? What did you do before all this?"

"Worked on a fishing boat out of Cullen Bay. Been doing it since I was sixteen—over fourteen years now." There was pride in her voice, the kind that came from hard work and mastery of a difficult craft.

"That's actually useful. More useful than knowing workplace safety regulations." Alexander adjusted the crossbow on his back and started walking again, his limp more pronounced than ever.

"You'd be surprised. I know boats, I know the coast. And your risk assessment skills might help us avoid danger." Aileen fell into step beside him, shortening her stride to match his compromised pace.

They continued walking, the afternoon sun beginning its slow descent toward the western horizon. In the distance, perhaps two or three miles ahead, they could see smoke rising in thin columns from what must be Cantsford. The gray plumes climbed into the pale sky like questions without answers.

"That doesn't look good," Aileen said, her hand unconsciously moving to the hilt of the sword at her back.

"Could be chimney smoke. People keeping warm." But Alexander's tone suggested he didn't believe his own optimistic interpretation.

"Or it could be buildings burning."

They walked in silence for a moment, each lost in their own thoughts about what they might find ahead.

"You mentioned your parents lived in Braelinwoodshire. How long since you'd seen them?" Alexander asked, his voice gentle.

Aileen's expression clouded, pain flickering across her features. "About six months. We had a falling out over… well, it doesn't matter now, does it?"

"I'm sorry. For what it's worth, your father seemed like a good man. Stubborn, but good."

A small, sad smile touched Aileen's lips. "That sounds like him."

As they drew closer, Cantsford resolved itself from a distant smudge into a proper village—a cluster of stone cottages arranged around a small church with a square tower. The architecture was typical Highland: thick walls built to withstand centuries of wind and weather, slate roofs, small windows. Several buildings showed obvious fire damage, their roofs collapsed and walls blackened with soot. But others appeared intact, their windows still whole, their doors still closed.

Alexander stopped at the crest of a low hill, holding up a hand to halt Aileen beside him. They stood in silence, watching and listening.

"No movement. No sounds," he observed, his eyes scanning the village systematically, checking windows and doorways for any sign of life—or unlife.

"Could be empty. Or could be a trap." Aileen's fishing experience had taught her caution—the sea punished those who didn't respect its dangers.

"Fourteen years on fishing boats—you must know these waters like the back of your hand?" Alexander glanced at her, a calculating look in his eyes.

"Well enough. If we can get to the coast, I might be able to find us a boat. Get you to your island." She met his gaze steadily, understanding the unspoken question in his words.

Alexander loaded a fresh bolt into his crossbow, the mechanism clicking softly as it locked into place. The sound seemed loud in the afternoon stillness.

"Only one way to find out what's in there. Stay close, and if I say run, you run." His voice had taken on the firm tone of someone accustomed to being obeyed—the voice he probably used when telling construction workers to wear their safety harnesses.

Aileen gripped the hilt of her sword, feeling its weight, still unfamiliar but somehow reassuring. "Understood. And Alexander? Thank you. For telling me about my parents. And for letting me come with you."

"We'll get through this. Both of us." He said it with a conviction he didn't entirely feel, but sometimes conviction was all you had.

They approached the village cautiously, keeping to the shadows cast by the stone walls that lined the road. Their footsteps were soft, deliberate, each one placed with care. The afternoon sun slanted across the abandoned streets, painting everything in shades of gold and shadow, beautiful and terrible in its emptiness.

The first cottage they passed had its door hanging open, swaying slightly in the breeze with a rhythmic creaking that set Alexander's teeth on edge. Inside, they could see overturned furniture and dark stains on the floor. They moved past quickly, neither wanting to investigate further.

The village held its breath around them, waiting to reveal its secrets.

Alexander and Aileen moved carefully along the ancient stone wall that bordered the village, their bodies pressed close to the weathered granite, using its bulk as cover. The stones were cool against Alexander's palm, worn smooth by centuries of Highland weather, each one fitted perfectly to its neighbour without mortar—the old way, the way that lasted.

The smoke they had seen from a distance revealed its source: a partially collapsed cottage whose roof had caved inward, leaving blackened timbers jutting toward the sky like broken ribs. Thin streams of gray smoke still rose from the wreckage, suggesting the fire had burned recently, perhaps within the last few hours.

The streets appeared empty, but the evidence of recent violence was everywhere. Rubbish bins lay overturned, their contents scattered across the cobblestones. Windows gaped like missing teeth, their glass shattered into glittering fragments that crunched underfoot. Dark stains marked the ancient cobblestones—rusty brown patches that formed trails leading toward buildings or simply ending in the middle of the street, as if whoever had left them had simply ceased to exist.

"You mentioned your family earlier," Aileen whispered, her voice barely audible above the whisper of wind through the empty village. "Your wife and daughter—what are their names?"

Alexander continued scanning the area as he answered, his eyes never stopping their systematic sweep of windows and doorways. "Ailsa and Magsy. Ailsa's my wife, Magsy's only two years old."

"How long since you've seen them?"

"Seven days." The words came out tight, compressed by emotion he was working hard to contain. "We live on Druichmachon—that's where they are now. I had to come down to the mainland for a work conference in Loonswrath." He paused, checking a narrow alley between two cottages before continuing. "I was supposed to fly back home four days ago, but then all this started."

He gestured around at the devastation—the broken windows, the bloodstains, the terrible silence where life should have been.

"Do you think they know what's happening down here?" Aileen asked, careful to keep her voice low.

"I hope not. The island's pretty isolated. Maybe the infection hasn't reached there yet." But even as he said it, Alexander could hear the desperate hope in his own voice, the need to believe rather than the certainty of knowledge.

They reached the edge of the village proper, where the narrow lane opened onto the main street. A few cars were parked along the curb, apparently abandoned—doors closed, windows intact, as if their owners had simply walked away and forgotten to return.

"What's Magsy like?" Aileen asked, sensing that talking about his daughter might give Alexander something to hold onto, some reason to keep pushing forward despite the pain in his ankle and the horrors surrounding them.

Alexander's face transformed, breaking into the cheesiest, biggest grin despite their dire circumstances. The change was startling—years seemed to fall away from his weathered features, replaced by pure, uncomplicated joy.

"Oh, Magsy's incredible. Stubborn as her mother. Into everything, never stops moving. She's just started talking properly." He looked down at his crossbow, the grin somehow growing even wider, as if the weapon reminded him of something amusing. "Her first word was dada. She always had the biggest smile for me ever since she was born. I know they said it was just wind and not a smile but… I know it was one."

His voice had taken on a quality Aileen hadn't heard before—soft, tender, filled with wonder at the small miracle of his daughter's existence.

"She has never stopped smiling since the day she was born and she had this mischievous little giggle that could light up every dark part in the world." He looked around at the devastation, his smile faltering slightly but not disappearing entirely. "Even moments like this."

"What about Ailsa? What's she like?" Aileen found herself genuinely curious, drawn in by the warmth in Alexander's voice when he spoke of his family.

Alexander's expression softened even further, if that was possible. His eyes took on a distant quality, as if he could see through the ruins of Cantsford to a small island cottage where a red-haired woman waited.

"Ailsa…" His voice became tender, almost reverent. "She has this beautiful red hair that glows like a sunset, especially when she's standing by the window in the evening light. And her smile—it can light up any room she walks into. She's got this way of making everything seem possible, you know? Even when things are tough, she just… she makes it better."

He paused, lost in the memory, his eyes unfocused as he lived in that moment rather than this one.

"She's the strongest person I know. Gentle, but fierce when she needs to be. Magsy gets her stubbornness from her mother, but she gets her kindness from her too."

His grip tightened on his crossbow, knuckles whitening against the worn wood.

"I just hope they're safe. I hope they're sitting by the fire right now, Ailsa reading to Magsy, wondering when daddy's coming home."

Aileen smiled at his obvious pride, at the fierce love that radiated from every word. "They both sound lovely."

"They are. That's why I have to get to them. They are my world and I have no world without them." The words were simple, absolute, spoken with the conviction of fundamental truth.

They approached the first abandoned car—a small blue hatchback with mud splattered along its sides. Through the window, Alexander could see the keys still dangling from the ignition, glinting in the afternoon light like a small promise.

"Come on…" Alexander murmured as he opened the driver's door and slid behind the wheel, his injured ankle protesting as he positioned it near the pedals. He turned the key.

The engine turned over once, twice, then caught with a rough but steady rumble.

"Finally." Aileen's relief was palpable, her shoulders dropping as tension she hadn't realized she was carrying released.

"We'll need fuel, but this should get us closer to the coast." Alexander adjusted the mirrors, checking angles, making sure he could see what might be coming from any direction. Old habits from his health and safety work—always assess the risks, always have an exit plan.

Aileen kept watch as he worked, her hand resting on the hilt of her sword, her eyes scanning the empty windows and shadowed doorways that surrounded them.

"Alexander?" Her voice was hesitant, as if she was afraid of the answer. "When we get to the coast… when you find that boat to your family… there'll be room for one more, won't there?"

Alexander looked at her, really looked at her—this woman who had lost everything in the span of minutes, who had chosen to run north into uncertainty rather than stay with the certain death of infection. His expression was steady, sincere.

"Of course. You've got nowhere else to go now."

"Thank you." The word was simple, but it carried the weight of everything—gratitude for the weapon, for the companionship, for the hope of a future that extended beyond the next few hours.

Suddenly, they heard it—a low moaning sound coming from one of the nearby cottages. It wasn't the wind. It wasn't an animal. It was something human, or something that had once been human, making a sound of mindless hunger.

"Get in. Now." Alexander's voice was quiet but commanding, brooking no argument.

They both climbed into the car as the moaning grew louder, joined by a second voice, then a third. Through the cracked windscreen, they could see movement in the shadows of a cottage doorway—jerky, uncoordinated motion that was nevertheless purposeful.

Alexander's hand went to the gear shift, ready to drive, his other hand gripping the steering wheel so tightly his knuckles had gone white. Aileen pulled her door closed as quietly as she could, the click of the latch sounding unnaturally loud in the confined space.

The moaning grew closer, and with it came the shuffle of feet dragging across cobblestones.

Alexander's hand moved decisively to the gear shift, slamming the car into drive as the moaning from the cottage swelled into a chorus of inhuman hunger. The vehicle lurched forward, tires spinning briefly on the slick cobblestones before finding purchase.

Through the rear window, framed in the grimy glass like a nightmare portrait, they could see a figure stumbling out of one of the damaged buildings. It was an Aimless—its movements slow but horribly deliberate, drawn toward the sound of the car engine like a moth to flame. The figure had once been human, that much was clear from its general shape, but something fundamental had been stripped away. Its head tilted at an unnatural angle, and even from this distance, they could see the milky quality of its eyes.

"Keep your eyes open for more of them," Alexander said, his voice tight with concentration as he navigated carefully through the village. The narrow street was littered with debris—broken furniture, scattered belongings, the detritus of lives interrupted and abandoned.

They passed several more abandoned vehicles, some with doors hanging open as if their occupants had fled in panic. Damaged storefronts lined the street, their windows shattered, merchandise spilled onto the pavement. A pharmacy's sign swung on a single hinge, creaking rhythmically. A bakery's display window was smashed, and they could see loaves of bread now covered in mould, untouched even by the birds.

A petrol station came into view ahead, its familiar red and white colours somehow incongruous against the backdrop of destruction. The windows were smashed, shards of glass glittering on the concrete forecourt, but the structure itself appeared intact. The pumps stood like sentinels, their digital displays dark.

"We should check that for fuel," Aileen suggested, leaning forward in her seat.

"Good thinking. We'll need all we can get." Alexander began to slow the vehicle, his foot easing off the accelerator.

But as they approached the petrol station, Alexander's trained eye—honed by years of assessing workplace hazards—caught something wrong. Movement in the shadows between the pumps. Not the random flutter of debris in the wind, but purposeful motion.

"Wait. Something's not right," he said, his foot moving toward the brake.

Two more Aimless emerged from behind the station building, drawn inexorably by the car's engine noise. They moved with that characteristic shambling gait, their limbs not quite coordinating properly, as if their bodies had forgotten how to walk efficiently. But their heads turned with disturbing precision, tracking directly toward the vehicle with single-minded focus.

"There's more of them," Aileen breathed, her hand instinctively moving to the sword at her side.

Alexander's mind raced through the risk assessment: unknown number of infected, confined space with limited exits, both of them exhausted, his ankle compromised. The calculation took less than a second.

"We'll have to come back for fuel later. Right now we need distance."

He pressed the accelerator, and the car surged forward past the petrol station. As they drove, more infected began to emerge from various buildings—from doorways and broken windows, from behind overturned vehicles and collapsed walls. They appeared like terrible flowers blooming in the afternoon light, drawn by the promise of living flesh.

In the rearview mirror, Alexander could see at least six Aimless now following the car, their arms reaching forward with desperate, grasping motions. But they quickly fell behind, unable to match even the modest speed of the vehicle. Their moaning faded gradually, replaced by the rumble of the engine and the crunch of tires over broken glass.

"How far to the coast from here?" Aileen asked, watching the infected recede into the distance.

Alexander glanced at the fuel gauge, its needle hovering uncomfortably close to the empty mark. "About fifteen miles. This tank should get us there, just barely."

They left Cantsford behind, the village growing smaller in the mirror until it was just another smudge on the horizon. Ahead, the road stretched westward toward the coast and, hopefully, safety.

21

Cauldhame

Spotify Apple Music Amazon Music

Track: CAULDHAME

The landscape began to transform as they drove west, the character of the land changing with each passing mile. The rolling hills that had dominated the interior gave way to increasingly rugged terrain—rocky outcrops thrust up through the earth like bones through skin, and patches of purple heather spread across the slopes like bruises.

The afternoon sun hung lower in the sky now, painting everything in shades of amber and gold. And in the distance, visible through gaps in the hills, they could catch glimpses of the sea—a thin line of blue on the horizon that seemed to promise escape, freedom, hope.

"There—you can see the water," Aileen said, pointing ahead, her voice carrying a note of relief mixed with longing. The sea was her element, the place she understood. On the water, she would no longer be helpless.

"Finally. How much further do you think?" Alexander's own relief was palpable. The island. Ailsa. Magsy. Each mile west brought him closer to them.

"Maybe five miles to the actual coastline. Depends on where we can find a harbour or beach to launch from." Aileen's fishing experience made her the expert now, and she studied the landscape with a practiced eye, mentally cataloging potential launch points.

The fuel gauge needle hovered dangerously close to empty, trembling with each bump in the road as if it might tip over that final edge at any moment.

As they crested a hill, the view opened up before them. A small village spread out on the hilltop ahead, its stone buildings clustered together like sheep seeking mutual protection. Smoke rose from several chimneys—thin streams of gray that spoke of warmth, cooking, life. The buildings were arranged around what looked like a village green, a patch of grass at the heart of the community.

"That looks promising. Signs of life," Alexander said, hope blooming in his chest.

Aileen leaned forward, studying the village with a more critical eye. "At least we might be able to get supplies there, maybe more fuel."

Suddenly, the car engine began to sputter, its steady rumble fragmenting into an uneven cough. The vehicle lurched slightly, and Alexander's hands tightened on the steering wheel.

"Come on, not now," he muttered, willing the machine to continue.

The engine coughed once more, a death rattle of mechanical protest, then died completely. The sudden silence was startling after hours of engine noise. Alexander tried to restart it, turning the key repeatedly, but nothing happened. Not even the turning-over sound. Just dead silence and the ticking of cooling metal.

"We're out of fuel." Frustration and resignation warred in Alexander's voice.

They coasted to a stop about half a mile from the village, the car rolling to a gentle halt on the shoulder of the road. Through the windscreen, they could see their destination tantalizingly close but still distant enough to require effort.

"We'll have to walk the rest of the way," Aileen said, already reaching for her pack.

Alexander gathered his crossbow and did a quick inventory of his remaining bolts—six left, he noted with concern. He reached down and quickly rubbed his ankle, feeling the heat and swelling through his boot. The brief rest in the car had allowed it to stiffen, and he knew the walk ahead would be painful. He opened the door and stepped out, testing his weight gingerly.

"At least we can see our destination. What's that village called?"

Aileen checked a weathered road sign they had passed, its paint faded but still legible. "Cauldhame. I know this place—it's about five miles east of Presthaven."

Alexander's head snapped toward her, excitement flooding his features. "So we're almost there! Presthaven's just beyond this village?"

"Should be." Aileen shouldered her pack, adjusting the straps and the sword on her back. "Depends on who's still alive down there."

They began walking toward the hilltop village, their shadows stretching long beside them in the late afternoon sun. Alexander's limp was pronounced now, but he set his jaw and pushed forward. Half a mile. They could manage half a mile.

Alexander and Aileen approached the hilltop village with the caution that had become second nature over the past few days. Every building could hide infected. Every shadow could conceal danger.

The stone cottages were arranged around a central green, a roughly circular patch of grass that served as the heart of the community. At one end stood a small church, its square tower rising above the other buildings, a Celtic cross visible at its peak. At the other end sat what looked like a pub, its sign—The Shepherd's Rest—swinging gently in the sea breeze.

Several vehicles were parked haphazardly around the village—some clearly abandoned, with doors open and possessions scattered, but others suggesting recent use. A Land Rover was parked neatly outside one cottage. A pickup truck sat with its bed loaded with supplies covered by a tarp.

"Looks more organized than the other places we've been through," Alexander observed, his eyes cataloging details, assessing the situation the way he would assess a construction site for hazards.

"Look—there's laundry hanging out. Fresh laundry." Aileen pointed to several washing lines strung between cottages, where sheets and clothing flapped in the breeze. The fabric looked clean, recently washed, not the grimy, abandoned remnants they'd seen in other places.

They could see movement in some of the windows—brief flickers of shadow that suggested people looking out, watching. The smoke from chimneys wasn't the thin, dissipating streams of dying fires, but thick, healthy plumes that spoke of active hearths, of communities still functioning.

"Should we just walk in, or…?" Alexander began, unsure of the protocol for approaching a possibly hostile settlement in the middle of an apocalypse.

Before Aileen could answer, a voice rang out from behind a stone wall to their left, sharp and commanding.

"That's far enough! State your business!"

A man in his fifties emerged from behind cover, rising from a crouch where he'd clearly been watching their approach. He was stocky and solid, with gray hair cut short and a weathered face that spoke of years spent outdoors. He wore practical clothing—work boots, heavy trousers, a thick jumper—and he held a shotgun in capable hands. Notably, he wasn't directly aiming it at them, but the weapon was ready, positioned across his body where it could be brought to bear in an instant.

"You're not infected, are you? No bites, no scratches?" His voice carried the accent of the Highlands, vowels stretched and consonants hard.

Alexander raised his hands slightly, making himself appear non-threatening while keeping his crossbow visible. "No, we're clean. Just trying to get to the coast."

"We're not looking for trouble. Just need supplies, maybe fuel if you have any," Aileen added, her voice steady and reasonable.

Gordon studied them for a long moment, his eyes moving from Alexander's crossbow to Aileen's sword, assessing their condition, their body language, their threat level. Whatever he saw must have satisfied him, because he lowered his weapon slightly.

"Where have you come from?"

"Muir of Howis, by way of Cantsford," Alexander replied.

Gordon's expression darkened. "Cantsford's gone then?"

"Overrun. We barely got out," Aileen confirmed.

Gordon nodded grimly, as if this confirmed something he'd already suspected. He fully lowered his shotgun, though he kept his hand on it. "I'm Gordon. We've got about thirty people here, holding the village. You can come in, but you'll need to speak to our leader first."

"Fair enough. I'm Alexander, this is Aileen." Relief flooded through Alexander. A functioning community. Organization. Maybe even help.

"Follow me. And keep your weapons visible but lowered—people are jumpy." Gordon's tone made it clear this wasn't a suggestion but a requirement for entry.

He turned and began leading them toward the village center. As they walked, Alexander could see other faces in windows, watching their progress. A woman with two children peered out from behind a curtain. An older man stood in a doorway, arms crossed, expression neutral but alert. These were survivors who had organized, who had created something resembling safety in a world gone mad.

The village green opened before them, and Alexander could see more people now—some tending to a communal fire pit, others carrying supplies, a few standing guard with various weapons. All of them stopped what they were doing to watch the newcomers.

They had reached sanctuary, or at least something close to it. But Alexander knew from experience that every sanctuary came with its own price.

Gordon led Alexander and Aileen into the heart of the village, and what they found there was nothing short of remarkable. The green was bustling with purposeful activity—a functioning community that had somehow maintained itself despite the collapse of the world around it.

People tended to cooking fires that sent fragrant smoke spiraling into the evening air, the smell of stew and fresh bread somehow incongruous in a world of death and decay. Children played under watchful eyes, their laughter a sound Alexander hadn't heard in days, so normal it almost hurt to listen to. Adults sat in small groups maintaining weapons and equipment—sharpening blades, checking firearms, repairing tools—all with the practiced efficiency of people who had adapted quickly to new necessities.

Barricades had been constructed at the main entrances to the village, impressive structures built from overturned vehicles, timber beams, and whatever else the community had been able to scavenge. Sentries were posted at key points around the perimeter, their silhouettes visible against the darkening sky, weapons ready but postures relaxed enough to suggest no immediate threat.

"Margaret! Got two more survivors here!" Gordon called out, his voice carrying across the green.

A woman in her forties approached from the direction of the church, moving with the confident stride of someone used to being obeyed. She had dark hair pulled back in a practical bun, and sharp eyes that missed nothing. She wore sensible clothing—

sturdy boots, jeans, a thick cardigan—and carried herself with an air of natural authority that needed no uniform or title to establish itself.

"You both look like you've been through hell," Margaret said, her eyes traveling over their disheveled appearance, the dirt on their clothes, the exhaustion etched into their faces.

"It's been a rough few days," Alexander admitted, the understatement almost absurd.

"I'm Margaret. I was the village doctor before all this started. Now I suppose I'm whatever passes for leadership around here." Her tone was matter-of-fact, neither proud nor apologetic about her role.

"I'm Aileen, this is Alexander. We're trying to get to Presthaven," Aileen said.

Margaret's expression shifted, concern flickering across her features. "Presthaven? That's not good news, I'm afraid."

Alexander felt his stomach drop. "What do you mean?"

"We had refugees come through yesterday. Said the town's been overrun," Gordon explained, his tone sympathetic.

"What's so important in Presthaven?" Margaret asked.

"My family. They're on Druichmachon Island. I need to find a boat." The words came out more desperately than Alexander intended, betraying the fear he'd been trying to contain.

Margaret exchanged a meaningful look with Gordon, some unspoken communication passing between them.

"That's going to be difficult. The harbor's crawling with those things now," Margaret said carefully.

"What about other ways to the coast? Smaller harbors?" Aileen pressed, her fishing knowledge making her think in terms of alternatives, backup plans.

"There are a few fishing coves, but they're harder to reach. And more dangerous."

A young boy, no more than eight or nine, ran up to Margaret and tugged on her sleeve with the unselfconscious urgency of childhood. “Margaret, Mrs. Henderson says the radio’s picking up something new.”

Margaret’s attention sharpened. “You two look like you could use food and rest. We’ll talk more after we hear what’s on the radio.”

Margaret led Alexander and Aileen into a small community hall that had clearly been converted into a command center of sorts. Maps were pinned to walls, supplies were organized in neat stacks, and several villagers were gathered around an old radio that crackled with static.

An elderly woman with steel-gray hair and nimble fingers was adjusting the dial with the practiced movements of someone who’d been doing this for decades. “It’s coming through clearer now,” Mrs. Henderson announced.

Static crackled and popped, then a voice emerged from the interference like a drowning man breaking the surface of water.

“…this is Harbor Master Thomson broadcasting from Presthaven. Can anyone hear me? Over.”

Mrs. Henderson quickly grabbed the radio microphone, her movements surprisingly spry. “This is Cauldhame. We can hear you, Thomson. What’s your situation? Over.”

“Margaret, is that you? Thank God.” The relief in Thomson’s voice was palpable even through the tinny speaker. “Listen, I’m sending another group of survivors your way. About eight people, including two children. They should reach you by nightfall. Over.”

Margaret took the microphone from Mrs. Henderson. “This is Margaret. We can accommodate them. What’s the situation down there? Over.”

There was a pause, long enough that Alexander wondered if they’d lost the signal. Then Thomson’s voice returned, heavier now, weighted with exhaustion and fear.

"Not good. We've lost the entire village. I'm holed up in the harbour office with a few others, but we can't hold much longer. Over."

The room fell silent except for the static hiss of the radio. Everyone leaned in, hanging on every word, desperate for information from the world beyond their small sanctuary.

"Margaret, I need to warn you about something else. We've had reports of boats mysteriously going down in the waters around here. Good boats, experienced crews. Something's not right out there. Over."

Alexander and Aileen exchanged concerned glances, a new fear adding itself to the already substantial collection.

"Any idea what's causing it? Over," Margaret asked, her doctor's training making her seek symptoms, causes, diagnoses even in situations like this.

"No clue. Just… be careful if anyone tries to make a sea crossing. Thomson out."

The signal faded back into static, leaving only the whisper of electromagnetic noise and the sound of worried breathing.

"That's all we're getting for now," Mrs. Henderson said quietly, her fingers still on the dial as if she might coax more information from the device through sheer will.

"So Presthaven's falling, but at least we know there might still be boats there," Margaret said, ever practical.

"There's also the old smuggler's cove about three miles north of town. Might be safer than the main harbor," Gordon offered.

"I know that cove. Used to shelter there during storms. It's accessible, but it's a rough walk through the hills," Aileen said, her mental map of the coastline already calculating routes and distances.

"What do you think about those boats going down?" Alexander asked, his risk assessment mind immediately cataloging potential hazards.

Aileen considered the question thoughtfully. "Could be anything. Engine failures, panic, maybe even those things getting onto vessels somehow."

"You'll need to stay the night," Margaret said to Alexander, her tone brooking no argument. "It's getting dark, and those hills are dangerous enough in daylight."

"I appreciate the offer, but I need to keep moving. My family's waiting for me." Alexander could hear the restlessness in his own voice, the desperate need to be in motion, to be doing something rather than waiting.

"Alexander, she's right. We can't navigate those hills in the dark," Aileen said gently.

"Every hour I delay is another hour they're wondering where I am. What if something happens to the island? What if—" The fear he'd been containing threatened to spill out.

"Mate, I've lived here my whole life," Gordon interrupted, his voice firm. "Those hills will kill you in the dark. Loose rocks, hidden drops, boggy ground. You'll break your neck before you get halfway there."

"And if you get injured, you'll never reach them at all," Margaret added, her medical experience lending weight to the argument.

"But they're so close. Presthaven's only five miles away." Alexander felt trapped between urgency and reason, knowing they were right but hating the delay.

"Alexander, listen to me." Aileen's voice carried the authority of her years at sea. "I've sailed these waters for fourteen years. Night crossings are dangerous even in good conditions. In the dark, with whatever's happening out there, it's suicide."

"We'll give you supplies, a proper meal, and you can leave at first light. You'll make better time well-rested than stumbling around in the dark," Margaret said.

"I just… I promised them I'd be back days ago." The words came out almost as a whisper, the guilt of broken promises heavy in his chest.

"And you will be. But you need to be smart about it. One more night won't make a difference if it means you actually make it there alive."

Alexander looked out the window at the gathering darkness. The sun had dipped below the horizon, painting the sky in shades of purple and deep blue. The hills to the west were already lost in shadow, their contours invisible, their dangers multiplied by darkness.

"Alright. First light. But we leave at dawn, no matter what." The concession felt like defeat, even though he knew it was the right choice.

"Agreed. Gordon, can you find them somewhere to sleep?" Margaret asked.

"Aye, there's space in the church hall," Gordon confirmed.

22

Dawn

Spotify Apple Music Amazon Music

Track: DAWN

The village had transformed as darkness settled over it. What had been a bustling centre of activity now took on a softer, more intimate atmosphere. Cooking fires provided warm light that pushed back the darkness, and people gathered in small groups, sharing meals and quiet conversation. The sound of voices mixed with the crackle of fires and the distant bleating of sheep penned somewhere beyond the barricades.

Sentries patrolled the perimeter with lanterns, their silhouettes moving along the fortifications like ghostly guardians. The discipline was impressive—these people had organized quickly, had recognized what needed to be done and done it without the need for military training or outside authority.

"We've got sleeping bags and blankets set up in the hall. Not luxury, but it's warm and dry," Gordon said, leading them toward the church.

"Mrs. Campbell's made a pot of stew. You both look like you could use a proper meal," Margaret added, walking alongside them.

Alexander kept glancing toward the western edge of the village, where the road led to Presthaven. Five miles. So close. Ailsa and

Magsy might as well be on the moon for all the good that proximity did him tonight.

"Alexander, they'll still be there in the morning," Aileen said softly, noticing his restlessness.

"I know. It's just… being this close and having to wait." The frustration in his voice was palpable.

The hall had been efficiently converted into a communal sleeping area. Families had claimed corners with their belongings, creating small islands of privacy with improvised barriers of backpacks and blankets. Children were settling down for the night, their voices gradually quieting as exhaustion claimed them.

Gordon showed them to a quiet area near the back, away from the families with young children. "There's space here. I'll bring you some food."

Alexander sat heavily on one of the sleeping bags, his body finally acknowledging the toll of the day. His ankle throbbed with every heartbeat, and every muscle ached with accumulated fatigue. But his mind refused to settle, racing with worry and plans and fears.

"Tell me about the island. What's it like?" Aileen asked, sitting beside him, sensing that talking might help ease his restlessness.

Alexander's expression softened immediately, the worry lines easing as his mind travelled across the water to home. "It's beautiful. Small—you can walk across it in about an hour. There's a little harbour, maybe twenty houses, a shop that's only open three days a week."

He pulled out his phone, its battery nearly dead but still clinging to life. He showed her a photo—a scenic view of white cottages around a hilltop, the grass impossibly green, the sky vast and clear.

"That's our house, the blue door. Ailsa painted it that colour because she said it reminded her of the sea."

"It looks peaceful," Aileen said, studying the image of a world that seemed impossibly distant from their current reality.

"It is. Was. Magsy loves the beach near there. She's always collecting shells and chasing the waves." Alexander's voice carried a mixture of love and longing that made Aileen's chest ache.

Gordon returned with two bowls of steaming stew, the aroma making Alexander realize how hungry he actually was. "Get this into you. You'll need your strength tomorrow."

Alexander accepted the food gratefully but continued looking toward the windows, where full darkness had now fallen.

"How early is first light?"

"About six this time of year. But I'd wait until seven—gives you enough light to see the path properly," Gordon advised.

"Seven it is," Alexander said reluctantly, as if committing to the delay physically hurt.

The hall gradually quieted as families settled their children for sleep. Soft murmurs replaced conversation, and the sounds of shuffling and settling replaced movement. Alexander ate mechanically, spooning the stew into his mouth without really tasting it, his mind clearly elsewhere. Aileen watched him with growing concern.

"You're not going to sleep a wink, are you?"

Alexander sighed, setting down his spoon. "Probably not. I keep thinking about what Ailsa must be going through. She'll know something's wrong by now."

"She sounds like a strong woman. She'll be keeping it together for Magsy."

"She is strong. Stronger than me, probably. When Magsy was born, there were complications. Ailsa was so calm through it all, even when the doctors were worried." He set down his empty bowl, his fingers tracing the rim absently. "I was a wreck, but she just kept saying everything would be fine. And it was."

"What about you? What do you do when you're not attending conferences?" Aileen asked, trying to keep him talking, to keep his mind occupied.

"Health and safety consulting, mostly for offshore companies. Ironic, really—I spend my days writing reports about risk assessment, and here I am in the middle of the biggest risk of my life."

A child nearby started crying softly, and they could hear a mother's gentle shushing, the universal sound of comfort that transcended even apocalypse. Aileen noticed a young boy watching them from across the hall—eyes red from recent tears, clutching a worn stuffed animal. She offered him a small smile, and he inched closer, eventually sitting near enough to listen to their quiet conversation.

"Do you think… do you think my parents suffered?" Aileen's voice was small, vulnerable.

Alexander turned to her, his expression gentle. "I don't think so. It was quick. Your father was still trying to help people even at the end."

"That sounds like him. Always putting others first." She wiped her eyes with the back of her hand. "I should have visited more. Should have called."

"You couldn't have known this would happen."

The young boy shifted closer, and Aileen noticed he was shivering slightly despite the blankets. Without thinking, she reached over and adjusted his blanket around his shoulders. The boy looked up at her with grateful eyes and whispered, "Thank you."

"What's your name?" Aileen asked gently.

"Jamie," he said quietly. "My mum… she didn't make it here."

Aileen's heart clenched. "I'm sorry, Jamie. That's really hard."

The boy nodded, then settled himself near Aileen, as if her presence offered some small comfort in a world that had become incomprehensibly frightening.

Gordon approached with extra blankets, his footsteps quiet on the stone floor. "Gets cold in here at night. These should help."

"Gordon, that radio contact—Harbor Master Thomson—how well do you know him?" Alexander asked.

"Known him for years. Good man. If he says there are boats going down mysteriously, I'd believe him."

"Any theories about what might be causing it?"

Gordon lowered his voice, glancing around to make sure nearby children weren't listening. "Could be those infected getting on board somehow. Panic sets in, people make mistakes. Or maybe one of those big creatures—like the one you described from Muir of Howis—could easily capsize a small boat if it got aboard."

"A Bullseye on a fishing boat would be a disaster. The weight alone would destabilize it," Aileen said, her fishing experience making her understand the physics involved.

"So we need to be extra careful about what boats we choose, and make sure they're clear before we set off," Alexander said.

Gordon nodded grimly and moved away to check on other residents. Alexander lay back on his sleeping bag, staring at the ceiling where shadows danced in the dim light from the few lanterns still burning.

"Seven o'clock can't come soon enough."

Spotify Apple Music Amazon Music

Track: PARTING WAYS

The first light of dawn broke over the hilltop village like a promise being kept. The sky lightened gradually from black to deep blue to pale gray, stars fading as the sun climbed somewhere beyond the eastern horizon.

Alexander was already awake—in truth, he'd barely slept more than an hour or two, his mind too busy with worry and planning to fully surrender to rest. He sat outside the church hall with his gear packed, watching the eastern horizon bloom with colour, waiting for enough light to justify departure.

Aileen emerged from the hall, also ready to go, her pack on her back and the sword Alexander had given her secured in place. But something in her posture suggested hesitation, uncertainty.

"Couldn't sleep either?" she asked, sitting beside him on the stone steps.

"A few hours. You?"

"Same. Alexander, I've been thinking…"

Before she could continue, Jamie burst from one of the nearby cottages and ran toward them. The young boy had tousled brown hair and eyes still red from last night's tears. He launched himself at Aileen and hugged her leg with the desperate grip of a child who'd lost too much already.

"Aileen, are you really leaving?"

Aileen knelt down to his level, her hands gentle on his shoulders. "I have to, Jamie. But you'll be safe here with Margaret and Gordon."

Margaret approached with a small backpack, and Gordon followed carrying what looked like additional supplies wrapped in oilcloth.

"I've packed some medical supplies, food for the journey, and water purification tablets," Margaret said, handing the pack to Alexander.

"Margaret, you mentioned needing help with organizing supplies and defences…" Aileen began, still at eye level with Jamie.

Alexander understood immediately. "You want to stay."

"These people need help. Jamie here lost his mum yesterday, and there are others who…" She paused, searching for words. "I feel like I could actually do some good here. I know about boats, about the coast—I could help with planning escape routes if things go bad."

Jamie looked up at Alexander with pleading eyes. "Please don't take Aileen away. She helped me when I was scared."

Alexander felt something shift in his chest—not disappointment, but understanding. Aileen had found something here that she'd lost when her parents died. Purpose. Connection. A reason to keep going that extended beyond mere survival.

"You don't have to come with me, Aileen. You've already done more than enough."

"But you need someone who knows boats, who knows the waters…"

Gordon handed Alexander a hand-drawn map, its lines careful and detailed despite being sketched in pencil on the back of an old envelope. "I've drawn you a rough map of the route to the smuggler's cove. About three hours to reach it if you keep a good pace."

"Stay. Help these people. I can manage from here," Alexander said to Aileen, smiling despite everything.

Gordon glanced at Alexander's ankle, clearly wanting to object, but seemed to recognize the futility of trying to stop a man on a mission.

"Are you sure?" Doubt flickered in Aileen's eyes.

"You've got your own family to look after now." Alexander nodded toward Jamie, who still clung to Aileen's hand.

Aileen looked down at the boy, seeing in his face all the children here who needed protection, guidance, hope. She'd spent the night talking to families, learning their stories, and something had taken root—a sense of belonging she hadn't expected to find.

"Take care of yourself, Alexander. Give Ailsa and Magsy my love when you see them."

"I will. Thank you, Aileen. For everything." He meant it—for the company, for pulling him from the rubble, for the conversations that had kept him sane during the darkest hours.

They embraced briefly, two strangers who'd become allies in the span of a day and a half, now parting to follow their separate paths.

"The survivors from Presthaven confirmed there are boats in the smuggler's cove. Small fishing vessels, a couple of pleasure craft," Margaret said.

"That's all I need." Alexander shouldered his pack, testing the weight, adjusting the straps. His ankle protested but held.

The sun was climbing higher now, painting the village in shades of gold. Alexander headed toward the western edge of the village alone, his silhouette gradually shrinking as he followed the rough track that led toward the coast. Toward Presthaven. Toward home.

Aileen watched until he disappeared over the first rise, then turned back to the village where Jamie still held her hand, where Margaret was already organizing the day's tasks, where life continued in defiance of the death surrounding them.

Both of them had found what they needed. Now they just had to survive long enough to keep it.

23

The Coast

Spotify Apple Music Amazon Music

Track: ROLLING HILLS OF ALBANY

Alexander followed the narrow path that wound through the rolling hills like a thread stitching the land together. The morning air was crisp and clear, each breath sharp and invigorating in his lungs, carrying the faint scent of heather and damp earth. Patches of mist clung to the valleys below like sleeping ghosts, slowly burning away as the sun climbed higher.

His injured ankle made the journey harder than he'd anticipated. What should have been a steady pace became a careful, measured progress, each step requiring conscious effort to avoid aggravating the swelling. He found himself stopping more frequently than he'd like, leaning against rocks or trees to take weight off the damaged joint. The path was well-worn, suggesting centuries of use by shepherds and smugglers and all manner of people with reason to travel between the hills and the sea. But it was steep in places, demanding careful footwork as it wound between rocky outcrops and through patches of purple heather that brushed against his legs—and every misstep sent sharp pain shooting up from his ankle.

He consulted Gordon's hand-drawn map periodically to ensure he stayed on course, using these navigational pauses as excuses to rest without admitting to himself how much he needed them.

The solitude was both blessing and curse. Without conversation to distract him, his mind was free to spiral through worry—images of Ailsa trying to explain to Magsy why daddy hadn't come home, of the infection spreading to the island, of arriving too late. But the physical exertion and the constant management of his injury kept the worst of the anxiety at bay, forcing him to focus on the immediate challenges of navigation and endurance.

After about three hours of walking, Alexander's legs burning and his breath coming in controlled gasps, he reached the old shepherd's hut marked on Gordon's map. The journey that Gordon had estimated at two hours to this point had taken him three—his injured ankle slowing him more than he'd wanted to admit. The hut was a small stone building with a slate roof, perched on a ridge that offered a commanding view of the surrounding landscape. The structure was ancient, its stones weathered by countless Highland winters, but it stood solid and permanent against the elements.

Alexander practically collapsed against the cool stone wall, finally allowing himself to acknowledge his exhaustion. He carefully lowered himself to sit on a flat rock beside the hut entrance, taking the weight off his ankle with a grimace of relief. The joint was hot and swollen inside his boot, and he knew he should probably take the boot off to examine it, but he was afraid that if he did, he wouldn't be able to get it back on.

He checked his bearings against the map, orienting himself by the landmarks Gordon had carefully noted.

From this vantage point, the view was spectacular. He could see the coast in the distance—a thin line of blue water beyond the undulating hills, the horizon where sea met sky barely distinguishable in the morning haze. And there, closer, rising from what must be Presthaven, were columns of smoke. Not the thin, white streams of cooking fires, but thick, dark plumes that spoke of destruction and chaos. The reports of the town being overrun were clearly accurate.

Alexander pulled out a water bottle and took a long drink, the liquid cool and refreshing on his dry throat. He studied the map again, tracing the remaining route with his finger.

"About an hour to go," he murmured to himself, the sound of his own voice oddly comforting in the vast silence. Though at his current pace, it might be closer to ninety minutes. The thought of another hour and a half on his damaged ankle made him want to weep, but he pushed the feeling aside. So close. He was so close.

As he was about to cap the water bottle and force himself to continue, he heard a sound behind him—the crunch of footsteps on gravel, irregular and hesitant. Alexander turned sharply, his hand moving instinctively to his crossbow, fingers finding the familiar grip with practiced ease. The sudden movement sent fresh pain lancing through his ankle, but he ignored it.

A figure emerged from behind a rocky outcrop—another survivor, a woman in her thirties. She looked utterly exhausted, her clothes torn and dirty, her face pale beneath streaks of grime. Her eyes were wide with fear and desperation, and she moved with the unsteady gait of someone at the absolute limit of their endurance.

"Please… are you heading to the coast?" Her voice was breathless, cracking with exhaustion.

Alexander kept his crossbow ready but not raised threateningly. "Depends. Where did you come from?"

"Presthaven. I've been walking all night. The town… it's gone." The words tumbled out, raw with recent trauma.

She collapsed against the stone wall of the hut, her legs simply giving out beneath her. Her hands trembled, and Alexander could see the tracks of dried tears on her cheeks.

"I saw you from the valley. Please, I just need to get away from here."

Alexander lowered his crossbow, recognizing genuine desperation when he saw it. "You're safe for now. What's your name?"

"Sarah. Sarah Mitchell. I was a teacher in Presthaven before… before all this." She seemed to need to anchor herself to her former identity, to remember who she had been before the world ended.

"I'm Alexander. Listen, Sarah, I can't take you where I'm going, but there's a safe place not far from here." He pulled out Gordon's map and, with some effort, shifted his position to crouch beside her, keeping his weight off his injured ankle. He spread the map out so she could see.

"Follow this path back the way I came—about three hours' walk if you take it steady. There's a village called Cauldhame on the hilltop. They've got about thirty survivors there, good defenses, food."

Sarah looked at the map with eyes that struggled to focus, her exhaustion making even this simple task difficult. "Three hours? I don't know if I can make it."

"You can. Just follow the path, it's well marked. When you get there, tell them Alexander sent you. Ask for Margaret—she's the leader. They'll take you in." His voice was firm, encouraging, the tone of someone who expected to be believed.

He handed her his water bottle. "Take this. And here…"

He pulled an energy bar from his pack, one of the supplies Margaret had given him. It wasn't much, but it might make the difference between Sarah making it to Cauldhame or collapsing somewhere along the path.

"This should help keep your strength up."

"Thank you. But where are you going?" Sarah asked, accepting the offerings with trembling hands.

"To find a boat. My family's on one of the islands."

Sarah's expression shifted, worry flickering across her exhausted features. "The coast's not safe. I saw things… boats in trouble."

The warning echoed what Harbor Master Thomson had said over the radio, adding weight to concerns Alexander was already carrying. But it didn't change anything. It couldn't change anything.

"I have to try. Sarah, you need to get moving. The longer you stay out here alone, the more dangerous it gets."

Sarah nodded, gathering her strength with visible effort. She pushed herself away from the wall, testing her legs, finding they would still support her weight. "Cauldhame. Ask for Margaret. Tell them Alexander sent me."

"That's right. Good luck."

Sarah began walking back along the path toward Cauldhame, moving slowly but with determination. Alexander watched her for a moment, making sure she was steady on her feet, then pushed himself upright with a grunt of effort. The brief rest had allowed his ankle to stiffen, and the first few steps were agony. He gritted his teeth and turned toward the coast. The smoke from Presthaven rose dark against the morning sky, a pillar of destruction marking his destination.

Spotify

Apple Music

Amazon Music

Track: STEEP PATHWAYS

The path began to descend more steeply as Alexander approached the coast, the angle forcing him to lean back slightly to maintain balance. His injured ankle screamed in protest with each downward step, the descent somehow worse than the climb had been. He found himself moving sideways at times, taking the steepest sections at an angle to reduce the stress on the damaged joint. He used his crossbow as a makeshift walking stick on the worst sections, grateful for its solid construction.

The sound of waves grew louder, a rhythmic crashing that spoke of power and permanence. The salt smell of the sea filled the air, sharp and clean, cutting through the lingering scent of smoke and decay that had haunted his journey.

The landscape changed character as he descended. The open moorland gave way to rockier terrain, gorse bushes with their yellow flowers and vicious thorns lining the narrow track. Wind-bent trees, sculpted by centuries of coastal gales, grew at impossible angles, their branches all pointing inland as if fleeing from the sea.

The path became increasingly treacherous, loose stones threatening to turn his already injured ankle with every step. Alexander moved with painful care, testing his footing, knowing that one wrong step could end his journey here, leaving him crippled and helpless on this windswept hillside. Sweat beaded on his forehead despite the cool air, and his jaw ached from clenching his teeth against the pain.

The sound of waves grew from a distant murmur to a constant roar, and he could taste salt on his lips. The sea was close now. So close.

Then, finally, as he rounded a bend between two massive boulders, he saw it—the smuggler's cove below, a small sheltered inlet carved into the rocky coastline by millennia of patient erosion.

The sight of it sent a surge of adrenaline through Alexander that momentarily overrode his exhaustion and pain. Almost there. Almost.

Alexander carefully picked his way down the final stretch of path to the water's edge, his boots sliding occasionally on loose scree. Each jarring impact sent fresh pain through his ankle, but he barely noticed anymore—his entire focus was on the boats below. The cove was perhaps fifty meters wide, protected by high rocky walls on three sides that rose like natural fortifications. The fourth side opened to the sea, but even there, submerged rocks broke the waves into manageable swells rather than allowing the full force of the ocean to penetrate the inlet.

And there, exactly as Margaret had described, were the boats. Several vessels were moored or beached in the shallow water—two small fishing boats with their hulls painted in fading colors, a white pleasure craft that looked out of place among the working vessels, and what appeared to be an old rubber dinghy half-deflated on the shore.

Alexander surveyed the vessels with a critical eye, his risk assessment training kicking in automatically despite his exhaustion. Hull condition, size, seaworthiness, fuel capacity—all factors that could mean the difference between reaching Druichmachon and ending up as one of Harbor Master Thomson's mysterious boat casualties.

He approached the nearest fishing boat cautiously, crossbow ready, alert for any sign of infected or other threats. The boat appeared abandoned but intact—about twenty feet long with an outboard motor mounted on the stern. Its blue hull showed signs of hard use but no obvious damage.

"This could work," Alexander muttered to himself, the sound of his voice almost lost in the crash of waves.

He waded into the shallow water, the cold immediately soaking through his boots and making him gasp. The shock of the cold water on his swollen ankle was almost unbearable—but then, paradoxically, the cold began to numb the pain, providing relief he hadn't felt in hours. The water was clear enough that he could see the rocky bottom, and he checked carefully for any submerged hazards before approaching the boat.

Examining it more closely, the hull seemed sound—no visible cracks or damage, no signs of rot. And there, almost unbelievably, were keys hanging from the ignition, glinting in the sunlight. Someone had abandoned this boat in a hurry, fleeing from something and never returning.

Alexander climbed aboard, the boat rocking gently under his weight. The movement required him to put full weight on his injured ankle for a moment, and he had to bite back a cry of pain. Water sloshed in the bottom—rainwater probably, not a leak. He found the bilge pump and gave it a few experimental strokes, feeling resistance that suggested it still worked.

Then he turned the key.

The engine turned over but didn't catch, making a grinding sound that echoed off the cove walls.

"Come on…" Alexander's frustration bled into his voice. He couldn't have come this far, pushed through this much pain, only to be stopped by a reluctant engine.

He tried again, pumping the throttle slightly. This time the engine sputtered to life, caught for a few seconds, then died with a coughing sound.

On the third attempt, giving it more throttle and holding his breath, the engine started and stayed running. The rough rumble steadied into a more even rhythm, and blue smoke puffed from the outboard.

"Thank God." Relief flooded through Alexander, so intense it made his hands shake and brought tears to his eyes. He'd made it. Against all odds, despite everything, he'd made it.

As he checked the fuel gauge—half full, enough to reach the island with some to spare—he heard a sound from the rocky shore that made his blood run cold. The unmistakable moan of an Aimless, that wet, gurgling sound of mindless hunger.

Alexander's head snapped up to see a figure stumbling down the path he had just used, its movements jerky and uncoordinated. Then another appeared behind it. And another.

"Time to go." The words came out urgent, sharp with adrenaline.

He quickly untied the mooring rope, his fingers fumbling slightly in his haste, then pushed the boat away from shore with an oar. The vessel drifted backward into deeper water, and Alexander gunned the engine.

The boat lurched forward, cutting through the calm water of the cove. Behind him, he could see at least six infected stumbling down toward the water's edge, their arms reaching forward even though he was already beyond their grasp.

Then, at the top of the path, a massive shape appeared. A Bullseye, its enormous frame barely fitting on the narrow track, its body covered in those terrible armored plates of mutated flesh. It opened its mouth and let out a bone-chilling roar that echoed off the cove walls, the sound so powerful Alexander could feel it vibrating in his chest even over the engine noise.

The creature began descending the path, each of its steps sending small avalanches of stones cascading down. The same path Alexander had just navigated so carefully, the Bullseye covered in mere seconds, its massive weight and lack of regard for injury allowing it to move with terrible speed.

Alexander didn't wait to see if it would actually enter the water. He pushed the throttle to full, and the small fishing boat responded, its bow lifting as it accelerated toward the open sea.

The mouth of the cove approached rapidly, and then he was through, bursting out into the open water where waves immediately began buffeting the hull. Behind him, Presthaven burned. Ahead, somewhere beyond the horizon, lay Druichmachon Island.

Ailsa. Magsy. I'm coming.

24

The Island

Spotify Apple Music Amazon Music

Track: FINALLY HOME

Alexander looked back over his shoulder, his hand still gripping the throttle, to see the Aimless gathered at the water's edge like a collection of broken marionettes. They stood in the shallow surf, the waves lapping at their legs, but they came no further. Whatever drove them—hunger, instinct, the virus—it didn't give them the capacity to swim or the understanding to commandeer a boat.

The Bullseye paced back and forth on the rocky shore, its massive bulk making the ground tremble with each step. It was clearly frustrated, its small eyes fixed on the retreating boat, its roars echoing across the water even as Alexander increased the distance. The creature's rage was palpable, but impotent. The sea had become an impassable barrier.

Alexander turned his attention forward and checked the boat's compass, a simple mechanical device mounted on the console. The needle swayed with the motion of the waves but held steady enough to give him his bearing. He adjusted his heading, compensating for the current and the wind. Druichmachon Island should be about twenty miles northwest of his current position—perhaps an hour's journey in this boat under these conditions.

The sea was relatively calm, a blessing he hadn't expected. The light chop that textured the surface was well within the fishing boat's capabilities, and the hull cut through the waves with the steady confidence of a vessel built for these waters. The engine purred reliably beneath the housing, its rhythm steady and reassuring.

Alexander settled into the routine of navigation, one hand on the throttle, the other on the wheel, his eyes scanning the horizon for landmarks and hazards. Sitting took the weight off his damaged ankle for the first time in hours, and the relief was almost overwhelming, though he could still feel the heat of inflammation pulsing beneath the bandage Margaret had wrapped. For the first time in days—since this nightmare had begun—he allowed himself to feel something that approached hope. He was on the water. He was heading home. Nothing stood between him and his family now but distance and time.

"I'm coming, Ailsa. I'm coming, Magsy," he said, speaking to the wind, to the sea, to whatever deity might be listening. His voice was torn away by the breeze, scattered across the waves, but saying the words aloud made them feel more real, more like a promise he could keep.

Spotify Apple Music Amazon Music

Track: HOME THROUGH THE SHADOWS

About twenty minutes into the journey, when the coast had receded to a dark line behind him and the island was not yet visible ahead, Alexander noticed something in the water. Debris floating on the surface—pieces of wood, what looked like a life jacket bobbing in the swell, other unidentifiable fragments scattered across perhaps fifty meters of ocean.

As he got closer, the truth became apparent. These weren't random pieces of flotsam. This was the remains of a boat, and recently too—the wood wasn't waterlogged or covered in marine growth, the colours of the life jacket were still bright.

This must be one of the mysterious sinkings Harbor Master Thomson had mentioned over the radio.

Alexander slowed his engine and carefully navigated around the wreckage, his eyes scanning the surface for any sign of survivors, though he knew in his heart what he would find. Nothing. No one. Just debris and the indifferent sea.

He could see no obvious cause for the sinking. No rocks broke the surface here—the water was deep, perhaps forty or fifty meters. No signs of fire or explosion. But as he maneuvered around a larger piece of hull, he noticed something that made his blood run cold. The boat appeared to have been torn apart rather than simply capsized. The wood showed jagged breaks, splintered edges, damage that spoke of violence rather than accident.

"What the hell happened here?" The question was directed at no one, but it hung in the air, unanswered and deeply unsettling.

Alexander increased speed, suddenly eager to put distance between himself and the wreckage. Whatever had happened here, he didn't want to linger long enough to find out if it might happen again.

Alexander continued northwest, the wreckage now far behind him, hopefully far enough that whatever had caused it wouldn't be a concern. The sun climbed higher in the clear sky, and he could feel its warmth on his face despite the cool sea breeze that carried the salt spray. It was almost pleasant—under any other circumstances, this would have been a beautiful day for a boat trip.

In the distance, gradually resolving itself from the haze where sea met sky, he began to make out the silhouette of Druichmachon Island. A dark shape on the horizon, familiar and beloved, the place where his heart lived. His pulse quickened at the sight.

"There it is," he breathed, emotion thickening his voice. Relief, hope, love—all tangled together in those three words.

As he got closer, covering the miles with agonizing slowness despite the steady speed of the boat, the familiar features of the island became clearer. The small harbour on the southern shore. The cluster of white cottages that made up the main settlement of Braelin. The lighthouse on the eastern point, its red and white stripes visible even from this distance.

But something was wrong.

Spotify Apple Music Amazon Music

Track: DRUICHMACHON

Alexander's trained eye, honed by years of risk assessment, caught the details even before his conscious mind wanted to acknowledge them. There was no movement visible on the docks. No boats coming or going. The usual activity of a small island community—fishing boats departing or returning, the ferry making its rounds, people moving between buildings—was completely absent.

As he drew closer still, more disturbing details emerged. Several boats were scattered around the harbour in unnatural positions—some capsized, their hulls pointing skyward, others run aground on the rocky shore where no competent sailor would ever beach a vessel.

Alexander throttled back as he approached the harbour, his heart sinking with each detail that resolved itself from distance into horrible clarity. The pier was damaged, with entire sections collapsed into the water. The wooden structure, which he had walked across a thousand times, which had been solid and well-maintained, now looked like it had been subjected to tremendous violence.

Dark stains marked the wooden planks that remained standing. Not the honest brown of weathered wood or the green of algae, but rusty, ominous stains that could only be one thing. Debris was scattered everywhere—overturned crates, tangled fishing nets, personal belongings left where they'd fallen.

No one came to greet his arrival. In a community this small, the sound of an approaching boat engine was always noticed, always brought people to the dock to see who was arriving. But now there was only silence—terrible, complete silence broken only by the lap of waves against hulls and the cry of seabirds.

Alexander tied his boat to what remained of the pier with hands that trembled, his fingers fumbling with the knot. He climbed onto the dock, testing each board before trusting it with his full weight. The structure creaked ominously beneath him.

The smell hit him immediately—the stench of death and decay, sickeningly familiar after his journey through the mainland. But here, on his island, in his home, the smell was a violation so profound it made his stomach heave.

"No… no, no, no…" The words came out as a whispered horror, a denial of what his senses were telling him.

He ran toward the village, his crossbow ready but his hands shaking so badly he wasn't sure he could aim if he needed to. The first cottage he passed had its door torn completely off the hinges, the wood splintered as if something massive had simply smashed through it. Dark stains covered the white walls, splashed in patterns that spoke of violence and terror.

Bodies lay scattered in the street. Some were clearly torn apart, dismembered with the casual brutality of the Bullseyes. Others showed the telltale signs of infection—the milky eyes, the grasping hands frozen in death, the mouths open in silent moans.

Alexander's mind couldn't process it all. His worst fears, the nightmare scenarios he'd tried not to imagine during his journey, were laid out before him in terrible detail. The infection hadn't just reached the island—it had devastated it.

He moved through Braelin like a ghost, his boots echoing on the cobblestones, past buildings he'd known his entire adult life. Mrs. Campbell's bakery, its windows shattered, flour spilled across the floor like snow. The pub where he'd celebrated Magsy's birth, its door hanging open, chairs overturned, dark stains on the wooden floor. The small shop where Ailsa bought groceries, its shelves ransacked, goods scattered and trampled.

A few Aimless wandered between the buildings, their movements sluggish and purposeless. They turned toward him as he passed, their milky eyes tracking his movement, but he was past them before they could react, his focus singular and desperate.

Not here. They're not here. Please let them not be here.

He ignored his now-throbbing ankle—the pain that had been a constant companion suddenly meaningless—and sprinted through the town, evading the Aimless that wandered between buildings.

Alexander ran along the familiar path that led from Braelin toward Thrainshaw, the smaller settlement on the northern side of the island where his cottage with the blue door stood. The coastal village behind him lay in ruins, but ahead the landscape looked more hopeful—untouched, peaceful, normal.

The path wound through rolling green hills dotted with ancient stone walls and patches of purple heather that released their scent when his boots crushed them. His breath came in ragged gasps, his chest burning, but he didn't slow. Couldn't slow.

About half a mile from Braelin, Alexander passed the old MacLeod farm, its whitewashed walls bright in the afternoon sun. The farmhouse appeared abandoned—door closed, no smoke from the chimney, curtains drawn. But the sheep were still grazing peacefully in the fields, their woolly bodies moving slowly across the green grass. A strangely normal sight that gave him a flicker of irrational hope. If the sheep were fine, maybe…

"Keep going… keep going…" he panted, pushing his exhausted body onward.

He followed the path as it curved around a small loch, its dark water reflecting the sky like polished obsidian. On the far shore, he could see the remains of what looked like a makeshift camp—tents and belongings scattered as if people had left in a hurry. But there were no bodies, no signs of violence. No blood staining the grass. Just abandoned possessions, as if the occupants had simply vanished.

Evacuation? Did people evacuate?

The thought gave him hope even as his rational mind tried to temper it. If there had been an evacuation, where had people gone? To another island? Back to the mainland? And why hadn't Ailsa contacted him?

At the highest point of the path, where the track crested a small hill, Alexander paused to catch his breath. His lungs burned, his legs felt like lead, and his ankle had progressed from pain to a numbness that was probably more concerning.

From this vantage point, he could see both settlements. Behind him, Braelin lay devastated—smoke rising from several buildings, the harbour a scene of destruction. And ahead, the small cluster of buildings that made up Thrainshaw, perhaps fifteen or twenty cottages clustered around the northern bay.

But something was wrong. There was no smoke rising from the chimneys, and it was a cold afternoon—everyone should have their fires lit. No movement between the buildings. No signs of life at all. The settlement looked completely deserted, as empty as a photograph, as still as a grave.

"No… please no…" The words were torn from him, a prayer to an unresponsive universe.

He started running down the hill, using the steep descent to build momentum, his feet pounding against the packed earth of the path. His injured ankle throbbed with each impact, sending sharp pains shooting up his leg like electric shocks, the temporary numbness from the cold seawater long since worn off. The pain should have slowed him, should have forced him to stop. But it didn't.

If anything, it drove him forward, the physical pain somehow easier to bear than the terror of what he might find.

"Come on… come on…" he gasped, more to himself than to his failing body.

The path wound steeply downward through patches of heather and over stone walls that had stood for centuries. Alexander vaulted over the walls without breaking stride, without even slowing, his ankle screaming in protest with each landing. Each leap was agony. Each step was torture. He didn't care.

The closer he got to Thrainshaw, the more obvious the desolation became. Doors hung open, moving slightly in the breeze. Windows were dark, their glass eyes reflecting nothing. Nothing moved. No smoke. No sound. No life.

His cottage with the blue door was somewhere in that silent village. Ailsa and Magsy were somewhere in that silence.

Alexander ran faster.

Spotify Apple Music Amazon Music

Track: RACING SHADOWS

Alexander reached the edge of Thrainshaw, his chest heaving with exertion, his breath coming in ragged gasps that tore at his throat. He bent forward, hands on his knees, trying to force air into his burning lungs while his mind catalogued what his senses were telling him.

The silence was complete—oppressive in its totality. No voices calling to neighbours. No footsteps on the cobblestones. Not even the sound of animals—no bleating sheep, no barking dogs, no chickens scratching in yards. Just silence, thick and suffocating, broken only by the distant crash of waves and his own laboured breathing.

He limped quickly through the empty streets, his ankle now a constant source of agony. Each step sent sharp bolts of pain radiating up his leg, but the physical discomfort was nothing compared to the terror squeezing his heart. He pushed forward, driven by desperate hope—the irrational but necessary belief that somehow, impossibly, his family had been spared.

Then their cottage came into view, and his breath caught in his throat.

The one with the blue door that Ailsa had painted two summers ago, laughing as Magsy—just a baby then—had grabbed at the brush with paint-covered hands. Unlike many of the other buildings he'd passed, it appeared intact. The door was closed. The windows unbroken. No blood on the whitewashed walls. No signs of violence.

Hope surged in his chest, painful and powerful.

Alexander burst through the blue door, his crossbow clattering against the frame in his haste. "Ailsa! Magsy!" His voice echoed through the empty rooms, bouncing back at him from the familiar walls.

Silence answered him.

He moved through the cottage frantically, his eyes taking in every detail with desperate intensity. The sitting room was tidy—cushions arranged on the sofa, Magsy's toys in their basket by the fireplace. A half-finished cup of tea sat on the side table, a thin film across its cold surface.

In the bedroom, he threw open the wardrobe with trembling hands. All of Ailsa's clothes were still there, hanging neatly on their hangers—her favourite green cardigan, the floral dresses she wore in summer, the practical jumpers for island winters. He ran his hand along the fabric, feeling the textures she had touched, and his throat tightened.

Magsy's dresser was full—none of her little clothes appeared to be missing. The tiny jeans, the colourful shirts with cartoon characters, the pink dress she insisted on wearing every day. All there. Well, almost all. He realized with a jolt that the pink princess dress—the one she insisted on wearing constantly, the one Ailsa had to hide sometimes just to get her into other clothes—was missing.

"They didn't pack…" Confusion mixed with his fear. If they had evacuated, if they had fled to safety, surely they would have taken clothes, supplies, essentials. But if they'd just gone out for the day…

He rushed to the kitchen, his boots loud on the tile floor. He checked the hook by the back door where Ailsa always hung her purse. Gone. The empty hook sent his heart racing again.

Through the kitchen window, he could see the small shed where they kept Magsy's buggy—the three-wheeled all-terrain pram that Ailsa used for walks along the coastal paths. The shed door hung open, and even from here he could see the empty space where the buggy normally sat.

"They just went out. Maybe to the shop, or to check on neighbours." He said the words aloud, needing to hear them, needing them to be true. His voice sounded strange in the empty cottage—hopeful and desperate in equal measure.

Of course. They had just gone out for errands. Ailsa had probably seen the trouble starting and decided to stock up on supplies at the village shop. She was practical like that, always thinking ahead. They would be somewhere in the village, safe, waiting.

Alexander emerged from the cottage and looked around the deserted village with new purpose. If they had just gone out for errands, they might have gone to the village shop—Morrison's Post Office and General Store, the small building that served Thrainshaw's daily needs. It was Ailsa's usual destination for quick errands—a short walk, easy with the buggy.

He limped quickly through the empty streets, his ankle throbbing with each step but his hope renewed, pushing back the fear. Morrison's was just two streets over, its weathered sign visible above the low stone buildings.

The shop door stood open, swinging slightly in the breeze, and Alexander approached cautiously, his crossbow raised. The interior was dim, lit only by the gray daylight filtering through the windows. As his eyes adjusted, he could see that the shelves were still full of goods—canned food, bread, milk cartons, boxes of cereal—as if the shop had been abandoned suddenly in the middle of a normal day.

But there were clear signs of struggle. Items had been knocked off shelves, a wire display rack lay overturned, its contents—magazines and newspapers—scattered across the floor. Scattered groceries created an obstacle course down the aisles. A smear of something dark stained the counter.

Alexander stepped inside, the floor creaking beneath his weight. “Ailsa? Magsy?” His voice was quieter now, instinct warning him to be careful.

As he moved deeper into the shop, navigating around the fallen displays, he rounded the corner of one of the aisles.

At the far end, perhaps ten meters away, stood a small figure with her back to him.

Alexander’s heart stopped, then restarted with painful force.

Even from behind, he recognized everything about her. The blonde curls that Ailsa brushed every morning. The little pink dress—her favourite, the one she called her “princess dress.” The tiny white shoes on her feet.

“Magsy!” The word burst from him, breathless with relief so intense it was almost painful.

The figure didn’t respond or turn around. She stood perfectly still, facing away, her small shoulders motionless.

Alexander ran down the aisle, his crossbow forgotten, his caution abandoned, his heart pounding with joy that pushed aside everything else—the pain in his ankle, the fear, the horror of the past days. None of it mattered. She was here. She was alive.

“Magsy, sweetheart, it’s Daddy!”

25

What Remains

Spotify Apple Music Amazon Music

Track: WHAT REMAINS

He reached her and scooped her up in his arms, spinning her around, tears streaming down his face, hot and relieving and born of pure, overwhelming relief.

"Oh thank God, thank God you're okay. Daddy's here now. Daddy's here, baby girl. Everything's going to be alright. I'm so sorry it took so long, but I'm here now—"

But Magsy didn't respond. She didn't wrap her little arms around his neck the way she always did. She didn't press her face into his shoulder. She didn't say "dada" in that delighted voice that made his heart melt.

She felt wrong in his arms.

Her little body twitched unnaturally, the movement jerky and inhuman. The weight was right, the size was right, but something fundamental was wrong.

Then, in a voice that sounded like hers but somehow distant—hollow, as if coming from the bottom of a well—she spoke.

"Daddy?"

Her head twitched to the side with a sharp, birdlike motion that no child should make.

Alexander pulled back to look at her face, dread already pooling in his stomach like ice water.

Her skin had an unnatural orange tint, glowing faintly with its own light. It felt cold to the touch, like marble, not the warm softness of a child.

"Magsy? Are you… are you okay?" His voice cracked, hope and horror warring in his chest.

Something was wrong. Something was terribly, fundamentally wrong.

He gently set her down on the floor, his hands shaking, his mind refusing to process what his eyes were seeing.

Magsy turned around to face him with slow, deliberate movements.

Alexander's heart stopped.

Her eyes—her beautiful blue eyes that had looked at him with such love and joy—were gone. In their place glowed an eerie orange light, like embers in a dying fire, surrounded by dark rings that looked like bruises. Her skin had that same orange luminescence, pulsing faintly like a heartbeat.

She looked up at him with those alien eyes, and her head twitched again, that unnatural jerking motion.

"Daddy…" Her voice was hollow, wrong, missing some essential quality that made it hers. "Hungry…"

Alexander stumbled backward, his legs hitting a shelf, cans tumbling to the floor with crashes that sounded impossibly loud. His world was crashing down around him, the hope that had sustained him for days shattering like glass.

His baby girl—his Magsy, his little princess with the mischievous giggle and the biggest smile—was gone. This thing wearing her face, inhabiting her body, using her voice, was not his daughter.

"Magsy… sweetheart… it's Daddy…" The words came out broken, desperate, a plea to whatever might be left of her inside that terrible transformation.

Magsy's orange eyes fixed on him with predatory hunger, and her small body began to change. She dropped to all fours with unnatural fluidity, her joints bending in ways that human joints shouldn't bend. Orange goo dripped from the side of her mouth, viscous and glowing faintly, pooling on the floor.

Then she opened her mouth—opened it wider than any child should be able to—and released a piercing, high-pitched screech that seemed to come from something far larger than her tiny body. The sound echoed through the shop, bouncing off the walls, vibrating through Alexander's bones with physical force. He covered his ears, wincing, but the sound penetrated anyway, seeming to bypass his hands entirely and drill directly into his skull.

The screech was a call. A summons.

A tall, gaunt figure emerged from around the corner, moving with eerie silence despite its size.

Ailsa.

"No…" The word was barely a whisper, all the air driven from Alexander's lungs.

She had been beautiful—his beautiful Ailsa with the red hair that glowed like sunset, with the smile that lit up rooms, with the gentle strength that had carried their family through every hardship.

But she had been transformed into something nightmarish.

Her once-beautiful red hair hung in matted strands around her face, which had been marked with thick orange goo. The substance covered the entire top half of her face like a grotesque mask, seeping into her skin, glowing with that same terrible luminescence. Her fingers had stretched unnaturally long, the joints wrong, and the most horrifying thing of all—

She was completely blind. The orange goo had sealed her eyes shut, or consumed them, or replaced them with something that couldn't see light the way humans did. But her head snapped toward the sound of Alexander's breathing with terrible precision.

She moved with eerie silence despite her size, feeling her way along the shelves with those elongated fingers.

Magsy began to circle Alexander on all fours, moving with frightening speed, her movements predatory and alien.

"Ailsa… Magsy… please… it's me…" Tears streamed down Alexander's face, his voice breaking. "Please… I came back for you… I came back…"

Magsy suddenly burst forward with incredible speed, far faster than any child should move, far faster than Alexander could react.

He dove to the side on pure instinct, crashing into a display of canned goods. Tins exploded across the floor, rolling and clattering, and Ailsa's head snapped toward the sound.

She reached out with those elongated arms, her fingers ending in sharp, bone-like protrusions that gleamed in the dim light. The fingers whistled through the air where Alexander's head had been a moment before.

Alexander scrambled for his crossbow, his hands shaking so badly he could barely grip it. His heart was breaking, shattering into pieces with each movement, because he knew—God help him, he knew—what he had to do.

"I'm sorry… I'm so sorry…" The words were sobs, torn from somewhere deep in his chest.

Magsy leaped at him from behind a shelf, her small body airborne, her mouth open showing teeth that seemed too sharp, too many. Alexander rolled away just in time, feeling the displacement of air as she passed. She crashed into the wall with a sound that should have hurt her, should have made her cry, but she simply immediately began scaling it, climbing up toward the ceiling with spider-like agility, her fingers and toes finding purchase on the painted surface as if it were a ladder.

Ailsa moved closer, guided by the sounds of the struggle, her head cocked at an angle, listening.

Then, from above, from the shadows near the ceiling where Magsy clung, came a voice in perfect imitation of how she used to sound—sweet and small and terrified.

"Daddy, help me please…"

The mimicry was perfect. Exactly her voice, exactly her inflection, the way she had sounded a thousand times when she was scared or hurt or needed him.

For a moment—just one terrible moment—Alexander hesitated.

That hesitation nearly cost him his life as Ailsa's clawed hand swiped through the space where his head was a second before. He felt the wind of its passage, felt one of those bone protrusions graze his shoulder, tearing through fabric and skin.

Alexander raised his crossbow with shaking hands, tears blurring his vision until the world became a watercolor painting of grief and horror. He aimed at Magsy as she clung to the ceiling like some terrible spider-thing, her small body defying gravity, her orange eyes glowing in the shadows.

His finger rested on the trigger, but it wouldn't move. The muscle simply refused to obey his brain's command.

"I can't… I can't do this…" His voice broke into pieces, each word a jagged shard of anguish.

Magsy dropped from the ceiling with predatory grace, landing behind him with barely a sound. Alexander spun around and fired wildly, the movement desperate and uncontrolled. The bolt flew wide, embedding itself harmlessly in a shelf of cereal boxes with a soft thump.

Ailsa lunged toward the sound of the crossbow's release, her clawed hands swiping through empty air with whistling precision. Alexander stumbled backward, frantically trying to reload, but his hands were shaking so badly the bolt slipped through his fingers. It clattered to the floor and rolled away, disappearing under a shelf.

"Daddy's home! Daddy's home!" Magsy's voice rang out, sweet and innocent, exactly as it had sounded a thousand mornings when he'd returned from business trips.

The mimicry was so perfect it stopped Alexander cold, freezing him in place for a critical second.

Magsy charged at him on all fours, moving with inhuman speed. Alexander fired again in pure panic, not even properly aiming. The bolt flew over her head, shattering a jar of pickles that exploded in a shower of glass and brine.

Magsy leaped at his chest, her small body airborne, and her claws—when had her fingernails become claws?—raked across his jacket. Alexander threw himself sideways, the impact driving the air from his lungs as he crashed into another display. Bottles and jars tumbled around him.

Ailsa moved silently toward the commotion, her elongated arms sweeping the area like a blind person reading Braille on the air itself. Alexander rolled away just as her bone-tipped fingers scraped the floor where he'd been lying, the sound like nails on a chalkboard, leaving deep gouges in the wooden planks.

He scrambled to his feet, loading another bolt with trembling fingers that felt thick and clumsy. "Please… please stop… it's Daddy…" The plea was pathetic, irrational, directed at things that were no longer capable of mercy or recognition.

Magsy screeched again from somewhere in the shadows, that terrible high-pitched sound that seemed to bypass his ears and resonate directly in his skull. Alexander spun toward the sound and fired. The bolt hit nothing but empty air, clattering uselessly against the back wall.

He was down to his last few bolts, and his family was closing in.

Alexander backed against the shop counter, his chest heaving, his last bolt loaded with fingers that wouldn't stop shaking. He could feel splinters from the counter digging into his back through his torn jacket.

Magsy emerged from behind a shelf, moving slowly now, deliberately, on all fours. Her orange eyes locked on him with the focus of a predator that knows its prey has nowhere left to run.

Ailsa approached from the other side, her blind face turned toward his ragged breathing. Her head cocked slightly, listening, tracking.

They were coordinating perfectly—cutting off his escape routes with the practiced efficiency of pack hunters.

"Daddy… I missed you so much…" Magsy's sweet voice, her head twitching with that unnatural motion, the words so innocent and the thing speaking them so alien.

Alexander raised the crossbow, aiming at Magsy. His finger found the trigger. All he had to do was squeeze. Just pull. Just end this.

But his finger froze.

"I can't… she's my baby… I can't…" The words came out as a sob, his entire body breaking down, the crossbow wavering.

Ailsa suddenly lunged forward with frightening speed, far faster than something her size should be able to move. Her clawed hand raked across Alexander's arm, tearing through fabric and flesh. He felt the sharp, burning pain and cried out, firing reflexively without aiming.

The bolt went wide again, punching through a window. Glass exploded outward, letting in a gust of cold air.

Alexander dropped the crossbow, clutching his bleeding arm. Hot blood seeped between his fingers, running down to drip from his elbow.

Magsy pounced, using his moment of distraction. She landed on his chest, her small weight driving him to the ground. His head cracked against the floor, stars exploding across his vision. Her small face hovered inches from his, those glowing orange eyes studying him with terrible intelligence.

"Daddy… you're bleeding…" She tilted her head, and for just a moment—just one cruel moment—the gesture was exactly like his Magsy used to do when she was curious or confused.

Alexander looked into those eyes—his daughter's eyes in shape and position, but not his daughter. Not anymore.

Ailsa loomed over them both, her elongated arms reaching down, her fingers spreading.

Alexander's peripheral vision caught a glint of light. A broken piece of glass from the shattered pickle jar, lying just within reach. With his good arm, he grabbed it, the sharp edge immediately cutting into his palm. Blood welled up, but he held tight, his grip desperate.

"I love you, Magsy. I love you, Ailsa. I'm so sorry…" The whisper was meant for them, for who they had been, for the ghosts of his family that deserved a better ending than this.

He drove the glass shard upward into the base of Magsy's skull, into the soft vulnerable spot where spine met brain.

She made a small, surprised sound—almost like his real daughter would have made if she'd stubbed her toe or been startled by something. The familiarity of that sound nearly destroyed him.

Her orange eyes flickered once, like a candle in the wind, then went dark.

She collapsed on his chest, suddenly just a small, still weight. Just a little girl again, not a monster.

Ailsa's head snapped toward them, her entire body going rigid. She sensed something had changed, some connection severed.

She let out a blood-curdling screech that shook the entire shop, that rattled the remaining glass in the windows, that seemed to come from somewhere deeper than lungs—a mother's anguished cry for her child. The sound was deafening, primal, filled with rage and loss that transcended species or infection.

"AAAAAAHHHHHHHHH!"

She waited, her body trembling, listening desperately for Magsy's response—for the answering call that always came, that had to come.

When none came, when the silence stretched into impossible emptiness, her blind face contorted with fury.

Alexander pushed Magsy's body aside—God forgive him, pushed his daughter's body aside like an object—and scrambled to his feet. His legs barely held him, weak with shock and grief.

Ailsa charged at him with terrifying speed, her elongated arms sweeping wildly, destroying everything in their path. Shelves toppled. Products exploded.

Alexander dove behind the counter as her claws raked deep gouges in the wood, tearing through it like paper.

She vaulted over the counter with spider-like agility, her body folding in ways that shouldn't be possible, landing directly in front of him.

Alexander rolled away as her bone-tipped fingers slammed into the floor where his head had been a second before. The wooden planks splintered under the impact.

He grabbed a heavy can of soup—the mundane absurdity of it almost making him laugh hysterically—and hurled it at her with all his strength. It struck her shoulder with a solid thunk, but she didn't even flinch. Didn't acknowledge the impact at all.

Ailsa swiped at him again, her claws catching his jacket and tearing it open, the fabric shredding like tissue paper. Alexander stumbled backward, his eyes frantically scanning for another weapon, any weapon.

He spotted a knife behind the deli counter—a proper butcher's knife with a long blade.

Ailsa followed the sound of his movement, her head tracking him with terrible precision, never more than a second behind.

Alexander lunged for the knife just as Ailsa's elongated arm swept across the counter in a horizontal arc. Her claws missed him by inches—he felt the displacement of air, felt how close death had come.

He grabbed the knife and spun around, the handle solid and reassuring in his grip.

Ailsa was already there, having moved with silent precision, her blind navigation more effective than sight.

Her clawed hand wrapped around his throat, lifting him off the ground with strength that shouldn't exist. Alexander's feet kicked uselessly, finding only air. His vision began to darken at the edges as her grip tightened, crushing his windpipe.

With his free hand, the one holding the knife, he drove the blade into her arm with every ounce of strength he had left.

She released him with a shriek of pain that echoed off the walls.

Alexander hit the ground hard, his knees buckling, gasping for air that burned as it entered his crushed throat. Each breath was agony.

Ailsa pulled the knife from her arm, dark blood oozing from the wound—not the bright red of human blood, but something darker, thicker, with an orange tinge that glowed faintly.

But even as Alexander watched, the gash began closing. The flesh knitting itself back together, the wound healing before his eyes with impossible speed.

She advanced on him again, her blind face somehow still finding him, always finding him.

Alexander backed against the shop window, the cold glass pressing against his shoulders. No more room to retreat. Nowhere left to go.

Ailsa raised both arms, preparing to strike, to end this.

Alexander's hand found a heavy glass bottle on a nearby shelf—whisky, his mind noted absurdly, expensive single malt.

As Ailsa's claws came down in a killing strike, he grabbed the bottle and smashed it against her head with all the force of desperation.

Glass exploded everywhere, showering them both. The sharp smell of alcohol filled the air.

Ailsa staggered, momentarily stunned, her movements uncoordinated for the first time.

Alexander saw his chance—perhaps the last chance he would ever have.

He grabbed the largest shard of glass, its edges wicked and sharp, and with a cry of anguish that came from the deepest part of his soul, drove it deep into Ailsa's temple.

She convulses once, her elongated body trembling, every muscle spasming. Her mouth opened, but no sound came out.

Then she collapsed beside her daughter, her long limbs folding beneath her, her blind face finally at peace.

Spotify

Apple Music

Amazon Music

Track: NAE REST FUR THE FALLEN

Alexander fell to his knees among the wreckage, surrounded by the bodies of his family. His hands were covered in a thick orange blood—theirs. The floor was slick with it, with pickle juice, with spilled groceries, with the whisky that should have been celebration but had become a weapon.

Alexander knelt among the scattered groceries and broken glass, his body shaking with exhaustion and grief so profound it felt like a physical weight crushing his chest. Blood dripped from his wounded arm and from the cuts on his hands, each drop hitting the floor with a soft pat that seemed impossibly loud in the new silence.

He stared at the still forms of Ailsa and Magsy, barely recognizable now as the family he had loved more than his own life. The orange glow had faded, leaving behind something that looked almost human again, almost like the people they had been.

The shop was eerily quiet after the violence—only the sound of his ragged breathing and the distant crash of waves against the shore. No more screeching. No more unnatural movements. Just silence and death and the ruins of everything he had fought so hard to reach.

"I'm sorry… I'm so sorry I wasn't here to protect you…" The whisper was broken, barely words at all, just sounds of grief given voice.

He reached out with a trembling hand to touch Magsy's blonde curls, now matted and lifeless. The orange glow had faded from her eyes, leaving them empty and gray—not her blue, not anything, just the absence of life.

Alexander pulled off his torn jacket with movements that felt distant, as if his body belonged to someone else, and gently covered both bodies. It seemed important, somehow, to give them that dignity. To not leave them exposed.

He sat back against the counter, staring at nothing, his eyes unfocused. The weight of everything—the journey from Edinburgh, the desperate hope that had sustained him, the loss, the horror of what he had just done with his own hands—crashed down on him all at once.

Outside, the wind picked up, rattling the broken window, making the door creak on its hinges.

Alexander looked around the destroyed shop—his family's final resting place. Canned goods scattered everywhere. Broken glass catching the dim light. Blood on the walls, dark and drying.

This wasn't how it was supposed to end.

He was supposed to come home to hugs and laughter. To Ailsa's smile that made everything better. To Magsy's excited babbling about everything she'd done while daddy was away. To normalcy and love and the simple joy of being home.

Instead, he had come home to a nightmare. Had been forced to kill the two people he loved most in the world. Had failed in the one job that mattered most—keeping them safe.

Suddenly, he heard something that made his blood freeze in his veins.

Magsy's voice, giggling and laughing. Clear as day. Real as anything.

But it was coming from somewhere behind the counter.

"Mummy, can we get the biscuits?"

Alexander's head snapped up, his heart racing, hope and terror warring in his chest. Was it possible? Had he been wrong? Was she—

He followed the sound behind the counter and found a damaged CCTV monitor and recorder, somehow still functioning despite everything. The screen flickered with static, lines of interference rolling across the image, but he could make out figures moving.

It was Ailsa and Magsy, shopping in this very store.

They were alive on the screen—laughing, talking, completely normal. Completely human. Completely them.

Alexander stared at the monitor, tears streaming down his face, cutting clean tracks through the grime and blood. A smile broke across his features despite everything, unbidden and helpless, as he watched Ailsa help Magsy reach for something on a high shelf.

"Careful, sweetheart. Let Mummy get that for you." Ailsa's voice, recorded and tinny but unmistakably hers.

Alexander reached toward the screen with blood-stained fingers, as if he could touch them, as if he could reach through time and warning them, protect them, change everything.

“My girls…” The whisper was reverent, broken, filled with love and loss.

Suddenly, a loud CRASH echoed from the recording, the sound distorted by the cheap speakers but unmistakable.

Alexander leaned closer to the screen, his breath catching.

On the flickering screen, Ailsa and Magsy jumped at the sound of the crash, their faces transforming from shopping-day contentment to terror in an instant. They ducked down behind the counter—the same counter Alexander was leaning against now—seeking shelter that would prove meaningless.

Alexander watched in horror, his breath caught in his throat, as a figure walked into frame.

A bald man, about six feet tall, with skin that had a gray, corpse-like pallor. But it wasn’t dead—pulsing orange veins were visible beneath the surface, a network of glowing corruption that seemed to have its own heartbeat. His chest glowed with an eerie orange light, as if something inside him was burning. Thick orange residue dripped from his mouth in viscous strings, pooling on the floor.

Behind him, several figures in dark clothing entered the frame—security personnel wearing tactical gear, their faces obscured. Professional. Military. One of them held a long chain attached to a collar around the creature’s neck, handling it like a dangerous animal being led to a feeding.

An unknown man’s voice spoke from off-camera, calm and clinical, with an accent Alexander couldn’t quite place.

“Release it. Let’s see what the Projen can do.”

The security team unleashed the creature, removing the collar with practiced efficiency before stepping back to safe positions.

Alexander watched in absolute horror, his hands gripping the sides of the monitor hard enough that his knuckles went white, as the Projen’s chest began to glow brighter. The orange light intensified, pulsing faster, building to something.

A wet, hissing sound filled the audio—organic and terrible, like flesh tearing or lungs collapsing.

On screen, Ailsa pulled Magsy closer, both of them trembling behind the counter. Ailsa's body was positioned protectively over their daughter, trying to shield her with her own flesh.

"Alexander! ALEXANDER, HELP US!" Ailsa's voice was terrified, raw with fear, calling out for him, trusting that he would come, that he would save them the way he always had.

"DADDY! DADDY, WHERE ARE YOU?!" Magsy's small voice crying out for him, needing him, her daddy who had promised to always protect her.

The Projen's mouth expanded grotesquely, the jaw unhinging like a snake's, opening far wider than any human mouth should. And then it spat—a stream of bright orange, gelatinous goo that arced through the air with terrible precision.

The screaming that followed was unbearable.

Ailsa's voice, high and agonized, the sound of someone experiencing pain beyond comprehension. Magsy's screams, shrill and terrified, the cries of a child who doesn't understand what's happening, who only knows fear and hurt and wanting her daddy.

Alexander pounded his fists against the monitor, the plastic cracking under the impacts.

"NO! NO, I'M HERE! I'M HERE!" His screams matched theirs, separated by time but united in anguish. "I'M HERE! AILSA, I'M HERE!"

But he could only watch, helpless, as his family's agonized cries filled the tinny speakers. He was there, but he wasn't there. He had arrived too late. Days too late. The tape showed him his failure in excruciating detail.

The screaming went on for what felt like an eternity—probably only seconds in reality, but time had lost all meaning. Each second was its own lifetime of suffering. He could hear the exact moment when Ailsa's screams changed, when the pain transformed into something else, when the infection took hold. He could hear when Magsy's cries became confused, then distant, then something not quite human.

Finally, the screaming stopped.

The silence that followed was somehow worse.

The unknown voice spoke again, still calm, still clinical, as if commenting on the weather rather than the murder of innocents.

"Good. It's done its work. Recapture it."

A figure in a long white lab coat walked into frame, but the camera angle—mounted high on the wall—only showed him from the chest down. Expensive shoes. Pressed trousers beneath the pristine white coat. He moved with the confidence of someone accustomed to authority, to obedience.

He knelt beside the bodies of Ailsa and Magsy, examining them clinically, checking pulse points, lifting eyelids, observing with the detached interest of a scientist studying specimens rather than a human being looking at victims.

Then he began to laugh.

It started as a chuckle, then built into full-throated laughter—a maniacal, chilling sound that echoed through the shop both in the recording and in the present, as if the walls themselves remembered and were replaying it.

"Perfect! Absolutely perfect! It's time!" The words were punctuated by laughter, genuine delight in his voice. Whatever results he was seeing, they pleased him immensely.

The figure in the lab coat stood and walked off camera, his laughter fading as he moved away, leaving behind the bodies of Alexander's family like discarded experiments.

The recording flickered, jumped, then cut to static—harsh white noise and rolling bars of interference.

Alexander stared at the blank screen, the static reflected in his eyes, his world completely shattered in a way that went beyond the grief of loss. That grief had been unbearable but comprehensible—a tragedy of circumstance, of being in the wrong place at the wrong time, of a world falling apart.

But this…

This was different.

His family hadn't just died in some random outbreak. They hadn't been unlucky victims of a spreading infection. They were murdered. Deliberately. Experimentally. Used as test subjects by someone who laughed at their suffering, who found their transformation "perfect."

The infection wasn't a natural disaster or an accident.

It was a weapon. And someone had unleashed it on his family to see what it would do.

Alexander's hands clenched into fists, his nails digging crescents into his palms. Blood welled up—he was already bleeding from so many wounds that a few more didn't matter.

"I'll find you. Whoever you are… I'll find you." His voice was low, filled with a rage and grief that went beyond words, beyond screaming. It was a promise made to the static on the screen, to the bodies beneath his jacket, to the memory of screams that would haunt him forever.

The man in the white coat. The voice giving orders. The security team that had unleashed that thing on innocent people shopping for groceries.

He would find them all.

And he would make them pay for every second of his family's suffering.

Spotify Apple Music Amazon Music

Track: LAST STAND

APPENDIX 1

Soundtrack & Audio Experience

Music is the heartbeat of Undead Revelations.

Each track mirrors a moment in Alexander's journey, shaping the tension, fear, triumph and loss of his story.

Scan the codes within each chapter to listen as you read, or experience the full soundtrack once your journey is complete.

FULL PLAYLIST

Listen to the full soundtrack on Spotify, Amazon Music, YouTube, Apple Music, and more!

Spotify | Apple Music | Amazon Music

Playlist: ALL TRACKS IN STORY ORDER

FULL PLAYLIST

1. Ailsa
2. Scottish Joy
3. Departure
4. Highlands Farewell
5. Distance Between Us
6. Conference Harmony
7. Conference Blues
8. Awakening
9. The Screecher
10. Bullseyes' Pursuit
11. Reflections in the Shadows
12. Finding Sanctuary
13. Shattered Hope
14. Sanctuary Lost
15. Whispers of the Woods
16. Echoes of the Bullseye
17. The Farm
18. Echoes of Home
19. Approaching Darkness
20. Belnahouthie Ferry
21. Solitary Seas
22. Auld Strathdee
23. Alexanders Escape
24. Glencore
25. Fylie Castle
26. The Armoury
27. Muir of Howis
28. Survival bonds
29. Whisper of the past
30. Aileen
31. Survival Bonds
32. Winding Paths of Cantsford
33. Cauldhame
34. Dawn
35. Parting Ways
36. Rolling Hills of Albany
37. Steep Pathways
38. Finally Home
39. Home Through The Shadows
40. Druichmachon
41. Racing Shadows
42. What Remains
43. Nae Rest Fur The Fallen
44. The Last Stand

Printed in Dunstable, United Kingdom

77952835R00153